Religion and Leisure
in America

Samuel D. Hemphill
6-10-80

Nashville   ABINGDON PRESS   New York

ROBERT LEE

RELIGION and LEISURE

in AMERICA

A Study in Four Dimensions

RELIGION AND LEISURE IN AMERICA

Copyright © 1964 by Abingdon Press

ISBN 0-687-36001-3

Library of Congress Catalog Card Number: 64-15758

SET UP, PRINTED, AND BOUND BY THE
PARTHENON PRESS, AT NASHVILLE,
TENNESSEE, UNITED STATES OF AMERICA

TO

Robert E. Fitch
Arthur L. Swift
John C. Bennett

For
Stimulus, encouragement,
and friendship along
the way

FOREWORD

This generation thinks of itself as immune to the shocks of rapid change, and yet we are continually confounded by the unbelievable contrasts that appear before us.

A large percentage of our population has to fight for its civil rights and to take to the streets and jails to move the nation to consider its second-class citizenship. Poverty and crime are immediate neighbors to many.

At the same time, our technological genius has produced a standard of living for many millions far beyond the hallucinations of kings in the immediate past. Automation and its allies have created vast new blocks of free time for us all. Add the unemployment figures to the time freed by mechanized work patterns, and you get a population with time on its hands.

Far more significant than the statistical measures of men and women not engaged in employment are the not so easily detected changes in the life goals of people who are not obsessed with work.

In the midst of a revolution in life style, characterized by frantic entertainment on the one hand and feelings of emptiness on the other, Christian insight must be applied to assess the meaning of the changes insofar as it is now apparent.

For some years the changing patterns of American leisure have been a concern of a small group of churchmen. A Christian Ministry in the National Parks, first a program in the

Department of Evangelism of the National Council of Churches, and now a part of that Council's Division of Home Missions, is an expression of that interest. For over two years, a committee of the Department of Evangelism has struggled to expand our understanding of the nature of the new leisure.

Dr. Robert Lee and his colleagues in the Institute of Ethics and Society at San Francisco Theological Seminary carried on a research program to furnish that committee with a summary of the information and interpretation currently available. This research furnished the background for Dr. Lee's reflection on the deeper issues involved, both sociological and theological. This book is a first fruit of that reflection. It marks an important beginning for future thought and action in the life of the Christian man in a new leisure society.

ROBERT W. SPIKE

General Secretary for Program
United Church Board for
Homeland Ministries
Chairman, Leisure Time Witness Study
National Council of Churches

PREFACE

A new day is dawning on the American scene. Never before have so many had so much free time on their hands. Modern Americans stand at the threshold of a revolution in leisure time that is full of promises and yet pregnant with perils. In order to gain some understanding of the new shape of the developing leisure society, the Department of Evangelism of the National Council of Churches instigated a twofold study: (1) To survey the extant literature and alert church leaders to some of the best current research and writing in the field, and (2) to develop a volume that would provide perspective on the problem of leisure from a contemporary, historical, and theological standpoint.

This book carries out the second task envisaged by the Leisure Time Witness Study Committee of the National Council of Churches. Needless to say, one author, much less one volume, can hardly be expected to do justice to a subject of such scope and intricacy as is leisure. This is clearly a topic that defies narrow conceptualization. Since leisure is necessarily related to all of life, it cannot be comprehended easily by any single approach or method of specialized study. Hence the reader will fail to find here a study that conforms strictly to the boundary lines staked out by any particular discipline.

In view of the magnitude and breadth of the leisure field, I have chosen to discuss the subject in four dimensions: Width, depth, length, and time. These dimensions comprise the four parts of this book, and although each may be read separately, there is a sense in which each part grows out of and builds upon the previous one. Thus the theologically minded reader may want to turn immediately to Part IV, which deals with time as a theological resource for leisure. Other parts should not be neglected in his reading, however.

A further word concerning the subtitle—"A Study in Four Dimensions"—the four dimensional schema of width, depth, length, and time adopted by this study is meant to cover contemporary, social-psychological, historical, and theological aspects of the leisure question. These dimensions should be taken as part of an open-ended discussion. None exhausts the reality it depicts, and much more could be said concerning each. Thus again, Part IV is confined to a treatment of only one theological resource for viewing leisure. It does not presume to confront the whole range of theological categories in formulating a "theology for leisure."

I cannot resist making several personal observations. First, it has been a pleasure to work on a study of leisure. My friends have understandably had great sport in teasing me about spending my leisure working so hard on a book about leisure!

Second, I must register a demur against the "leisure-ho-ho-what's-that" response of many friends who discovered I was writing on this subject. I fear that underlying this reaction is a deeply imbedded notion that leisure is a frivolous, trivial, or slightly amusing concern that really can't be taken seriously. Though widespread, this is a distorted perspective. Leisure cannot be so lightly dismissed with a shrug or a smile. The burden of this book is to establish the seriousness and significance, indeed, the decisiveness, of the leisure situation facing us in contemporary life. By putting the discussion of leisure in a new perspective, perhaps this book will help us to think differently about the many facets of our emerging leisure society.

Third, it must be emphasized that this book is written for everyone—not just for those whose working hours have been shortened, but also for those who think they have no leisure. The latter are apt to labor under a false impression that identifies leisure with after-work time. Our redefinition of leisure conceives of it not merely in relation to time or work, but as an attitude of mind. Thus leisure is not so much a period of time, as it is a state of mind. To those who would charge that the issues of work have been slighted I can only reply that we have written about *leisure,* not work, and that this book seeks to free leisure as an independent variable from its agelong subservience to work. The fact is, we have so exalted work that we find leisure difficult to face. In this respect we are more related to the nineteenth century—if not, indeed, to the sixteenth century—than we are to the decade of the sixties in twentieth-century America. In the last section of this volume, we seek to depict a Christian style of living that is relevant to the new leisure society.

Fourth, the problem of leisure is not merely a social one "out there" to be studied in scholarly detachment, but it is also a deeply personal problem. If I trace the intellectual roots of my concern for this subject, I have to confess that this is not just America's problem, but it is profoundly my own problem—not so much in the way that it strikes many, as an abundance of free time, but rather, the inability to take time for leisure. Thus as preachers occasionally preach to themselves, authors sometimes must write to themselves.

My appreciation goes to many people who have helped close the gap between the dream and the reality of this volume: President Theodore A. Gill of San Francisco Theological Seminary provided the necessary leisure time for study and reflection by granting a much-appreciated study leave which freed me from academic and administrative responsibilities. The Leisure Time Witness Study Committee has been most helpful, especially its chairman, Robert W. Spike; its staff co-ordinator,

Ralph M. Holdeman; and committee members, Warren Ost, Lauris Whitman, Cameron Hall, Colin Williams, Robert Dodds, and Al Roberts, all of whom were instrumental in getting the study project off the ground. Also, much thanks goes to four denominations and their evangelism departments for providing the bulk of the funds for the study—United Presbyterian Church, U.S.A.; United Church of Christ; American Baptist Convention; and Evangelical United Brethren.

I am grateful to Robert Thomas of the Division of Lay Education, Board of Christian Education, United Presbyterian Church, for hospitality and an opportunity to expose and test these ideas in a "Seminar on Religion and Leisure" with a group of discerning laymen and clergymen at Ghost Ranch, New Mexico.

Finally, my deepest appreciation goes to the members of the research team of the Institute of Ethics and Society. They labored long and hard in surveying the field and digesting the literature in the form of "Research Notes" which were distributed to church leaders and libraries. The work of William G. Doty, Ted Harrington, and Marjorie Casebier makes this book a product of team effort. I wish particularly to acknowledge the services of Miss Casebier, who stayed with the project longest as research assistant. She has provided valuable insights and deserves credit for many of the volume's virtues. Its limitations, however, are solely the responsibility of the author.

And now, off to some "creative loafing!"
ROBERT LEE

CONTENTS

PART ONE
Width: The Scope of Leisure in America

1. The Problem and Meaning of Leisure 17
2. The New Leisure Society: Facts and Trends 36
3. The Play Element in Contemporary Life 53

PART TWO
Depth: Leisure in Relation to Play

4. Leisure and the Spirit of Play 71
5. Children at Play 91
6. Play and Delinquency: The Tragic
   Use of Leisure 106

PART THREE
Length: Some Historical Roots of Leisure

7. From Holy Days to Holidays 127

13

8. The Puritan Influence 151
9. The Sabbath Tradition 174

PART FOUR

Time: A Theological Resource for Leisure

10. Perspectives on Time 199
11. Time as God's Creation 218
12. Time, Life, and Leisure 237

Selected Bibliography 265

Index 269

PART ONE

Width: The Scope of Leisure in America

1

The Problem and Meaning of Leisure

"What is the gravest crisis facing the American people in the year ahead?" Many answers were given when this question was posed to a group of distinguished news commentators on an end-of-the-year roundup television program. One person suggested heightened cold-war tensions, another thought Latin America, another said the independent nations of Africa, and a fourth felt Berlin would provoke the gravest crisis. Around the table the discussion went, until it came Eric Sevareid's turn to comment. In striking contrast to the others, Sevareid stated that he thought the most dangerous threat to American society is the *rise of leisure* and the fact that those who have the most leisure are the least equipped to make use of it.

The Problem of Leisure

This acute observation is both startling and prophetic. It is startling because few Americans are yet consciously aware of leisure as a "problem," far from its being a grave social crisis. Who would have thought, in the decade of the twenties and thirties, that someday leisure would supplant labor as an issue of national significance? It is striking to contrast the labor movement's struggle for recognition to bargain collectively with its current national drive for a shorter workweek.

Sevareid's comment is prophetic because Americans are now standing on the threshold of a revolution in leisure time. At this juncture the contours of this revolution can be but dimly perceived. Its full consequences, however, are bound to reshape the social and moral visage of American life. The idea that the rise of leisure poses a crisis is prophetic in still another sense—judgment and warning, hazard and opportunity.

Students of history have voiced the vague but ominous notion that there is more than a tenuous connection between how a people use or abuse their leisure and the decline or survival of their civilization. It may seem rather farfetched to a single, solitary individual that the future of civilization hangs on the balance of how he uses or misuses his leisure. It stands to reason, however, that the corporate, communal uses of leisure could well make or break a culture, reveal the moral worth of a nation, and have an impact upon the nation's destiny in terms of cultural degeneration or cultural flowering in the years to come. As Ida Craven aptly expressed it:

Leisure is not only the germinating time of art and philosophy, the time in which the seer attains glimpses of the values and the realities behind ordinary appearance; it is also the opportunity for appreciation, the time in which such values get across into common experience. The quality of a civilization depends upon the effectiveness of the transmission of such values.[1]

How a nation uses its free time, then, tells much about the texture of its society and provides portents for the future. Thus in the final analysis, the real threat to a civilization's decline is the enemy within. Its name is not subversion or revolution, but misspent time.

Next to the abundance of *things,* the most significant characteristic of the American scene is the abundance of *free time.* A century ago the industrial workweek was seventy hours. Now with new labor-saving devices in factory, office, and home, and with the onset of automation, we are becoming a new leisure society. No longer is our work day dictated by the rising and setting sun. The twenty-five or thirty hour workweek is more

[1] "Leisure," *Encyclopedia of the Social Sciences,* edited by Edwin R. A. Seligman and Alvin Johnson (New York: The Macmillan Company, 1933), p. 405.

than a wild dream—it is a definite threat. Sir Thomas More had visions of a nine hour workday, a sixty hour workweek, in his *Utopia,* published in 1516. From a leisure standpoint we are already living in Utopia. Suddenly Edward Bellamy's utopian vision in *Looking Backward,* that people retire at the age of forty-five in the year 2000, becomes less visionary and less fanciful. Perhaps a token of things yet to come may be glimpsed in a report that the Russians have invented a new sleep machine called the "electrosone" that will pack a full night's deep, restful sleep into just two hours or less. Imagine the revolutionary implications for leisure time once this device, now being tested in American medical centers, is perfected!

There is a new leisure although, of course, leisure itself is not new. Every society has had a "leisure class." Our forefathers too knew of a privileged leisure class as spelled out classically by Thorstein Veblen's *Theory of the Leisure Class,* written in 1899. Traditionally membership in this class has been a privilege shared by very few. Now leisure has been extended to the masses. A rewrite of Veblen's work would have to be entitled *Theory of the Leisure Masses.*

Leisure is no longer confined solely to a social and aristocratic elite. Although leisure has always been a fringe benefit in the history of mankind, now it is moving into the center of life, threatening to replace work as the basis of culture. Literally a revolution has occurred—a turning around—for what was on the periphery is now at the heart of man's daily existence.

One of the traditional images of America is that of a toiling, sweating nation in its shirt-sleeves. Ours is a nation of workers who have labored frantically to achieve leisure as a kind of utopian yearning. Although pockets of poverty still remain, the vast majority of Americans have left behind the eat-sleep-work routine, where they have to eat to gain strength to work hard in order to earn money to have enough to eat. If you ask the proverbial man-in-the-street why he works so hard, his likely answer is "In order to have more leisure." Throughout the ages, man has dreamed of achieving a state in which he would be liberated from the burdens of labor. But now that the yearning for leisure has been largely fulfilled, we are in a quandary. We don't know quite how to face this new situation of living in a leisure society. We have so glorified labor that we find it difficult to live with leisure. Ironically, we approach with anxiety and restlessness a subject which is more appropriately associated with ease and relaxation.

Russell Lynes likens our situation to a primitive society that has known only stone tools and then suddenly is presented with mechanized farm equipment. Its work is quickly done, its fields are tilled by a few men with a few machines, while others stand around and watch. It seems the millennium has arrived. Then the watchers grow increasingly restless and feel useless and distrustful. They have to change their tribal rites, revamp their moral codes and their social customs, or else fly apart as a community.[2]

As a people, we are accustomed to the struggle against poverty; this is a noble and self-justifying kind of crusade. Mankind has never had to ask what comes after the defeat of this enemy, for total victory was never in sight. We are all familiar with the term "poverty stricken." But have we ever thought of being "leisure stricken"? Our culture seems to value the machine above music and labor above leisure. After leisure, what? This is the disturbing question. How does one engage in battle with this new, enigmatic foe? This is our blissful, and yet desperate plight.

Many and varied are the ways of appraising and evaluating the problems which a new leisure society poses. One approach—thus far largely neglected—is to consider the moral problem and the role of religion and theology in relation to leisure.

If morality may be interpreted in a broad sense as the critical study of human behavior, with particular focus upon

[2] Russell Lynes, "The Pressures of Leisure," *What's New* (Winter, 1958), 1.

the choices that man makes in his individual and social life, then the rise of mass leisure should command the attention of the moralist and challenge him to contribute to an understanding of the problem. Leisure involves that realm of human action where man is constantly making free decisions. It provides a valuable clue to the basic questions of human existence: Who am I? Where do I want to go? How am I related to my culture?

The moral problem is not simply one of taste—that is, the concern that the masses are overindulging in stultifying, unedifying, or moronic pastimes. Of course, it may be true that a kind of Gresham's Law is at work in which bad currency tends to drive out good currency from circulation, or lower tastes—say in television viewing—pre-empt the field and drive out good taste.

Far more seriously, however, the moral problem is that of drift, of a "group think" mentality that merely follows a leaderless crowd. It is one of forfeiting the right of choice, of emptiness in what should be life's satisfactions. Triviality is not as much the problem as is self-surrender and self-resignation in a field where the possibilities for choosing have enlarged spectacularly. As a consequence we are faced with an erosion of meaning ("anomie"), a great emptiness that haunts modern man as he drifts along by chance or by circumstance. The inner impoverishment of the individual in our age and the pervasiveness of boredom ("ennui") are symptomatic of our inability to cope with the problem of leisure. Professor Robert M. MacIver expressed the moral mood with poignancy:

Back in the days when unremitting toil was the lot of all but the very few and leisure still a hopeless yearning, hard and painful as life was, it still felt real. People were in rapport with the small bit of reality allotted to them, the sense of the earth, the tang of the changing seasons, the consciousness of the eternal on-going of birth and death. Now, when so many have leisure, they become detached from themselves, not merely from the earth. From all widened horizons of our greater world a thousand voices call us to come near, to understand, and to enjoy, but our ears are not trained to hear them. The leisure is ours but not the skill to use it. So leisure has become a void, and from the ensuing restlessness, men take refuge in delusive excitations or fictitious visions, returning to their own earth no more.[3]

Robert W. Spike summarized the paradoxical moral problem posed by leisure in this way: "There are two conflicting motifs that characterize American leisure time: first, a great sense of vacuity, of time emptied of meaningful activity; and second, an impression of determined frenzy to relax, to unwind, to do something different." [4]

The moral problem is complicated by the fact that while Christians, especially since the Protestant Reformation, have developed a sizeable body of literature to provide moral guidance with respect to work or vocation, any such doctrine or direction for our leisure or avocation is lacking. Modern Western industrial civilization has a work ethic, which, of course, is a curious compound of Puritan and bourgeois values. But when it comes to a morality or ethic of leisure, we face an alarming vacuum. We are confronted clearly with what might be called a "theological lag" in which theological and ethical thinking lags behind rapid social changes. This is obviously an instance in which the pace of historical, technological, and social change has far outrun the pace of theological and ethical thought.

American society is shifting from a primary focus on work to one on leisure, from production-oriented to a consumption-oriented economy. As Protestants who seek to be relevant to contemporary culture, we dare not reman silent about our

[3] *The Pursuit of Happiness* (New York: Simon and Schuster, 1955), pp. 54-55. Used by permission of the author.
[4] *To Be a Man* (New York: Association Press, 1961), p. 55.

new leisure society. The newly found freedom for leisure should mean an extension of personal choice and decision making. Instead, the typical response to so much of the new leisure opportunities is not one of discriminate judgment and selectivity, but is an increasingly mechanized response; one that is routinized and compartmentalized; one that denies man's self-transcendence and makes him a plaything of mass conformity to current moods and fads.

No wonder modern man is plagued by *boredom* when he flees from the drudgery of work to the meaninglessness of leisure. As Paul Elmen noted:

The bored man needs a world which will distract him to seek out the noisiest and most gaudy entertainment. The last thing he wants is to be part of a world where free men make their desperate decisions. Instead he cowers in his ennui, much as a child wishes to return on occasion to the safety of the womb. Those few who are eager for life cast about them for some expression equal to their desire, and listen to One who has said, "I am come that ye might have life, and have it more abundantly." [5]

One often hears it said about a particularly active person that he died from overwork. With the shifting focus from work to leisure, is it possible that men now die of boredom, that they die from overleisure? We have barely begun to explore the moral dimensions of boredom. Near the turn of the century Rudyard Kipling put his finger on the problem when he wrote to William James that "the curse of America is sheer, hopeless, well-ordered boredom; and that is going someday to be the curse of the world." One suspects there was a twinkle in Clifton Fadiman's eyes when he suggested that the Crusades were stimulated "in part by the love of God, in part by the love of loot, in part by the tedium of daily life." In casting an eye

[5] From *The Restoration of Meaning to Contemporary Life* by Paul Elmen. Copyright © 1958 by Paul Elmen. Reprinted by permission of Doubleday & Company, Inc. P. 47.

to the future, however, Fadiman was hardly joking when he depicted highly industrialized nations in such a state of boredom that release comes only through mass aggression: "Wars may be fought less between nations than between rival systems of ennui. The hyper-bomb of that day will have lost meaning as a weapon. . . . That being the ultimate logic of the situation, we may contrive to kill boredom and ourselves at one and the same time." [6]

The distraughtness that disturbs contemporary man is expressed in the revealing phrase "killing time" in discussing leisure. It implies that we find leisure difficult to face. To kill time is to kill leisure—and ultimately, as we shall have occasion to see, to deny God. Killing time is an expression of modern man's self-alienation which he refuses to acknowledge. Instead, he either escapes into a world of feverish activities or indulges in idleness in order to fill the void. The delinquency of the young and the despair of the aged reveal something of the albatross about the neck of those for whom leisure means little but idleness.

Another dimension of the moral problem we face is that many Americans approach leisure with a sense of guilt or of pride—guilt when they have too much leisure and do not know what to do with it or feel they must justify it ("I really needed this rest; I was plumb worn out"), and pride when they regard themselves as such busy, important people that they couldn't possibly have leisure ("Why I haven't taken a vacation in twenty years," or "The only vacation I had was on my honeymoon").

There are those who refuse to take a vacation or who face the prospects of a leisurely weekend with neurotic fear. They are unable to relax or actually have a fear of relaxation. If a vacation is taken it is filled with tension and torment. Their ailment might be termed "acute leisure-itis." A noted psy-

[6] "Boredom, Brainstorms, and Bombs," *Saturday Review of Literature* (August 31, 1957), p. 9.

chiatrist, Dr. Alexander Reid Martin, has observed that most suicides occur during weekends, holidays, and vacations.

The inability to relax is found among those beset by "severe after-work irritability" and in those who suffer from "weekend neurosis." Ironically this fear of leisure is found frequently among prominent, highly respected individuals, regarded by the community as success symbols. Perhaps they are victims of their own success. As Dr. Martin noted,

In the last analysis, the individual who is afraid of relaxation and leisure and who misuses recreation in the service of compulsion, lacks faith in himself and his fellow man and denies mankind's interdependency. He is afraid to depend on others and has the illusion of only depending upon himself when, in reality, he is depending on his compulsions. He is enslaved by them and has no freedom.[7]

It would indeed be tragic if the best that we can do with our new leisure opportunities is to impose a self-made hell upon human existence. Bernard Shaw must have had the leisure problem in mind when he coined this definition of hell: "Hell is an endless holiday—the everlasting state of having nothing to do and plenty of money to spend on doing it."

The problem of leisure is, of course, no less the problem of life. Leisure finds its significance in the total context of a meaningful life. Modern man's persistent myth is that leisure is a frivolity that is apart from the concerns of life that really matter. Nothing could be further from the truth. Leisure is a part of man's ultimate concern. It is a crucial part of the very search for meaning in life, inasmuch as the social malaise of our time has been diagnosed as anxiety and boredom, alienation and meaninglessness. Note that these categories of understanding the human situation, employed so searchingly by

[7] "A Philosophy of Recreation" (Chapel Hill: University of North Carolina, Second Southern Regional Conference of Hospital Recreation, 1955).

social critics in their analysis of the social crisis of our day, point unmistakably to a condition of the spirit. It is in the realm of free time that these conditions of the spirit will be brought into bold relief, bringing man to the depths of despair or to the heights of ecstacy and creativity.

Increasingly it is in our leisure time that either the meaningfulness or the pointlessness of life will be revealed. Leisure today may be a challenge or a threat, a hazard or an opportunity, a vice or a virtue, a bane or a blessing. Whether it will be a boring nuisance or an unmatched opportunity may well depend upon the perspectives and resources we bring to bear upon the problem. The choice before us is clear: A new age of leisure or a new barbarism!

The Meaning of Leisure

In order to understand more clearly this choice before us we must first define the meaning of leisure. One can find as many definitions of leisure as there are commentaries upon the word. It seems that every man has a glimmering of what leisure is (or half-jestingly denies he ever has enough of it), but, like the meaning of truth, he finds it difficult to spell out. Part of the difficulty inheres in the fact that leisure encompasses such a colossally varied assortment of behavior that it well-nigh defies conceptualization. We must seek the meaning of leisure, however, for "leisure cannot exist where people don't know what it is." [8]

Leisure in Relation to Time

Leisure is most commonly viewed in relation to time—free time, time not devoted to paid occupation, or time off from work. Perhaps the standard definition, suggested by George Lundberg and his associates, is that "leisure is . . . the time we

[8] Sebastian de Grazia, *Of Time, Work and Leisure* (New York: The Twentieth Century Fund, 1962), p. 8.

26

are free from the more obvious and formal duties which a paid job or other obligatory occupation imposes upon us." [9]

Such an attempt to define leisure by putting the stress on the time element—free time, spare time, left-over time, unobligated time—is bound to be misleading. This is basically a quantitative view of leisure, an arithmetic approach which simply subtracts the time devoted to work, sleep, and other necessities from the twenty-four hour day to derive the "surplus time." To be sure the time focus is necessary, yet it is not a sufficient condition of leisure. At best this is a minimal view, and at worst a distortion, for it fails to capture the depths of the meaning of leisure, the essentially inner and subjective quality of the experience.

The difficulty with this definition, which reflects a tradition probably dating back to the early stages of the industrial revolution, is that it is at once too broad and too narrow. It may be too broad if it refers to all the time we are not actually engaged in "making a living," and too narrow if it implies that leisure is merely the residual time after one has accomplished one's work *and* all the myriad duties which contemporary life imposes upon us. In the latter case there is virtually no such thing as leisure since there may be little residual time when "duty" in the sense of what is expected of one or one's role obligation is related to every area of a person's behavior and responsibility.

The focus on time free from the demands of work or duty, when advanced as the sole criterion of leisure, tells us nothing about the normative content of leisure. "If sociology has taught us anything," writes sociologist Bennett Berger, "it has taught us that no time is free of normative constraints." [10] Indeed

---

[9] Lundberg, Mirra Komarovsky, and Mary Alice McInerny, *Leisure: A Suburban Study* (New York: Columbia University Press, 1934), p. 2.

[10] "The Sociology of Leisure," *Industrial Relations: A Journal of Economy and Society* (February, 1962), 1, 38.

Berger argues that leisure refers precisely to those activities that are *most* constrained by moral norms. That is to say, free time may be more obligated because where commitments are voluntary they tend to carry with them a sense of responsibility.[11]

There is a still more serious limitation of viewing leisure simply as free time or spare time. Free time is not really synonymous with leisure. The unemployed or the confined may have free time but not necessarily leisure. Not everything one does in one's free time qualifies as leisure. Of course free time may be converted into leisure time. Hence *free time is only potentially leisure time*. Noncommitted or free time may well be idle time. The mood of leisure is affirmative, whereas the mood of idleness is negative. Idleness must not be confused with leisure, for idleness renders leisure impossible. Indeed the problem we face in contemporary American life is that too many people have too much time and too little leisure.

Leisure, then, is not merely a period of unengaged time. Rather than place the emphasis upon time itself, the focus should be upon the person. Leisure depends not only upon available time, but also upon the *freedom of the person* to use that time. Thus leisure represents the opportunity for a person to use a portion of time for ends which are designed by the person himself. Leisure is that time during which we are free to choose what we wish to do within the range of our personal freedom.

Leisure in Relation to Work

In a culture that is accustomed to extolling the virtues of work, perhaps the most prevalent juxtaposition of leisure is with work. Leisure is commonly seen as work-oriented—we

[11] *Ibid.* To illustrate this point the author cites the following example: "One finds it emotionally more difficult to beg off (for phony reasons) from a previously accepted invitation to a party given by a friend, than to call the boss to say one is sick and not coming to work. This suggests that leisure obligations are *more* thoroughly internalized than obligations to work."

rest *from* work, *for* the purpose of doing more work, or in order that our work will be more efficient. Many observers consider that leisure is "at bottom a function of work, flows from work, and changes as the nature of work changes." [12] Typical definitions view leisure as the antithesis of labor or as the time a man is free from work.[13]

Those who seek to define leisure in opposition to work fail to account sufficiently for the interpenetration of work and leisure, for the many ways in which work and play are suffused. Their views imply that leisure is a reward for sweat—something that must be earned through productive effort, much as a beast of burden deserves food and a night's rest as a reward for the day's toil. Leisure need not be viewed as subordinate to work or as a restorative for work, but may be seen as an end in itself, something valued for its own sake. "Strictly understood," contended Bennett Berger, "the conventional opposition of work and leisure is a false opposition because these terms characterize different orders of phenomena: leisure is a kind of time, whereas work is a kind of action." [14]

In setting leisure against work, the implication is that leisure is unproductive. Actually leisure is no less virtuous than work, nor is it necessarily opposed to work. Increasingly the distinction between the two has become tenuous. In fact modern society moves toward a fusion of labor and leisure. There is abundant evidence that work has become more like play and play has taken on the trappings of work. In her own pointed and whimsical way, the anthropologist Margaret Mead described a condition in modern home life that has become neither work nor leisure:

[12] Clement Greenberg, "Work and Leisure under Industrialism," in *Mass Leisure,* edited by Eric Larrabee and Rolf Meyersohn (Chicago: The Free Press of Glencoe, Ill., 1958) , p. 38.

[13] Cf. Nels Anderson, *Work and Leisure* (London: Routledge & Kegan Paul, Ltd., 1961) , p. 33.

[14] *Op. cit.,* p. 37.

If this home life really is to be classified as play, then it should be a good deal easier than it is. . . . Do-it-yourself with five children, besides being delightful, is strenuous, time consuming, backbreaking, nerve-straining, and confining—most of the things once characteristic of a good job which a man enjoyed. The job ouside the home, if not seen as recreation in the spiritual sense, is becoming recreation in the physical sense.[15]

Paradoxically we flee from leisure in order to find rest in our work.

At work there are the conventional and institutionalized— and interminable—morning and afternoon coffee breaks, the lunch "hour" among business and professional people (where wheels make deals over meals), the card games among night shift employees, the piping of soft background music into factories and offices. Off the job there is the irrepressible do-it-yourself movement for millions, the "customers" golf games for sales executives, the commuter-train conferences among executives—all these are indications of a blurring of the gap between labor and leisure.

This gap has narrowed in a more fundamental sense. Many professional people, including doctors, lawyers, teachers, and clergymen, scoff at the idea that they have any leisure. It is common in discussing the subject before such groups for someone to exclaim in somewhat offended and anxious tones, "What is this thing you're talking about; show it to me!" What these people don't realize is that they are living the life of leisure! Theirs is truly a "labor of love." Since they make a living doing what they most enjoy for its own sake, their leisure and their work have so intermingled that such persons have *leisure in work*. Research scientists, skilled craftsmen, seminary professors, statesmen, painters, actors, and musicians are others who may enjoy this happy combination of work and leisure.

[15] "The Pattern of Leisure in Contemporary American Culture," *Mass Leisure,* *op. cit.,* pp. 14-15.

30

Then there are the fortunate few of sufficient wherewithal who choose a highly satisfying vocation without regard for financial reward, or who may contribute their services to the public good. Unlike those who have leisure in work, they have *work in leisure*.[16] In view of this blurring of distinction between work and leisure, it is understandable why professional persons often work many more hours than are actually required for their compensation. They find it difficult to determine the point at which work ends and leisure begins. At any rate the traditional dichotomy between labor and leisure has been rendered obsolete for the many with "leisure in work" and for the few who "work in leisure."

A further assault on the antithesis of work and leisure is suggested by two French students of the problem. Joffre Dumazedier and Nicole Latouche have called an important group of activities, which arise from leisure but represent varying degrees of obligation, "semi-leisure." [17] Four types of semi-leisure may be distinguished: (1) Leisure activities of a semi-lucrative, semi-disinterested character, such as remunerative odd-job indoor work, participation in orchestras, et cetera; (2) domestic activities of a semi-utilitarian, semi-recreational type, such as gardening or "do-it-yourself"; (3) familial activities of a semi-distractive, semi-educational nature, such as playing with the children; (4) small, agreeable jobs, such as decoration, making small models of boats, et cetera.

The close liaison between work and leisure, so much a part of Western thought, has been dubbed rightly or wrongly the "Protestant view of leisure." [18] Now for an ampler sense of

[16] George Soule, "The Economics of Leisure," *The Annals* (September, 1957), 313, 21.

[17] Joffre Dumazedier and Nicole Latouche, "Work and Leisure in French Sociology," *Industrial Relations: A Journal of Economy and Society* (February, 1962), 1, 20-21.

[18] Berger, *op. cit.*, p. 35. From a contemporary Protestant standpoint, this allegation may seem unfair in that it doesn't sufficiently take into account the complexity of historical factors and circumstances in the rise of industrialism.

the meaning of leisure, we must turn from considerations of time and work to the classical or Greek tradition.

The Classical View of Leisure

A clue to the classical tradition is supplied by the Greek word for leisure which is "scole." In Latin the word is "scola." From these words, of course, we derive our term "school." Leisure thus conceived is an aspect of the educational or learning process. Indeed Aristotle has said that "the aim of education is the wise use of leisure." And Socrates paid high tribute to leisure when he called it "the best of all possessions." The term refers not merely to time but to the content of time, how one uses and what one should do with the time. Leisure cannot be adequately understood apart from man's response to it.

Our English word "leisure" comes from the French "loisir" and the Latin "licere," both of which have the root meaning "to be permitted," "to be free." Our words "liberty," "license," and "leisure" are all etymologically derived from the same Latin word. Freedom of choice is an important element in the meaning of leisure. Hence Cicero's remark, "He does not seem to me to be a free man who does not sometimes do nothing." In the context of true leisure, man exercises his freedom to do what he pleases. This quality of freedom is sensitively depicted by August Heckscher, Director of the Twentieth Century Fund and the first Special White House Consultant on the Arts:

A man's leisure was once supposed to be that part of his life which was most completely his own. At work he was compelled to heed the boss. If he was in business for himself he had to act as if the customer were always right, or accede to the impersonal dictates of the market. But in leisure his own mind was supreme. Guarded by a detached and smiling humor, ringed about by the smoke of a contemplative pipe, a man's leisure was a kingdom of its own.[19]

[19] *The Public Happiness* (New York: Atheneum Publishers, 1962, pp. 159-60.

If freedom and learning are twin attributes of leisure, then it is apparent why leisure should be considered the basis of culture. The choice of leisure time activities can give shape and meaning to our cultural configurations. The spirit of leisure is the spirit of learning, of self-cultivation. In a sense the world of leisure is a great laboratory for learning. Leisure provides the climate for the growth of man's whole being—for contemplation of man's ultimate concerns, for activities which enrich the mind, strengthen the body, and restore the soul. Like education, leisure takes discipline, training, cultivation of habits and tastes, discriminating judgments. It is decidedly not something one drifts into.

Josef Pieper underscores this viewpoint in his important work, *Leisure, the Basis of Culture.* He maintains that leisure is a mental and spiritual attitude which is not simply the result of external factors such as spare time, a holiday, a weekend, or a vacation. "It is in the first place an attitude of mind, a condition of the soul . . . the occasion and the capacity for steeping oneself in the whole of creation." [20] Thus conceived, leisure is concerned with the edification of one's total being. It is not limited to intellectual cultivation, but embraces the mind, body, and soul of the living person. It has the potential for psychophysical restoration of the individual and thus relates him to the joy and possibilities of life.

Two shortcomings mark the classical view of leisure. The first is its association with a particular aristocratic or patrician class who share a disdain for work. Presupposed in the Greek tradition of leisure is the institution of slavery, which enabled the free man to engage in the "higher" cultural pursuits of philosophy, art, politics, and debate. We cannot erect a theory of leisure on the foundations of slave labor. In formulating a concept of leisure relevant for the contemporary scene, leisure must not be a privilege reserved for the dignified and well-bred

[20]New York: Pantheon Book, Inc., 1952, p. 52.

few. It is an opportunity for the many and knows no distinction of caste or class.

A second defect is that the Greek view tended to equate leisure with contemplation or intellectual pursuits. The ideal life of leisure for a Plato or an Aristotle was the life of contemplation, a life devoted to abstract thought and cultivation of the arts. Those following in the Aristotelian tradition, most notably Cardinal Newman and Josef Pieper, are likely to overstress the cultivation of the mind in their approach to leisure. The potential danger here is a flight from the real world, as revealed in the charming story Plato tells of the philosopher Thales of Miletus who fell into a well while gazing at the stars, while nearby stood a little maid, laughing at the sport. Moreover, Pieper's suggestion that contemplation is "pure nonactivity" is an effort to remove every trace of work from leisure. Without an element of work in it, contemplation may well turn into *accidie*—sloth, idleness, boredom, and despair.

Leisure cannot be confined to intellectual pursuits. It is not so much a question of the mind as it is a condition of the spirit. Man does not have a body and a mind which are in separate realms. Man must be seen as a whole person. To be at leisure, therefore, is not to be on vacation from reality. Leisure is part and parcel of contemporary man's world of real existence.

Leisure, then, is the time for discovery—or better, self-discovery. When I go on a vacation trip I find I get a renewed perspective on life. It is not the change of scenery that is so important, though this may be refreshing. Rather it is the freeing of the mind from immediate habitual concerns to a consideration of ultimate concern. It is a time for rediscovering the meaning and purpose of life, for seeing the pursuit of living in its wholeness. Leisure is the occasion for the development of broader and deeper perspective and for renewing the body, mind, and spirit. This is the kind of self-learning and self-understanding that forms the basis of true selfhood and provides perspective for the person's involvement in society.

Leisure is an end in itself, not merely toil in a different guise. Free time which has become so plentiful for so many may be filled with humdrum, monotonous activities—or it may provide the context and opportunity for creative leisure. In so far as the latter is possible, leisure may be viewed as part of the totality of man's activity, a part that is meaningfully related to the rest of his life. Since all of life must be regarded as a whole, it is artificial to compartmentalize leisure time from work or from the rest of the time. Yet faithful attention to the parts will serve to renew the sense of life's wholeness.

Leisure is the growing time of the human spirit. Leisure provides the occasion for learning and freedom, for growth and expression, for rest and restoration, for rediscovering life in its entirety. By its misuse the alternative to creative leisure is futility and despair, pointlessness and meaninglessness. Never before have so many had the opportunity to choose between the one or the other.

35

2

The New Leisure Society:
Facts and Trends

A resounding chorus of voices now proclaims that we are
headed toward an unprecedented era of leisure in American
life. By any reasonable calculus, and viewed simply as available
free time, the possibilities and prospects for leisure have risen
spectacularly. As baffling as the various efforts to define leisure,
however, are the attempts to pin down precisely the new shape
of the developing leisure society. The data are often confusing
and even contradictory. Let us turn, then, to a discussion of
leisure facts and trends.

Shorter Workweek

One dramatic way of expressing how leisure time has been
democratized is to cite the statistics on the shortened workweek among industrial and agricultural workers in America.
In the last century we have witnessed a steady decline in the
number of working hours of the laboring classes.

During the post–Civil War period the average workweek
was roughly seventy hours—the equivalent of a nearly twelve-
hour day, six-day week. This was reduced to a sixty-hour week
at the turn of the century. Just prior to the great depression in
1929 the workweek was down to fifty. John Kenneth Galbraith
notes that as late as the early 1920's the steel industry worked
a twelve-hour day and a seventy-two-hour week with an in-
credible twenty-four hour stint every fortnight when the shift
changed.[1]

[1] *American Capitalism* (Boston: Houghton Mifflin Company, 1956), p. 121.

Long-term trends indicate that since 1900 there has been an average reduction of four hours in the workweek for each decade. It is a striking fact to note that the working man of a century ago spent some seventy hours per week on the job and lived about forty years. Today he spends some forty hours per week at work and can expect to live about seventy years. This adds something like twenty-two more *years of leisure* to his life, about 1,500 free hours each year, and a total of some 33,000 additional free hours that the man born today has to enjoy!

Sometime in the mid-1950's the standard forty-hour week began to slip silently into history for nonagricultural industrial workers. Many employees in the garment and printing trades, the construction and rubber industries, have been working less than forty hours. Nearly half of the six million office workers queried by the Labor Department work less than the traditional forty hours, excluding, of course, time off for coffee breaks and the like. Several powerful labor unions are currently exerting strong pressures for a thirty or a thirty-five-hour workweek schedule.

Perhaps as a harbinger of things to come, the Electrical Workers Union, Local 3 of New York City, has successfully negotiated a contract calling for a five-hour workday and a twenty-hour workweek. Predictions of a four-day workweek are not uncommon. Indeed, with technological advances—particularly automation—just barely introduced, the shape of things to come is nearly a foregone conclusion.

Agricultural workers are similarly affected by these trends. In fact, since World War II the workweek on the farm has declined even more rapidly than in nonagricultural industries. Traditionally the workweek in farming has been considerably longer than in nonagricultural pursuits, but the gap has been narrowing. Between 1947 and 1956, the workweek declined by four hours in agriculture as compared with 1.4 hours in nonagricultural industries. The overall percentage decline of farm workers—from 70 per cent in 1850 to less than 12 per cent in 1950—has played an important part in the decline in average working hours for the economy as a whole. This trend is likely to continue. According to the U. S. Census Bureau the number of agricultural workers declined during the decade of the 1950's by 37 per cent, or from 7,047,000 to 4,415,000. During this same period the number employed in professional and related services soared by 58 per cent.

Roughly half the number of hours a week are devoted to work now as compared to a century ago. At the same time production has increased markedly, so that one worker now produces six times as much as his grandfather did for every hour he stays on the job. In 1900 one farm worker produced enough food and fiber for himself and seven others; now he supports himself and twenty-four others.

Today's shorter workweek—resulting in what *Life* has enthusiastically dubbed a "cultural explosion"—must be seen in the context of increased productivity; longer weekends (the half day of work on Saturday went out during the pre–World War II days); greater consumer buying power; more paid vacations, holidays, and sick leaves. Nearly all labor contracts now provide for paid vacations. A study of labor contracts covering six million industrial workers showed that 80 per cent received six or more paid holidays a year. Ninety per cent of all production workers enjoy paid vacations. Another study by the National Industrial Conference shows that 99 per cent of the companies surveyed give paid vacations to hourly employees as compared with only 46 per cent before World War II, and that the entire U. S. labor force received about sixty-five million weeks of paid vacation time in 1961, as against less than eighteen million in 1929. Altogether the number of paid vacation, holidays, and sick leave days in nonagricultural industries now average about twenty. Thus many workers not only have time on their hands, but paid time. In the future it should come as no surprise if something like the academic sabbatical is adopted as part of the way of life and leisure for both management and workers. As a harbinger of the future, the last steel wage pact calls for a thirteen-week vacation to be granted every five years to senior employees in major steel mills and can companies.

Although the facts concerning the declining workweek appear to be indisputable, several qualifications are in order. The first is the obvious one mentioned earlier, that not all the citizens of our society share equally in the benefits of a reduced workweek. Doctors, lawyers, educators, clergymen, small business proprietors, and business executives may well find that the hours of work, and especially the psychic demands of their tasks, have declined little, if at all.

As we have noted, some of these professionals find "leisure in work" as their work and leisure are happily integrated. Others, however, are simply dogged by work schedules of back-breaking proportions. This situation is partly of their own choosing, but it also results partly from a shortage of supply, particularly notable in the case of medical doctors. Ironically enough, the medical profession preaches the doctrine of rest, relaxation, and leisure for the health and well-being of patients, and yet doctors themselves find it exceedingly difficult to live by their own counsel.

In the long run, however, as the college ranks swell and a more ample supply of trained professional people become available, the problem of the overworked professional should be somewhat mitigated. Robert Bendiner has surmised that:

. . . doctors and lawyers can be expected eventually to follow the prevailing social pattern, even if it means making less money. Small groups of doctors, taking joint quarters and rotating off-hour duty, are even now able to enjoy long weekends and even midweek breaks. Some are acutely conscious of the heart attacks that carry off so many of their overworked colleagues before their time, and they prefer to make a little less of what they can't take with them. I have even heard the idea advanced that a way should be found to enable independent professionals to take sabbaticals, not only for the sake of rest but as an offset to the narrowness of an overtechnical education and a specialist's life.[2]

At the moment, however, as far as leisure is concerned, medical doctors, lawyers, and business executives are, paradoxically, victims of their own success. As long as their drive toward financial success remains relentless, they will not have the leisure that could be theirs, almost for the taking.

Secondly, there is the phenomenon of the dual or multiple job holder who has so much spare time that he goes out to find another job and works, as it were, by the light of the moon. "Moonlighting"—the holding of a second job in the after-hours of one's primary job—will surely cut down on the amount of an individual's free time.

It is difficult for obvious reasons to determine accurately how widespread the practice of moonlighting actually is. A 1950 study estimated that 1.8 million workers, or 3 per cent of the total work force, were engaged in moonlighting. At the end of 1959 the figures were three million, or about 5 per cent. There is good reason to believe that its practice is more widespread than these figures reveal.

Of course, Akron, Ohio, cannot be taken as a typical community as far as moonlighting practices go. But it is a known fact that from 16 to 20 per cent of Akron's rubber workers hold a second *full-time* job, and that another 40 per cent work part time on a second job. Apparently these workers prefer extra work to more free time.

Why do so many Americans want to, or feel they have to, work these extra hours? The reasons and motivations for moonlighting are many and mixed. Surely in an economy of abundance and prosperity the answer that they need money is oversimplified. To be sure, some are caught in the vicious circle—

---

[2] "Could You Stand a Four-Day Week?" *The Reporter* (August 8, 1957), p. 12. Copyright 1957 by The Reporter Magazine Company.

the more free time available, the more money is spent on the leisure market, and the more one spends, the more one must work in order to have additional money to provide for more expansive leisure enjoyment. Nevertheless, we cannot overlook the interpretation that many workers resort to moonlighting because they have not learned how to utilize their free time and find it difficult to face. Moonlighting is at least one response to avert the threat of leisure.

Take the case, which was actually reported, of the industrial workers in a southern California aircraft-parts factory who found themselves with a reduced four-day workweek. Instead of enjoying this newfound freedom, they soon discovered that it raised unanticipated problems. At first it worked out all right, but being around the house at odd hours, husbands soon found themselves fair game for domestic chores. They were subject to the so-called "honey-do days"—"honey do this, honey do that." Moreover, the longer they hung around the house, the more they seemed unable to keep out of their wives' way. The ensuing collision led to emotional disorder in the family. By comparison, the "escape from freedom" by assuming a second job was a relief and helped to restore family stability! Moonlighting may be a flight from the challenges of leisure to the solace of more work. The moonlighter escapes from work not looking for leisure but for some other kind of work.

A final qualification has to do with the journey to and from work. This, of course, is so much a necessary part of the job that it can hardly be treated as free time. As large segments of the populace increasingly move from central city areas to peripheral suburban communities, and out beyond to "exurban" locales, the time required for commuting has correspondingly lengthened. Some forty million Americans now reside in these mushrooming dormitory cities. In the next decade of the exploding metropolis this figure is likely to double.

Once upon a time, work, job, and family were in close proximity. Now, with the separation of job from home, long journeys are frequently involved to get to one's place of work. Indeed, one estimate has it that we spend 10 to 20 per cent of our working life commuting between home and work.

With all its snags and snarls, there is little hope for early improvement in the commuting situation, considering the obsolete modes of transportation facilities and the cluttered freeways that plague, if not choke, most of our metropolitan areas. One wit refers to cities in the motor age as dying from "artery-sclerosis." The hapless commuting suburbanite has been facetiously depicted as one whose life is divided into two parts —coming and going. Not so funny is the cartoon showing the suburban commuter who leaves his home and family while it is still dark outside and returns home when it is dark again, just in time to tuck his children into bed. This is reminiscent of the toiler whose workday lasted from dawn to dusk a century ago. In any case, time for leisure opportunities is curtailed if the demands of commuting are inordinate.

The three qualifications we have considered must be acknowledged. They tend to correct the exaggerated claims being made by some observers about the amount of available free time. Even when they are taken into account, however, the evidence still points to a long-term decline in the length of the workweek for the industrial and agricultural worker in America, and a subsequent rise in time free from work demands. Whether or not this free time is being used for leisure is another question. But the trend toward a shorter workweek shows no signs of abatement and is likely to continue.

The Leisure Market

Another way to assess the leisure trend is to ask how much money Americans spend on leisure time pursuits. To this seemingly simple question no clear-cut answer can be given. In fact, the discrepancies are so vast among different interpreters that one questions how disciplined the statistics are—not to speak of the statisticians. Estimates for leisure expenditures range all the way from $20,000,000,000 to over $218,000,000,000.

Of course, the crux of the problem has to do with what should be included in the accounting of leisure expenditures. For instance, how much is travel or dining out to be reckoned a leisure item or a necessity? To what extent should the "luxury" market be included? Is the sports car boom part of the leisure market? To indicate the difficulty of what should be "in" or "out," some studies include tobacco—a $7,500,000,000 item in 1960 as compared with $4,700,000,000 spent for all religious and welfare activities—since it is presumably a voluntary pleasure; yet other studies exclude smoking from the leisure accounting on the grounds of its compulsive nature!

In view of the varying estimates for overall leisure expenditures, it is difficult to say in any meaningful way what proportion of the household or national budget the leisure market commands. Figures have ranged all the way from 5 to 50 per cent.

Whatever the actual sum—why quibble between $20,000,000,-000 or $218,000,000,000!—it is a staggering figure, hardly imaginable several decades ago. The point is: The leisure market has become a gigantic economic force. By all odds leisure has become Big Business—geared to mass distribution and consumption of products. Leisure has become one of the largest, most complex, and perhaps fastest growing markets in the entire national economy.

A sizeable segment of the economy is now engaged in the mass production of entertainment, fun, and diversion. As a result new industries have emerged; for example, the outdoor power tool business; sporting equipment, notably skin diving; paperback books; model kits; and various do-it-yourself lines, including home carpentry, paint rollers, and wallpaper. It is reported that 500,000 people visited a commercial show catering to the do-it-yourselfers in Los Angeles and bought $1,000,-

000 worth of equipment and materials from 300 exhibitors over a five-day period.

Not only have new products developed, but without the increase in free time many of the older industries could not have risen to their present heights. As the society becomes more affluent the ability of Americans to spend more for fun increases. Symbolic of the affluent new leisure society are the private swimming pools that dot the landscape. It is said that a passenger flying north from Mexico can tell when he has crossed into the United States by the swimming pools which begin to appear below. No wonder David Riesman says of the new leisure society that America has moved from the melting pot to the casserole dish.

Families with incomes of $4,000 and more dominate the leisure market. Their numbers have expanded rapidly in recent decades so that the traditional pyramid of the social class structure now looks like a fat bulging diamond. Today's leisure dollars are being spent by many more people. Gain in real income is gain in purchasing power. And "extra leisure time tends to result in extra leisure spending." [3]

It may be instructive to turn to a number of selective leisure expenditures to indicate the general contours of the market: In a single year the value of equipment sold for the game of golf—once considered a pastime of the privileged classes—amounted to $39,500,000; the amount spent on flowers, seeds, and potted plants in 1960 was a blooming $985,000,000; the popularity of boating has pushed outboard motor sales to new highs with a gross of over $2,000,000,000, more than tripling the 1951 figure; vacation travel expenditures have been estimated as high as $21,000,000,000 and not below $12,000,000,000 annually; the sum spent on TV repairs in 1960 was a tidy $860,000,000, as compared to only $88,000,000 in 1945.

These overall trends should be sufficient to underscore what

[3] Editors of *Fortune*, "$30 Billion for Fun," *Mass Leisure*, edited by Larrabee and Meyersohn, p. 172.

everyone knows: From a commercial standpoint leisure has become Big Leisure. Surely the leisure market has contributed substantially toward the shift in our economy from a production to a consumption-oriented one. It has brought us to the brink of an orgy of consumption. Barring nuclear catastrophe or economic depression, the business of selling the life of leisure seems destined to continue to thrive. As the Editors of *Fortune* aptly suggest, "The leisure market may eventually become the dynamic component of the whole American economy. For while consumer appetites for necessities may become sated, where is the limit to the market for pleasure?" [4]

The Uses of Free Time

The shorter workweek, coupled with higher productivity and greater economic prosperity, has given Americans more time and money for leisure pursuits. How are they spending this time? What clues about the quality of American life may be detected through the leisure choice activities of its citizens?

In answering these questions one is immediately confronted with a tremendous variety of leisure options. At present the American's use of free time may include literally hundreds of choices. Chief among them are the following:

Watching television; listening to the radio; listening to records; reading newspapers, magazines, books; working around yard or in garden; pleasure driving; going to meetings or organizational activities; attending lectures or adult school; visiting; going out to dinner; going to the theater, concerts, opera, movies; participating in numerous sports (bowling, riding, skating, fishing, swimming, golf) ; sight-seeing; singing; playing musical instruments; dancing; going to government parks and amusement parks; attending sports events; placing pari-mutuel bets; spending time at the drugstore; playing cards; engaging in special hobbies (photography, stamp collecting) ; keeping pets; and playing slot machines.[5]

[4] *Ibid.*
[5] De Grazia, *Of Time, Work, and Leisure*, p. 105.

Extensive though this listing of free time activities may seem, it hardly begins to scratch the surface of the bewildering alternatives available to the leisure-bent person. One can expect to find the relaxing American tiling his bathroom, digging in his garden with a Rototiller, cooking shish kabobs on his outdoor grill, listening to Stravinsky on his hi-fi set, or traveling to distant places with his family.

Ten years ago some 676,000 Americans went abroad, whereas in 1960 more than a million and a half took such sojourns. Travel to Europe is no longer the special province of the rich, of businessmen, or of students. Today people with quite moderate incomes are making the grand tour. Indicative of the new trend is Trans World Airlines' experience of flying to Europe several planeloads of women—not society matrons but production workers from General Electric plants in Fort Wayne, Indiana. TWA gives this profile of the group:

Their average age is 38; their average income is $57 a week. Few of them have finished high school, none has ever been to Europe before. The tour will cost them anywhere from $879 to $1,022, depending on whether they elect to take the fifteen-day or the twenty-two-day excursion. Most of them—90%—have chosen the twenty-two-day tour, even though it involves time off without pay.

Traveling within the nation has also become a favorite pastime. In 1961 some 86,700,000 people visited the national parks and monuments as compared to 33,200,000 in 1950 and 20,000,000 in 1940. Visits to state parks have also been popular, having increased by 123 per cent during the past decade. In the same period the population of California increased 60 per cent, whereas visits to California's state parks went up 300 per cent, or five times as fast as the state's rapid rate of growth. "So much of this roaming is done by car," noted Robert Bendiner "that motels, hardly heard of before the war, are now twice as numerous as hotels and constitute a billion-dollar industry. Six thousand of them have sprung up just in the past two years, many of them luxuriously appointed and equipped with air conditioning, TV, playgrounds, and swimming pools." [6]

A survey conducted by the Opinion Research Corporation of Princeton showed that the ten most frequent activities done by people in their free time are: Watching television, visiting with friends and relatives, working around the yard and in the garden, reading magazines, reading books, going pleasure driving, listening to records, going to meetings or other organizational activities, special hobbies like woodworking and knitting, and going out to dinner. [7]

Lest one is entertaining the highbrow impression that the upsurge of leisure activities pertains only to the active or passive sporting field, this familiar charge may be countered by pointing out that twice as many people play musical instruments as did so twenty years ago—28,000,000, including 8,000,000 children. Hi-fi has grown by leaps and bounds and has become a multimillion dollar business. Over 700 home grown opera groups, 1,200 amateur symphony orchestras, 30,000 high school orchestras, and 20,000 bands may be found making a joyful noise in American communities. More money is now being spent on concert music than on baseball admissions. In summertime more than 2,000,000 Americans head for art colonies and workshops to play music, paint, dance, write fiction, and fashion pottery and poetry.

Doubtless the most time consuming and highly visible of the leisure time activities is spent with one or another of the mass media—television, radio, popular books and magazines, movies, and newspapers. It is a truism to say that we live in an age of

---

[6] *Op. cit.,* p. 13.

[7] "The Public Appraises Movies," *A Survey for Motion Picture Associates of America, Inc.* (Princeton, N. J.: Opinion Research Corporation) , December, 1957. For a statistical report of how people use their free time, see the Gallup Poll, "Recreational Participation" and "Recreational Spectatorship," 1959, reported by Associated Press (February 21, 1959) .

mass media.[8] Such was not always the case. The development of the mass media has been so rapid and pervasive in our daily living that it is a veritable mid–twentieth-century revolution. TV, radio, movies, mass magazines, book clubs, FM—these are all so commonplace today; yet fifty years ago they were either unknown or insignificant.

The average adult spends an estimated quarter of his waking hours involved with the mass media—either viewing TV or movies or reading newspapers, magazines, and books. This is equal to all the evening hours from the end of dinner until bedtime. No less than 59,000,000 newspapers are circulated each day, one for about every three persons. Over 99 per cent of the homes in America have one or more radio sets.

Television has by all odds become the most prominent of the mass media, dominating as it does the typical American home in the evening hours. Recall, however, that TV had its real beginning as recently as 1947 and is still regarded as "the lusty child of the arts." Today the average American viewer spends about four or five hours per day glued to his set. As of 1960, 88 per cent of all American homes had TV sets, with 11 per cent of the households owning two or more sets. Contrast this to 1950 when only 12 per cent of the homes had sets. Within urban metropolitan areas the rate of TV ownership is 91 per cent, compared to 82 per cent for rural areas. TV has become more pervasive than the bathtub! It has become a conventional part of the American way of life, and many now claim it as a right, the exercise of which is so prevalent that "life, liberty, and the pursuit of Gunsmoke" is the current declaration of many Americans!

So much time and attention is commanded by the mass media

[8] Note the recent development of "leisure departments" in such national magazines as *Time* and *Newsweek* as well as the creation of new mass periodicals such as *Holiday, Sports Illustrated, Playboy,* and, yes, *Leisure.* Also note how the leisure environment has become the ideal setting for advertisement—smoking a particular brand is featured not at work but in a leisure setting; you drink Pepsi to be "sociable."

that they have been called the "schoolmaster of our age," "a popular addiction," and an "adult pacifier." The media provide much of the context of information and understanding within which American attitudes and values are shaped and developed. As one astute student of leisure, Rolf Meyersohn averred:

> Not only because of their popularity but also because they deal in thought rather than devices, and stimuli for perception rather than tools for activity, the mass media are of greater importance than other commercial recreation forms. Since these stimuli range in content over all human activity and experience, they have greater consequences for the consumer's conception of the world, of reality, of the ranges in styles of life, and of the human experiences.[9]

It may be too early to determine the full impact of television viewing upon other leisure patterns. There is some reason to believe it has cut heavily into attendance at movies and spectator sports; radio listening and book reading have also suffered—the latter having lagged conspicuously behind the general advance in leisure expenditures.

In the world of sports, a significant feature of today's leisure trend is the shift away from passive-spectator type activities (once dismissed by Lewis Mumford as "one of the mass duties of the machine age") in favor of sports that involve active participation. Thus the old charge, thundered from speaker's rostrum and pulpit, that Americans are afflicted by the disease "spectatoritis" has begun to sound somewhat hollow. More impressive than the cheering crowds at football and baseball stadia is the large number who are eager to become players themselves in a variety of active sports—especially swimming, bowling, tennis, golf, skiing, skating, bicycling, and water sking (one of the fastest growing sports). A recent report of

[9] "An Examination of Commercial Entertainment," *Aging and Leisure,* edited by R. W. Kleemeier (New York: Oxford University Press, 1961), p. 251.

the Outdoor Recreation Resources Review Commission states that more than 90 per cent of all Americans engage in some form of outdoor recreation during the course of a year. Besides walking and swimming, fishing is one of the perennial favorites among outdoor activities. For the past ten years between 15 to 20,000,000 fishing licenses have been issued annually. It seems to be a universal sport with equal appeal to both sexes and to all age as well as income groups. Not far behind fishing is hunting, for which some 14,000,000 licenses are issued annually.

The spurt in active participation, not only in sports but also in the burgeoning do-it-yourself movement, has prompted some observers to claim that we have become a nation of players; instead of spectatoritis, we are now afflicted by "partici-pantitis." [10] Estimates for the amount of money spent on admissions to spectator sporting events runs in the neighborhood of $1,500,000,000. By contrast, the amount being spent on participant sports has zoomed to some $8,500,000,000.

Although the mass appeal spectator sports have barely managed to hold their own in attendance and receipts during the decade of the 1950's, the significant fact is their decline relative to other ways of spending the leisure hour and the leisure dollar.

Why the much-heralded shift to more active pursuits is not entirely clear. Perhaps a partial explanation is the compensation it provides for the sedentary existence that characterizes so much of the world of work. Labor saving devices have removed much of the drudgery of work, leaving the worker with sufficient energy to pursue vigorous offwork activities. If ours is indeed a "sedentary society" in which "sitting is the symbolic posture of the age of science and technology," [11] then partici-

[10] Norman M. Lobsenz, *Is Anybody Happy?* (Garden City, N. Y.: Doubleday & Company, Inc., 1962), p. 70. The do-it-yourself movement springs partly from an economic motive, but mostly it is done for pleasure.

[11] Herbert Collins, "The Sedentary Society," *Mass Leisure*, p. 19.

pantitis would seem to be a natural reaction after we have been satiated with viewing television and spectator sports.

This discussion has been devoted largely to the quantitative aspects of free time. We have reviewed the reduction in the workweek, the proportions of our leisure spending habits, and the various uses of free time. No effort was made to discuss the broader philosophical and theological implications of time, since this dimension of our topic will be considered later.

Obviously, an analysis of facts and trends of the new leisure society leaves out the question of meaning and significance. The search for the meaning of an activity cannot ignore either the quality of time or the inner share of action. The same activity cannot be viewed in a flat, unidimensional, quantitative way, but yields greater or lesser meaning for the individual.

Merely to know that 260,000,000 copies of paperback books were sold in a single year is interesting, but hardly enough. More important than the number sold is the qualitative question, "What is being read?" Is it ephemeral literature or reading that will stretch the imagination and increase aesthetic enjoyment?

Moreover, time or money consumed by an activity is not necessarily an index of its cultural importance. Take church participation as a convenient example. We may only spend an hour or so at church, but it would seem highly improper to assign the same value to this hour as an hour spent in commuting on the freeway or one spent drearily waiting out the late, late movie on television.

Nevertheless, it is important that we come to grips with the statistical and factual data if we are to have some understanding of the patterns and trends of the new leisure society unfolding in America. For example, the shorter workweek, with prolonged free time during weekends, will inevitably enable more extensive plans for leisure activities such as weekend travel (perhaps to a second home), and family-centered activities. Doubtless this will have serious repercussions on churches and their fixed Sunday worship patterns. As early as 1934 an elder in a suburban church complained, "I don't know what will happen to my church when the Parkway System is completed and people can drive even farther on Sunday." [12] Since that time parkways have proliferated! Other voluntary organizations try to adapt their program by not scheduling important meetings during weekends. It may well be in order for churches to experiment with varying patterns, times, and even places for worship and church school. If present trends continue the new leisure society may give practical relevance to the notion of a "scattered church," placing less emphasis on church buildings and more on new patterns of "church life" to be found in areas where millions of Americans will spend their longer weekends and vacations.

[12] Lundberg, et al., Leisure: A Suburban Study, pp. 216-17.

3

The Play Element in Contemporary Life

At the heart of a leisure society is the spirit of play. One of the typical responses to the question, "What do you feel about leisure?" is the sensation of play. In a real sense leisure time is play time. It is thus appropriate to probe the subject of play in a discussion of the scope of leisure in America.

Johan Huizinga concludes his *Homo Ludens: A Study of the Play Element in Culture* with the charge that in an increasingly industrial and technological society there is a decreasing place for the "play element" and for the traditional structures and modes of play which developed through the centuries and were themselves the original foundation for many other cultural manifestations of society.

Huizinga is essentially correct in maintaining that certain traditional forms of the play element were disappearing or being changed beyond recognition. At the same time, however, one has the feeling that he somewhat misses the mark. Doubtless he was influenced by the many depressing signs of European life he saw in the late 1930's, particularly in the political arena. This play element had begun to emerge in new ways. There were, as there are now, areas not sufficiently explored in his analysis in which the play element has become increasingly operative, rather than being "smothered by techniques of producton and organization."

At least this contention is worth exploring as we look at aspects of the play spirit in contemporary life. If our notion is sound it may illuminate the pervasive character of play and leisure in our society and the blurring of distinctions between play and other facets of social life. Let us, then, survey a number of areas in present-day American life where the play element is still alive and kicking. These will include sports, business and professional life, clubs and societies, the military, and everyday social interaction.

Sports

Huizinga complained bitterly about developments in the spritely world of sports. He insisted that the professionalization of many of the major sports in the last thirty or forty years has destroyed the basic play element originally found in these sports. To a large extent this is true of such spectator sports as baseball, football, tennis, golf, racing, wrestling, boxing, and basketball. In view of extensive subsidization of athletes—even in the colleges and amateur unions—Huizinga's analysis is relevant.

Yet he overlooks many other sports that have become increasingly popular in recent years. They are channels into which the original play element in man's nature has been moving, while its more traditional modes of expression have become commercialized and part of the "universal regimentation of life." These alternative sports which manifest a play spirit may be conveniently divided into four categories: (1) "Partially pure"; (2) "elite"; (3) "traditionalistic"; and (4) "imaginative" or "role playing."

1. In the first category of the "partially pure" exist those sports which have largely become corrupted—in Huizinga's sense—when played on the professional level. When pursued by students or by genuine amateurs, however, they partake of the original play spirit. One example is wrestling, if we turn from the television spectacles and look at the large number of wrestling competitors in colleges, private schools, and even high schools. Another good example is tennis, although the

institution of amateur rankings in this sport is a major step toward professionalization.

Soccer is an excellent example. In this country it is largely played by two groups—members of European ethnic minorities in large metropolitan areas and by students at private schools and colleges. As a result there are probably many more competent soccer players in this country than most people realize. Hockey has a similar following. Although played professionally in most of the land, there is a difference between the way the sport is played professionally in its major and minor leagues and the way it is approached in the schools and colleges. Among the nonprofessional players, few think of a career in hockey. They may play the game with less finesse, but they play with no less enthusiasm.

2. The so-called "elite" sports are squash, badminton, handball, lacrosse, crew, sailing, polo, and to a certain extent, water polo. Out of many people's financial range, these sports are most frequently played in smaller private clubs that tend to be selective. Moreover, they are selective in somewhat self-perpetuating style. That is, being played in few places or institutions, they are not usually learned by younger people unless their families belong to the clubs or unless they attend the schools where these activities are popular.

3. The third category comprises the "traditionalistic" sports, such as curling, which originated in Scotland. A similar game is lawn bowling, originating either in England or Holland. Another rare game is court tennis, which came from France. This is played with unusual balls and rackets in an indoor court specially designed with various types of banked walls. Due to its difficulty, the facilities needed to play, and the limited opportunities for learning it, this game is not widely known in the United States.

These games are more truly "games" than even the "elite" ones. They are generally played by nationals who have emigrated to these shores. A particular pride surrounds the ability to play these games. One is a member of a curious "elect," which, of course, would be impossible were these games more popular. Perhaps the best example of a "traditionalistic" sport is "hurling," or Gaelic hammer throwing. This game possesses all sorts of complicated rules and is played with a special "hammer." It was descended from a grueling and rough sport popular in Ireland early in the Middle Ages. A great deal of Irish nationalism is involved in being interested or even in being allowed to learn about this game.

There must be many similar games, descended from long traditions, not widely known, but played by many of the nationality groups in this country. Most of these would fit into our third category of sports.

4. The final category of games is the "imaginative" or role-playing variety. Although invented on the spur of the moment, these games may involve a series of elaborate rules. Literally constructed or invented from nothing, they become institutionalized and sometimes develop into popular fads. Actually these imaginative games may be divided into two types—the momentary fads and those that have longer currency. Momentary fads would include such activities as hula hooping, ice cube catching, crowding into phone booths, et cetera. Such games are approached with true aspects of the play element involved.

The second, longer-lasting variety is typified in a game called "frisbee." It is widely believed that frisbee was started at Dartmouth College in the late 1940's or early '50's. Now there exists the nationwide American Frisbee Players' Association which has chapters on over twenty college campuses and a membership reputed to number in the thousands. Yet this is no ordinary sport. Its origin, its combined strictness of rules with flexibility of playing area, and the expertise which can be attained (but is not necessary to play it) set this game in a class by itself. Frisbee serves as an excellent example of how the play element in culture manifests itself in new ways when its old avenues have been blocked or have become either mundane or overly professional.

Business and Professional Life

Not only in the sporting field, but also in business and professional life, the play element continues to thrive in many and often subtle ways. Certain professions lend themselves particularly well to the spirit of play. These are likely to involve a degree of manipulation of money, men, or materials for one purpose or another. Notable among these professions are advertising, communications and public relations industries, stockbroking and speculating, certain forms of sales work, and surely, politics.

To a degree all these pursuits involve the not-always-gentle art of persuading people to do certain things or to accept objectives that are self-defined. They are extremely competitive, but the game is often not won as in the more "mundane" professions by careful economic analysis, but by hunches, by salesmanship, by hitting the correct emotional or subjective factors in a presentation that will appeal to people or will create a mood response, enabling one to readily discern the best course of action to follow in selling his material or himself. These fields tend to attract men with articulate and quick minds, and, lamentably, some individuals with few scruples about deluding or taking unfair advantage of others.

Of course it can be argued that since the rewards are great in these businesses, many able men will be attracted to them. But rewards are great in many fields. There must be a special reason why people choose to work in these pursuits rather than in others. This reason may well be related to an aspect of the play element in the competitive structure of these businesses, namely, the sheer fun which is involved. Day after day, the salesman is willing to go out when he might be working at a more consistent and steady job. Perhaps his persistence is enhanced by the fact there is real challenge to sell more than the next individual, and there is sheer love of competition in his soul.

This topic could be pursued in its extensive ramifications in the public relations and the advertising industries. Here if one is not consciously involved in competitive "hoaxes," in "putting things over" on the public, then one is at least consciously trying to ascertain what will most likely impress or persuade. Of course there is a very fine ethical line to be drawn here; the basic procedures for the "honest" group when carried just one step further may become the gimmicks or the "rules of the game" played by the more unscrupulous group.

The stock market lends itself well to the play element. Many people invest in stocks with the intention of "playing the market." Since funds are being invested for a conscious purpose, however, the sheer fun of the game is seldom allowed to be the dominant attitude. Yet a number of people invest what they can "afford to lose" just to play the market for the fun of it. Many are small investors and members of "investors clubs," but, of course, there are men of means who engage in this same practice. Perhaps unconsciously the professional speculator is a disciple of the play element. Playing the market day after day can be a tedious and tense process. In many cases these men develop the "game" mentality so that their work becomes more endurable and challenging. Perhaps there is basically an element of the gambler and the gamesman in the men who choose this profession.

Politics is a field that illustrates the play element exceedingly well. We are not speaking here of the professional civil servant or even of the individual who dabbles in politics; rather, we have in mind the full-fledged politician, the professional at the game of winning and controlling large blocs of votes. One might venture the statement that the more keenly developed his sense of politics as a game, the more successful the politician. Men like Harry Truman, James Farley, James Curley, Carmine DeSapio, Mayor Daley of Chicago, Senator Everett Dirksen, the

Kennedy brothers, and Barry Goldwater are all astute players of the game of politics.

In his book *The Making of the President, 1960* Theodore White suggests that the mark of a great president is found in one who not only has power and knows how to use it, but who also *enjoys* using it. The seasoned politician enjoys the political process much as one would enjoy a contest. One political analyst has described revealingly the United States Senate as "A Cast of Characters, the Senate floor as a stage, and a visit to the Senate galleries as a great day of theater where one is likely to see the best show in town." [1]

Of course the spirit of play shines through during a political campaign. August Heckscher notes that the public expects a political speaker "to pour it on" and demands a "fighting campaign" but is happiest when there remains the suggestion that this is a tactic, almost a game. Thus the keynote speaker at a national political convention, with his sweeping charges of wickedness concerning the other party and virtue for his own, is enjoyed but never taken literally.[2]

New leisure opportunities, it has been surmised, will usher into the political arena newcomers who, at least on the local level, are turning from mill and factory to politics. Plain citizens who could not afford the luxury of spending time on public affairs in an earlier generation will increasingly play an ever-expanding role in the great game of politics.

Clubs and Societies

Membership in clubs and societies is another activity bound to profit from the increase in free time. Here is a field that also contains many evidences of the play spirit. Since de Tocqueville's time, America has been depicted as a "nation of

[1] Russell Baker, "The Senate: A Cast of Characters," *Show* (January, 1963), pp. 56 ff.
[2] *The Public Happiness*, p. 108.

joiners," a nation which possesses a proliferation of clubs and voluntary associations for its citizenry.

In view of the organizational revolution in American life there is more truth in this charge now than in nineteenth-century America. Membership in clubs and societies fulfills many functions for the person. Surely one of these is an outlet for the play factor.

What are the real reasons for the continuing appeal of secret societies and such clubs as the Masons, Knights of Columbus, Shriners, and similar groups which revel in rituals of various sorts? Is it because people have a love of ritual which is not being met in the religious and other areas of their life? Is it because people enjoy being selective and choosing their own friends and want to be "exclusive"? Then what is the reason for the success of less ritualistic and selective clubs, such as the Elks, Orioles, Moose, Rotary, and other fraternal orders? Is it because people need the social stimulus and fellowship, the satisfaction of belonging, or the business contacts which come from such affiliations? Doubtless all of these explanations are valid to some extent.

A key factor that often gets overlooked, however, is that belonging to these clubs and participating in their various antics involves one in a kind of formalized play in the traditional sense of Huizinga's usage. Are Americans so naïve that they do not basically see through and question the validity or meaningfulness of certain rituals and practices of these organizations? They are not.

Club members are willing to "play along with the game," as it were, because it is interesting and amusing; they enjoy some of the people they meet there; it offers a real change of pace from the daily round of activities; and it may offer escape from frustration or an anchor in a hostile environment. For the most part one finds responsible and serious men belonging to such groups. Many members by no means take the whole business as seriously as some of our social critics would imagine.

In most cases these clubs are taken with a grain of salt and entered into in the spirit of play.

Our analysis can be extended to one of the most traditional and widespread institutions on the American campus—the college fraternity. Fraternity row is a field for the operation of the play element par excellence. In many cases the large college fraternity initiates its members in secretive rituals originating in the mid-nineteenth century, with its great overlay of romanticism and pseudo-Christian imagery. Few mature men, looking in retrospect, do not take *cum grano salis* the activities they endured during "pledging" or in "Hell Week," or in the various rituals, songs, and individual fraternity traditions that they learned so solemnly and knew by heart so loyally. The nuances of social relationship with the various sororities in a co-ed school, the yearly activities such as the two or three large football weekends, or the winter or spring houseparties are all part of the great structure which is enacted in the spirit of play. Students go through the motions and have a wonderful time switching from the discipline of their studies to the sort of romantic play area in which "the House" may become an organic totality bigger and more all-encompassing than any other single unit in their lives. When older they look back at this period with nostalgia, because they realize they can never return to it. Nothing is more pathetic than the fifty-year-old "rah-rah boy" who tries to live in the undergraduate past. He has played out his game and now he must turn to other fields of play.

The Military

Another area in contemporary life where the play element is more prominent that one would normally suspect is that all-pervasive establishment, the military. In a sense the American army differs from many other large armies of great world powers. Here we face the paradox of a large military force, supposedly run along strict military lines, which nevertheless

must be ultimately responsible to the democratic processes of
the society. No matter how it may seem on the surface, this
means that ultimately the soldier remains in control of the
army in which he fights. Of course all the normal power
structures are there, but the soldier knows that basically his
rights are going to be protected. So consequently he is not really
deprived of his human dignity in any ultimate sense. Knowing
this enables him to play imaginatively and to think for himself,
actively working to get a "good deal" as long as he will go
along with the ostensibly typical, but really superficial, exterior
forms. Especially is this true of those who have no plans of
making the military a lifetime career.

Let not the exposé of soldiers serving cocktails for their
senior officers or taking care of their dogs strike the knowing
observer as a feat particularly offensive to the soldier. No doubt
he loves every minute of it and would much prefer to be doing
this than to be off sloshing through the mud somewhere with
the rest of the troops or polishing the overpolished woodwork
in his own barracks.

In a sense, life in the army is one vast game. It has its
pageantry, uniforms, flags, emblems, parades, music, and elaborate etiquette and ritual. Superficially, to the casual observer,
matters proceed with precision like clockwork and all is ship-
shape and orderly. Behind the spit and polish facade, however,
there is unlimited plotting and ploying taking place. For
those officers who are veterans and who can read between
the lines, there is probably no institution where more often
an individual says one thing and means it either in a secondary
sense or means something else entirely for those who have ears
to listen. The sergeant who prefaces any remark with "the
Captain says" is more likely than not indicating to the men
that if they do something contrary to what has been ordered
and the Captain does not catch them the sergeant will not do
much about it. Only a small percentage of the statements expressing ardent enthusiasm for anything military should be

taken seriously. They are meant to impress the right people that protocol is being followed on whatever level.

The military service, particularly the Army, may be viewed as just one vast series of impressions. Everyone is working as hard as possible to impress those immediately above him that he is doing his job in the right way. Yet he is palpably not in many instances—unless inspection time is at hand. Contrary to what one might expect, this system does not lead to excessive inefficiency, because those on top have generally come up through the system and because in most respects the sergeants, who are masters of the system, run the routine affairs of the army anyway. The officer who has not learned these facts or how to cope with this situation has simply not learned how to be an officer. If he is astute he knows the necessity of leaving hands off unless it becomes absolutely necessary to avoid disaster, or to please someone who is checking on *him*. Ultimately all is checked on by the American people, currently symbolized to the Armed Forces by the investigative powers of the Congress and the final authority of the executive branch of the government.

Thus the individual who learns the ropes will be involved day by day in a vast process of dissimulation. He must know the rules of the game, for he cannot afford to be caught, nor can those in charge of him afford to let him get away with breaking the pre-established rules of attitude and behavior as well as performance. But he is emphatically not asked to sell his soul to the organization, and efforts at so asking are themselves part of the vast game. He goes through his day-by-day existence playing the superficial game, meanwhile trying to obtain the best—that is, the easiest and highest-paying—job. The latter is in many cases not even a primary factor, due to routine and scheduled promotions. Indeed, playing the game is a means of alleviating the sheer ennui of daily existence, which would be deadly without the play element. He would continue to play this game regardless of tangible advantages, since it has become part of the way of military life.

Everyday Social Interaction

A final area in our accounting of how the play element is found in contemporary life is the everyday behavior of individuals as they go through the day in ordinary social relationships. There seems to be a tremendous propensity for role playing and for dissimulation in the human makeup, which is closely related to the play factor and which governs much more of normal social interaction than we would be willing to concede.

Shakespeare has said that all of life is a stage and each man plays his seven ages. Who does not find himself adopting many roles during a day? We know that we are obligated by role expectations or that certain reactions are expected of us in specific situations. Despite the possession of an independent mind, we find it impossibly tiring in normal social relations to respond to every new situation one encounters by calculating afresh the fitting response in light of one's conceptions of reality. Thus in many instances one finds oneself living up to the role prescribed or expected of him. In a sense this defeats the person who asks this requirement of conformity, since it illustrates knowledge of one's understanding of what is demanded so well that one is in a position to reject the expectation. Hence in his own secret way, by living up to it, he actually is criticizing it and emerging triumphant over the demands for conformity.

Or one can play many roles more or less unwittingly: The role of the suave sophisticate, the role of the intellectual, the role of the shocked citizen, the role of the person in a big hurry, the role of the busy do-gooder, the role of the person with no time for leisure, the role of a person with deep troubles who is to be pitied. Social role playing is not necessarily the fruit of education, although many intellectuals and college graduates make the mistake of assuming that they alone are capable of doing it best. Woe unto the "city-slicker" who thinks that the hayseed with whom he is dealing in a real-estate transaction is not merely playing the role of the dumb farmer— and loving every minute of it! Some of the slyest (and richest) farmers have been experts at this sort of dissimulation and would pull it off even were it not for the purpose of material gain, for it serves the ends of the game.

It is again a mistake to assume that these roles are indulged in for monetary gain alone. As an accompanying factor, yes; but the real satisfaction is involved in the secret knowledge that the game has been "pulled off." It is basically true that "the play's the thing" in and of itself, with or without the catching of the conscience of the king.

The literature best depicting this spirit of role playing in a most delightful manner is the series of works produced by Stephen Potter—*Gamesmanship, Lifemanship, Supermanship,* and *One-Upmanship.* Far from being merely humorous, they are really comprised of many amazing psychological insights into the human personality and its play patterns, for the spirit of play permeates the whimsical art of gamesmanship.

A specific area where this role playing and all of these imaginative poses and functions comes into focus is the ancient "game of love"—a subject probably more treated than any other in the history of world literature. The poses, the tricks that are played, are in one sense deadly earnest, but in another sense the process of courting prior to marriage involves a vast element of "play." Courtship would be difficult to understand apart from this play perspective. Surely, to alien ears the language of love spoken between a lover and his beloved appears nonsensical. This is a game only two people can play!

We need not dally here in detailing the obvious implications of our analysis for sex behavior. Suffice it to point out that in a provocative piece entitled "Sex as Play" sociologist Nelson N. Foote opined that "the view that sex is fun can . . . hardly be called the invention of immoralists; it is everyman's discovery." [3] Indeed one leading theologian has said that sex is far less important and far more fun than we have ever imagined.

Finally, to shift gears in our thinking, the area of worship and the Church's liturgy may be viewed as a kind of play. If Veblen in his *Theory of the Leisure Class* had viewed what he called the "ceremonial paraphernalia required of any cult" in the light of play, one wonders whether he would have consigned much of liturgy and worship to the doom of "conspicuous waste." The contention that liturgy is a kind of sacred game is best advanced by a Roman Catholic scholar, Romano Guardini. He suggested that prayers, gestures, garments, colors, holy vessels and other ritual forms are "incomprehensible when . . . measured by the objective standard of strict suitability for a purpose." [4] The liturgy, like child's play, is life pouring itself forth without an aim. The liturgy

speaks measuredly and melodiously . . . employs formal, rhythmic gestures . . . is clothed in colours and garments foreign to everyday life. . . . It is in the highest sense the life of a child in which everything is picture, melody, and song. It is a pouring forth of the sacred, God-given life of the soul; it is a kind of holy play in which the soul, with utter abandon learns how to waste time for the sake of God.[5]

To think of worship as a form of play is by no means to reduce it to a theatrical sham—quite the contrary. To view human activity as play from a divine standpoint is certainly not to deprecate such activity. Karl Barth recognizes this in his concept of *das Spiel* (play or sport), which provides a clue to our understanding of the Church's approach to culture:

Not from depreciation of the work of culture, but in highest appreciation of that toward which she sees all cultural work to be

[3] In *Mass Leisure*, edited by Larrabee and Meyersohn, p. 335.
[4] *The Spirit of the Liturgy* (New York: Sheed & Ward, 1937), pp. 95-96.
[5] *Ibid.*, pp. 101-6.

aimed. Not from pessimism, but from boundless hope. Not as a spoil-sport, but knowing that art and science, economics and politics, technology and education are really a sport (*Spiel*), a serious sport (or game) but still a sport; and that means an activity which in the long run does not have its meaning in its own achievable goals, but in what it means to play that much better and more objectively, because one knows the sport to be a reflection, and not the goal of life itself.[6]

In a real sense, man's play reveals that he is a child of God. In the eyes of God, are we not all children at play? Plato recognized this reality when he referred to men as the "playthings of the gods." In the book of Proverbs we find Wisdom saying: "The Lord possessed me in the beginning. . . . I was set up from eternity . . . I was with him forming all things; and was delighted every day, playing before him at all times; playing in the world" (8:22-23, 30-31).

In sum, one fails to understand human society without a profound awareness of the play element. Peter Berger stated it aptly:

One cannot fully grasp the political world unless one understands it as a confidence game, or the stratification system unless one sees its character as a costume party. One cannot achieve a sociological perception of religious institutions unless one recalls how as a child one put on masks and frightened the wits out of one's contemporaries by the simple expedient of saying "boo." [7]

Our survey of the play element has depicted various areas of life in which play persists. We have explored how characteristic a part of life play remains—in the field of sports, in professional and business relationships, in clubs and voluntary associations, in the military, in the roles we assume in daily social

[6] Quoted by Charles West, *Communism and the Theologians* (Philadelphia: The Westminster Press, 1958), p. 209.

[7] *Invitation to Sociology: A Humanistic Perspective* (Garden City, N. Y.: Doubleday & Company, Inc., 1963), p. 165.

interaction, and in the life of worship. In these and in other areas that will be examined subsequently the playful sense of life lives on and lends joy to living. All the pressures of modernity—with persuasive and pervasive mass commercialized appeal—cannot prevail against the stanch spirit of play in *Homo Ludens* (man the player).

Thus far we have looked at one dimension of our subject: The dimension of width. In doing so we have scanned the scope of leisure in America, the problem it raises in contemporary life, its meaning, the new shape of an emerging leisure society. and the pervasiveness of the play element. Now we are prepared to turn to a second dimension—that of depth.

PART TWO

Depth: Leisure in Relation to Play

4
Leisure and the Spirit of Play

As a means of exploring leisure in the dimension of depth we turn now to a further consideration of play—one of the primary manifestations of leisure. The present chapter is conceptual in nature and deals with some of the theoretical issues in delineating the play spirit and the relationship between leisure and play. Such background analysis is necessary if we are to discuss play seriously! Subsequent chapters will focus on more immediate and contemporary concerns.

Representing, as it may, everything on a spectrum from the infant's initial kicking to the terrifying machinations of a Ku Klux Klan rally, the concept of play is extraordinarily difficult to define. Play is often understood as referring specifically to the activities of children in contrast to the serious-minded work of adults, or it can be broadly inclusive in comprehending the nature of man, as in Huizinga's *Homo Ludens* or Schiller's statement that "man only plays when in the full meaning of the word he is a man, and he is perfectly human only when he plays."

The simple word becomes complex when one tries to analyze its varied and numerous meanings. It may be used as a noun or a verb: We can witness a play, but we can also play an instrument, play a game, play fair with the other fellow, play havoc with the state of things, or even play a prank on our neighbor. Perhaps no other word in the English language can be given so many meanings. To one person play may mean the romping and shouting of children in the park; to another, it may mean an afternoon at the races; to a third, it may mean experimentation with a homemade radio set; and to still another person, play is the very highest form of intellectual endeavor as found in literature, science, and art. Perhaps in its own playful way, play eludes precise definition!

Various theories and functions of play have been delineated —for example, the relation of the play spirit to personality growth and development or to the rise of culture and civilization. Play can be analyzed from the perspective of education, of training, or of rehabilitation. It has social functions; a "sociology of games" can be derived. The way a nation plays can suggest the character of its people. What one does in his play when he is free to do what he wishes, as he wishes, and with whom he wishes will reflect the kind of person he is.

Play satisfies human needs; its forms of expression vary with age and with physiological and psychological maturity. It can reflect the values and ideals of a particular cultural group. Our concern in this discussion of leisure and the spirit of play will retain its immediacy if we remember that the play life demands a certain amount of spontaneity, freedom of choice, and naturalness. Without the spirit of play, life and leisure are stripped of their vitality and bouyancy.

The Play Spirit in Relation to Culture

Johan Huizinga and Josef Pieper are two of the most profound students of leisure and the spirit of play. In a brilliant and provocative study of the function of play, Huizinga contends that civilization is, in its earliest phases, played. "Civilization arises and unfolds in and as play . . . genuine, pure play is one of the main bases of civilization." [1] Pieper argues that "culture depends for its very existence on leisure." [2]

These two scholars readily suggest the importance accredited

---

[1] *Homo Ludens* (Boston: Beacon Press, 1950), p. 5.
[2] *Leisure: The Basis of Culture*, p. 19.

to the spirit of play and to the place of leisure in creation and maintenance of culture. In Huizinga's view the "agonistic" (contest) function of play is primary. It reaches an apex of beauty before becoming smothered by techniques of production and the complexities of social organization as civilization increases in technical organization. Competition and contest: These two elements form and stem from the spirit of play. They are basic ingredients of social interaction. As civilization grows more "serious," however, the play element is accorded a secondary place. Competition remains the primary initiating factor of social exchange, but it is now disguised and hidden. What is the basis of the stock-market gambits or the fierce rivalry of Madison Avenue men but this primary spirit of competition?

Pieper's concern is more immediately to aim an angry finger at a world of vacuous activism, sounding at the same time a clarion call. He points to the element of contemplation as essential to civilization and to celebration as the essence of culture. Celebration becomes the basic content of the play spirit for Pieper, as does competition for Huizinga.

Celebration is possible only within a life based on divine worship, for it is this life which signifies the man who is at one with himself and the world. Leisure implies an attitude of calm, of being open to "hearing" the meaning of the universe which surrounds one. Pieper feels that the man whose life and leisure finds its foundations in "culture," specifically in the divine *cultus,* will enjoy this quality. To such a man, celebration of a feast, of the joy of life, implies a union of peace, contemplation, and affirmation of his fundamental accord with the world.

A third theorist who points to the importance of play for the development of culture is Roger Caillois, French sociologist and literary critic. His sociological analysis of culture is based on a study of the games men play. Play "is a parallel, independent activity, opposed to the acts and decisions of ordinary life by special characteristics appropriate to play." [3] Play is parallel to culture in the sense that what is expressed in play is no different from what is expressed in culture.

For Caillois play must be seen primarily as a *social occurrence*. He systematizes games on a spectrum from *paidia,* the free, "spontaneous manifestations of the play instinct," toward *ludus,* the refinement and disciplining of the spirit of play. *Ludus* relates to the primitive desire to find diversion and amusement in arbitrary, perpetually recurrent obstacles.

The classification of games on such a schema may indeed suggest a parallel to the culture: The transition of a social group to civilization as such may imply and be characterized by a change in the type of game—or play spirit—which is given primacy. Caillois contended that:

It is not absurd to try diagnosing a civilization in terms of the games that are especially popular there. In fact, if games are cultural factors and images, it follows that to a certain degree a civilition and its content may be characterized by its games. They necessarily reflect its cultural pattern and provide useful indications as to the preferences, weakness, and strength of a given society at a particular stage of its evolution.[4]

In the transitional process there is a gradual elimination of the predominance of *ilinx* (the desire for vertigo, the love of whirling or dancing about) and *mimicry* (simulation, make-believe) in combination with a subsequent substitution and predominance of the *agon-alea* (competition—chance, fate) pairing. This would suggest levels of cultural advance. Chess and bridge would most likely represent a highly civilized nation or social grouping, whereas a great love for torrid dances and the carnival crush might represent a comparatively lower stage of cultural development.

[3] *Man, Play, and Games* (Chicago: The Free Press of Glencoe, Ill., 1961), p. 63.
[4] *Ibid.,* p. 83.

74

Obvious limitations in this view should be apparent. The society with more free time may not be the more civilized; yet free time may be the objectively necessary prerequisite for development of refinements in the play spirit. A contextual factor must be introduced as well: Is it proper to yank the play spirit out of the cultural setting from whence it derives its meaning? Can the twelfth-century love of the *Chanson de Roland* be equally compared with modern Parisian "slick" love stories? Caillois' suggestions, then, must be viewed as tentative and somewhat too abstractly theoretical. His theory, however, does rightly emphasize that the types of gaming activity which are freely allowed and sponsored by a society provide a clue to understanding the quality of its people's cultural life.

These three analysts, Huizinga, Pieper, and Caillois (Dutch, German, and French), have delineated specific relationships of the play spirit to the development of man's culture. Huizinga's work is probably the most inclusive and broad formulation. Before we survey the reasons for the importance of play for modern man it will be advantageous to seek more precise definitions of play—play *as* leisure and play *in* leisure.

As we proceed, it will be well to remember the central line of thought thus far discussed: Play, as an element of man's leisure, is not a frivolous concern which we are attempting to justify or to elevate with profound expressions. It is important in the history of man's evolving civilization as an agent of culture building, as a means of transmission of cultural norms, mores, and values, and further as an indicator of the parallel social development and civilization which provides the framework in which play occurs.

In this sense, Marshall and Inez McClintock in their massive study *Toys in America* express an incisive understanding of the importance of play and play's artifacts—toys. They suggest that toys might provide insights about our entire society, that the amount of play and the number and nature of toys might reveal a great deal about any stage of history. "The more we learned, and the longer we worked, the more clearly we saw that toys and games were indeed accurate mirrors of the adult world. When grownups worked hard and enjoyed few amusements, children played little and owned few toys." [5] Toys reflect the adult world scaled down to child sizes, and games are "world-building activities." Students of social life use games as working models because they seem to display in a simple way the structure of real life situations. Play, then, is a way of reducing life to its liveliest elements.

The Concept of Play in Relation to Leisure

Webster's new Third International Dictionary requires no less than ninety-five separate entries to define play. As a working definition we may consider human play to be: An activity characteristic of all ages, occurring in a social setting. It is free and has none other than a self-directed aim; it is real only as a self-construct; it is happy, euphoric, rather than sad; it is structured, characterized by rules and regulations; it is meaningful activity.

Let us proceed to examine various aspects of this definition.

1. In contrast to the animal kingdom, *all ages* of humans *play,* whether adult or child. To grasp this is to be able to speak of the pervasiveness of a play spirit and implies rejection of earlier theories which equate play only with the affairs of children. It suggests further that a man never stops playing, although play forms may be modified. Play is an activity that may be expressive, dynamic, and educative for all ages.

2. Play activity occurs in a *social* setting, either directly within a social group or at least within a socially determined environment. As a recent pamphlet title suggests. "You Can't Be Human Alone!" Huizinga has noted that play tends to pro-

[5] *Toys in America* (Washington, D. C.: Public Affairs Press, 1961), p. 5.

mote the formation of social groupings which may surround themselves with secrecy. Play is social in the sense that there is no act without interaction.

3. Play activity is *free*. It is voluntary activity, although the environment may not be freely chosen, as in the case of a playground with its space limitations. No one can force another to play. In this sense, some "recess" provisions or controlled "recreation" must be considered sham or false play. As with leisure, play is an activity which is in itself free, aimless, amusing. There is a delightful quality of spontaneity about play.

4. The *aim* of play does not extend beyond the playing. There is no material-producing purpose. Of course, the view that no material interest is involved can be an overstatement. Note the financial aspects of gambling as incorporating a play element. Hobbies may take on a utilitarian goal. Yet play is essentially an end in itself.

5. Play is *real* within the construction of the play situation. It is real when one says, "Let's play," and it becomes unreal when one says, "Let's stop playing." The reality is self-assigned and self-ranked. "Mary, you play against George and May." Positions have been assigned and the world of the play activity, designated. When the reality of the play situation is absolutized in relation to the reality of the rest of life, then we speak of maladjustment of the society or of the unbalanced person.

6. Usually happy, *euphoric*, play may include a variation of emotions within it. Thus there may be sadness at losing a game or elation at winning; there may be resistance to participation or even dislike of the play form. This allowance for varied emotional response suggests that it is improper to define play simply as pleasurable activity. As Huizinga said, "The play-mood is one of rapture and enthusiasm, and is sacred or festive in accordance with the occasion. A feeling of exaltation and tension accompanies the action, mirth and relaxation follow." [6]

[6] *Op. cit.*, p. 132.

7. Play is *structured* within its own play world. This implies a freedom within bounds, for rules and regulations are necessary, but it does not imply a contradiction to the earlier characteristic that play is free activity. This structuring is necessary for socialization and happens after the to-play-or-not-to-play choice occurs. The structural element may be highly complex, as in chess; it may even come to represent the major factor, and so provide an escape in learning the rules or a flight from boredom. Moreover, as Huizinga points out, there is spatial structuring, whether it be the baseball diamond, the courtroom, or the sanctuary.

8. Play is *meaningful* activity. Play may serve as a possible means of self-expression, mutual enjoyment, release from tension or loneliness, or an attempt to adjust to reality. Some meaning is found—positive or negative—for the person engaged in play.

The definition of leisure must necessarily be broader than that of play. Perhaps it is sufficient to state that real leisure includes play—or that play is a function of leisure. Play occurs *in* leisure time and is significant *as* a leisure expression. Like leisure, play is done for its own sake for sheer enjoyment. Without play the growth of the life of leisure is stunted. August Heckscher reminded us that play is at the heart of life and leisure:

This should not seem strange; indeed it should seem very obvious —except for the fact that a genius for play has been conspicuously absent from modern leisure. This leisure has been marked by entertainment, amusement, and distraction. . . . All this is fine so far as it goes; it is all a part of the way people spend free time when it comes to them in quantity. But it will begin to pall—the hobbies, the travel, the television shows, the spectator and even the participant sports—unless beneath there is a sense that life itself is a kind of game.[7]

[7] *The Public Happiness*, pp. 176-77.

Play, like leisure, is built upon freedom. No matter what else we might say about play, we would acknowledge that it cannot be forced on another person. When a man plays he is doing what he wants to do; in a sense he is being most truly himself. For this reason anthropologists have discovered that one of the best means of examining a culture is through the way people express themselves in their play. Contemporary child therapists use play to discover and remedy certain personality problems of children.

Of necessity play deals with the whole person. As we have seen, leisure may be defined as freedom from some necessary obligation, with the result that leisure itself is oriented in terms of the obligation rather than established in its own right. On the other hand, leisure can be too closely associated with the mind so that it becomes pure contemplation and fails to concern itself with the body or with any physical activity.

With play, however, the situation is different, for play must be seen as requiring activity that absorbs our complete attention. It has its own goals and its own rewards. Although it stimulates the mind as much as it stimulates the body, it stimulates them together as a unity. Thus it allows the whole person to express himself. In play one has the opportunity to think about life and to live it at the same time. Since the interest and attention must be directed upon the play itself, play cannot be seen as having a utilitarian function. Although a psychiatrist might examine and help a child solve certain emotional problems through play therapy, if the child himself should recognize his play as therapy (and thus does not lose himself in his play) the therapeutic function is jeopardized.

Our concept of play should always recognize its totality rather than its isolated elements. We are in trouble when we try to define play by excluding all but one quality. The unity of play is taken from the dynamic concept of the phenomena of play itself.

That play has been used to serve other than its own end, however, is apparent throughout history. With the Roman state, for instance, young children were allowed to play as they pleased, but as soon as the state felt they were old enough they were taught to run, wrestle, and swim and to participate in activities which fitted them for warfare. Play was considered by the Romans as a means of educating for military purposes. In our own time we are familiar with Hitler's "Kraft durch Freude" program, or the "Hitler-Jugend" movement, which has its present-day parallel in the East German "Freie Deutsche Jugend." In this case play is considered as a means to an end because the focus of attention is directed toward the external military objective rather than upon playing itself.

At the other extreme, play can be viewed as purely the expression of exuberance, of an over-flowing enthusiasm for life itself (the *joie-de-vivre* theory). Remember that Huizinga saw the play element as the basis of culture and that Caillois considered games as independent but parallel to man's social order. If culture is the product of play, and if civilization has been enhanced by the play spirit, then it is fair to expect new cultural enrichment, new forms of relatedness, to emerge from the new leisure opportunities in American society.

Shakespeare has made immortal the saying that the theater ("playing," in his language) has as its main end "to hold, as 'twere, the mirror up to nature; to show virtue her own feature, scorn her own image, and the very age and body of the time his form and pressure." [8] Perhaps the play of which we speak is such a mirror to a man's person, reflecting his self-understanding, his ultimate values, his place in relation to others. "As a man playeth, so he is."

The Social Significance of Play

The social element of play has already been introduced in our earlier definition. As no man lives unto himself alone, we

[8] *Hamlet*, Act III, scene 2.

may say as well that no man plays to himself alone. We seek now to examine the special social aspects of groups which exist for play, including the restrictions and pressures that are brought to bear on the individual by the play group. It will also be seen that there is an important function of play in the formation and maintenance of any group. Then we shall explore how man's participation in a social setting influences his play.

1. The process of making and sustaining *rules and sanctions* is characteristic of the play group and thus makes it a source of ethical codes. Without rules there could be no sense of fairness or no repetition of a playform; participation in any given play situation would be anarchic, with little possibility for *all* individuals to participate and to find free self-expression. Caillois has pointed to this element (*ludus*), suggesting that the regulatory element grows in complexity with the maturity of the play group. Rules of relevance and irrelevance indicating the permissible boundaries are necessary for the players.

The rules of the group, then, function socially: (1) To screen out the irrelevant emotions and pressures of the "world outside" the sphere of the game; (2) to provide norms of conduct for the members, which include restrictions as to bringing in emotional concerns from "outside," and which provide sanctions or penalties or allowances for the person who does; (3) to assign role and status within the group; (4) to suggest the attitude of the group toward other similar or dissimilar groups; and (5) to provide standards for an ethical code beyond the immediate confines of the game. Fair play and sportsmanship are feelings developed through play, but have a much wider impact in serving as a model for life outside the game.

2. Activities by a social group may produce a feeling of *cohesiveness or oneness of group spirit*. Erving Goffman noted that,

shared spontaneous involvement in a mutual activity often brings the sharers into some kind of exclusive solidarity and permits them to express relatedness, psychic closeness, and mutual respect; failure to participate with good heart can therefore express rejection of those present or of the setting.[9]

It is this feeling of relatedness or "psychic closeness" which may lead to a partial explanation of the why of man at play. We play with others because we are created social beings. Play is a manifestation of human interdependence.

In the biblical perspective men are created as children of God to become brothers. Thus a major teaching of the Christian church is the emphasis on mankind's oneness in Christ. Of course it may be charged with some justification that there is often more "oneness" at the local softball game than in most churches, not to speak of denominational rivalries. On the other hand, note the element of play in the formal sense within the worship structure. Within the church setting the play spirit may reach lofty heights or it can sink to depths which devalue play. There are many churches which use play as a means of evangelizing. These sports-arena churches are decked out with barbells, tennis courts, and bowling alleys to "bring youth to Christ,"—what one wit has called the "basketballization of the church."

Games have a social significance and a great part of their pleasure—beyond satisfaction of personal motives—derives from the social feeling which they generate. Members who fail to contribute to group consciousness and that "friendly group feeling" may be cast out from the play group.

3. A third aspect of social play groups is the *relationship of the individual to the group*. We have noted that a person may be excluded from the group if he does not affirm the rules of the game, if he "floods out" in Goffman's terms. The group re-

[9] *Encounters: Two Studies in the Sociology of Interaction* (Indianapolis: The Bobbs-Merrill Company, Inc., 1961), p. 40.

stricts the deviant individual from participation in its activities, builds channels around his obstructing influence (such as referring to him in the third person or relegating him to menial tasks), or ignores him completely.

Ordinarily an extremely close relationship exists between the individual and the group—especially in primary groups, which most play groups represent. A great deal of interpersonal interaction and mutual stimulation takes place. The individual identifies with his group—"I'm a Silver Beaver," et cetera. The person and the group are individual and collective aspects of the same thing. In view of this close identification, the individual may grow in stature or maturity or status as the group does. So, too, the person may acquire the group's code of conduct and living standards. Ideals and standards of the play group may replace or supplant those of the home. We are all familiar with this pattern of conduct in children—"But, Mom, Silver Beavers don't have to wash their faces!"

Another facet of the individual's relation to the group is seen in what is known as crowd or collective behavior. Some of the characteristics of the crowd apply to the primary play group, and, of course, most of them apply to larger units or spectator audiences. Fads and crazes, devotion to popular political and religious leaders, fan clubs, and resistance-to-change groups may also share some of the aspects of crowd behavior. These behavior patterns include emotionalism, excitability, loyalty galvanized around a leader, and the release of impulses that are ordinarily held in check. In the contagion of crowd excitement the individual may lose his critical faculties and be swayed by objectives and standards set by the mass.

4. Finally, play has been socially significant in another sense in recent American life. It has provided a primary avenue for minority racial groups to *improve* their *social status*. The tremendous stride toward equality and opportunity in the enter-

tainment and athletic fields by racial minorities is not an end in itself but surely a by-product or an unintended result of play.

Recall that it was only in April, 1947, that Jackie Robinson became the first Negro to break into major league baseball. Important as the breaking of the barrier was, perhaps even more socially significant was the way in which Negro athletes subsequently became heroes on the basis of their skills. Think of the implications for racial acceptance when card pictures of stars such as Robinson, Roy Campanella, Willie Mays, Tommy Davis, and Maury Wills were being coveted and freely traded by card-carrying youngsters across the nation.

Vast improvements and progress toward inclusiveness in the sporting and entertainment industries have doubtless contributed to the reduction of racial inequality and prejudice in other areas of American life. Of course, this consequence was not a direct objective of play, but rather a latent function. Thus the leisure sphere has had an impact upon the stratification system of American society.

The Functions of Human Play

We have seen that the phenomenon of human play is complex. *Homo sapiens* plays in many different ways and for many different reasons. Play may be the elevation of the human spirit to the free sharing of itself with others in community, the free expression of one person before God, or the tortuous and confused conformity to the mass recreation market. Play may represent a man's attempt at self-expression or the pressure of a group to find meaning in interaction. It may occur as the response to physiological needs or to mental drudgery and boredom.

Just why man plays is indeed a complex question. A slightly easier question to analyze, and one which may provide clues to the motives for play, is to find the functions that play fulfills for the individual and for society. To a discussion of these functions we shall now turn.

1. Man plays for *self-expression* and *communication*. In play he may express natural ebullience and joy which is closely channeled and restricted in the normal course of life. He may also find in play the opportunity to "vent" either harmless or unhealthy emotions. This cathartic element was recognized even in Aristotle's time and is a major tenet of the current psychoanalytical understanding of play's functioning.

In play man may communicate for the sheer joy of sharing ideas with others, of doing things with others, of being with others. In so far as he is able to maintain his own self-identity as opposed to being submerged in the mass identity of the group, and to the extent that this participation is healthy or that he grows in his own self-understanding, we must see this function as extremely positive. It is a reflection of man's nature that he has been created a social being.

2. Man also plays for the *sheer joy* of play itself. The euphoric part of life is its highest form, in so far as it takes place within a context of concern and respect for others and for issues of social significance. The sheer indulgence of the individual in pursuits which only tend to separate him from his fellow men and to enhance his own selfish aims at the expense of the public interest must be rejected from a Christian perspective. But to see the natural desire for happiness as part of God-given human nature is to understand the spirit of the biblical writer who said:

A cheerful heart is a good medicine,
    but a downcast spirit dries up the bones. (Prov. 17:22.)

Joy in life itself, joy in beauty, joy in creativity and in social communion—these must rank for the Christian as fruits of the spirit. At the same time there is implied a responsibility that our efforts be directed toward assuring that same happiness for others. Our own national forefathers were so taken with the rationalistic ideals of the right for every man to have this happiness that they included the "pursuit of happiness" in the major founding document of our nation. Our modern interpretation of this statement tends to be less naturalistic and somewhat more realistic; yet the ideal of the American nation has always been and should always continue to be to express the belief that every man has the right, the sacred right, to find happiness and joy in this world. Our play must express this joy. When the "natural" joy of life bows and gives way to the conformity of a civilization that is solely economically or materialistically minded, then men must reaffirm their basic right to the "pursuit of happiness."

3. Play no doubt provides many people with a *security* that they fail to find in the rest of life. For others it may be an *escape from reality,* a flight to fantasy. To the extent that this is a universal phenomenon, it probably is not extremely dangerous. Our concern must be aroused when this is the sole reason that men play. The psychotic, the sports bum, whose entire way of life revolves around what is done in this escape from reality, however, must be the concern of a sane society which considers the total aspects of life as important for personality maturity.

Play also serves as a *substitute for work satisfaction.* It forms the best redress against the routine and monotony of life and work in a compartmentalized and fragmented industrial civilization. It gives the worker a sense of adventure which has disappeared from his working life. Competition may be disappearing from the worker's job, but in play and sports it lives on in full blast.

4. Play functions further in giving expression to the *desire for community* and relationship with other humans. Nothing seems to arouse and unite a community in a feeling of identity

like a successful sports team.[10] It is quite an experience to be in a city—other than New York, for obvious reasons—whose team has just won a World Series.

The quest for community is perennial and play groups help to satisfy this longing. Man has a desire to act in concert with others, to find in the group an expression of his own personality, to be part of a "community of experience," and to enjoy the mutuality of the situation. How natural and customary it is for persons to share in festive occasions, such as New Year's Eve, in group settings!

Group experience can be corruptive, but it can also be one of the noblest forms of the play spirit. The individual does not play alone but within social settings, whether this takes the form of the immediate play group or the total social configuration. So adult men and women—not just children and adolescents—play in groups; they attend social meetings and play social games; they play at pursuits which are socially oriented. Even in gardening in one's own backyard, it is almost impossible to escape the influence of the Joneses, whose "corn grew three feet last week, Harry!" As poor Harry wonders which fertilizer he has forgotten, he may also ponder whether his supposedly solitary preoccupation is just that at all.

When the social aspects of play lead to a denial of a person's ability to express his own individuality, then it must be suspect. In so far as persons are unable to enjoy authentic communication with others except through the medium of a play situation, modern drives and directions must be re-examined. Irving Crespi has written an interesting article on "The Social Significance of Card Playing." He notes that card playing is a group phenomenon, expressive of the natural urge to do things with others rather than a manifestation of social disorder. Grespi suggests that once we get beneath the moralistic overtones of

[10] In this connection, a study of the impact of the Green Bay Packers professional football team or of the Milwaukee Braves baseball team upon their respective cities would be most revealing.

card playing we can see that its prevalence reflects not moral degeneracy but the struggle of primary groups to maintain their viability in contemporary mass society in which human relations become fragmented and personal contacts become fleeting and superficial. At the same time, however, he notes the restrictive nature of this activity: "Eager for friendliness and easy congeniality, many Americans appear to be incapable of generating such relationships (closeness in primary groups) without the artificial stimulation of impersonal, competitive group games." [11]

In so far as play is an important feature of our humanity, therefore, it must be our constant concern to develop a perspective of play which will allow for the continued possibility for individual freedom and uniqueness while at the same time allowing for the genuine fellowship of the play group.

5. Play functions further to bring men a sense of *wholeness in freedom*. Both of these concepts—wholeness and freedom—have been touched on earlier. Perhaps, however, we are prone to forget the fact that freedom is a moral issue, that the possibilities for men to become their real selves in wholeness of life is a moral commitment of the Christian.

Of the many writings by Alexander Reid Martin during his service as Chairman of the "Committee on Leisure Time and Its Uses" of the American Psychiatric Association doubtless the most distinctive feature has been his recurrent emphasis on the need for a holistic approach to life. Leisure is not something that occurs on the fringes of consciousness; man's play is a reflection of his total personality, and the abortive extremes of behavior which we see in mentally ill persons often represent just one element of normal life which has become corrupted and dominating.

The immediate implication of Martin's work and the work

[11] *American Sociological Review* (December, 1956), 21, 721.

of recreationists and experts in the use and management of time within the perspective of a man's total life and personality is that future planning for leisure and for the play activity of man will include such a total view of personality. In its theological understanding the churches have pointed toward a holistic concept of man and human personality. In this perspective play will be viewed as a natural and good part of man's life, not to be lightly valued or entered into without adequate preparation during the formative years.

The moral dimensions of the situation are readily apparent. A conference sponsored by the Jewish Theological Seminary in America on the "Problems and Challenges of the New Leisure" makes this point clearly: "To be aware that there *is* a moral factor involved in the choices one makes in his personal freedom is itself the first moral responsibility in man's use of his leisure time." The moral factor includes the awareness of the purposiveness of life and that one should discriminate between those pursuits which benefit oneself and help others gain personal value and those which do not, but tend instead to devalue the human individual and to elevate one group or person at the expense of others.

The writers of the conference working paper suggest, further the moral obligation involved in pointing toward creative opportunities available in individual pursuits, in helping to shape new structures and relationships in the communities where men live. One fulfills the moral principle of giving of himself to the useful occupations of society, leaving the world a better place for his neighbors and his family than he found it. As for himself, to develop fully his own unique and inherent resources is the greatest single act of individual freedom. In this common quest leisure and the spirit of play are united.

As in many other areas of modern life, Walter Rauschenbusch, one of the great leaders of the Social Gospel movement in America, had a prophetic awareness of play, when he wrote:

The real joy of Life is in its play. Play is anything we do for the joy and love of doing it, apart from any profit, compulsion, or sense of duty. It is the real living of life with the feeling of freedom and self-expression. Play is the business of childhood, and its continuation in later years is the prolongation of youth. Real civilization should increase the margin of time given to play.[12]

In the chapters that follow we shall seek to explore play as the "business of childhood," and then turn to some tragic uses of play among delinquent youth.

[12] *Christianizing the Social Order* (New York: The Macmillan Company, 1912), p. 248.

5

Children at Play

Since leisure time is, in a sense, play time, the wonderful world of children's play can shed considerable light upon leisure. Childhood play is a laboratory for learning and a seed-bed for growth. In a sense childhood *is* playhood. Play is the peculiar prerogative of children, as play activities occupy the greater part of the youngster's life.

It has been estimated that the child has about 8,700 hours at his disposal annually. Approximately 3,000 of these hours he uses for sleep, and another 1,000 for eating, dressing, and caring for other necessities. This leaves over 3,500 hours for the pursuit of play. Within this enormously large frame of available time, the child has innumerable opportunities for leisure-time activities.

Childhood is the ideal time for enjoyment, for spontaneous play and fun. The American prototype of the playful child is portrayed in the classical figures of Tom Sawyer and Huckleberry Finn, who have uncommon resources for enjoying the pleasures and amusements of the moment. Yet many adults tend to think of the activities of children as trivial in meaning and unessential in nature—"kid-stuff" a phase to pass through before the child can develop sufficiently or settle down to undertake the really serious matters of life. The view that childhood play is nonsense makes sense itself only in the context of a society so dominated by a work ethos that non-work, even on the part of little children, needs some form of justification or rationalization.

Far from being a waste of time, play to the young child is his business of living and is as serious and necessary for him as are the preoccupations of adults. As the basis of life for the child, play assumes a dimension of reality that is quite spontaneous. Of course children cannot be expected to articulate the significance of play, as evidenced by their typical reply to that perennial parental question: "What did you do outside?" "Nothing."

Efforts to locate the exact borderline between fantasy and reality in the play life of a growing child are usually doomed to failure. Fantasy and reality run together in one big whirl that is a game world. Woe unto the parent who intrudes into the play life of his children with his rationalistic adult standards of reality. Small wonder that the literalist finds it difficult to appreciate the innocence and freshness of the make-believe play world as it comes to children.

A little child may trot downstairs for breakfast acting like a puppy, suddenly change into a menacing "Mighty Mouse" as he tears outdoors, where he successively becomes an Indian, a robber, a truck driver, a storekeeper, and a "Big Bad Wolf" during the day. When bedtime comes he zooms upstairs as an airplane —propelled perhaps by the heavy sigh of relief heaved by his parents!

My four-year-old daughter comes to me with a toy camera devoid of film and pleads, "Daddy, pretend there's film in here so I can take your picture." When I answer, "Naw, there's no film in there," she cries, "No, No, pretend there is." As I comply with her wish, she proceeds to snap my picture and then breaks out with a broad, contented grin, for I have entered into her world of reality. On another occasion the children are "playing ghost." They know the "ghost" is three-year-old Marcus, for they have seen him drape the sheet around himself. But as he advances toward them they all squeal and scream

92

with terror and delight. Children play their improvised parts with complete sincerity.

Play functions in a diversity of ways in the child's development. It may serve as a learning process, as a means of communication with others, or as a way of expressing the developing self-hood of the child. The child orients himself to his world and learns his role identification through play. Play is a means of experimentation with the outside world and a stage for the development of skills. Sheer joy may be expressed in play; emotional discharge is characteristic of the free play of children, as it may be for their adult mentors. In play a child attains status on the basis of his own capabilities and social adjustment; he attains a ranking as a good or poor sport, a good or poor playmate.

Play as Learning

Play is important to the child at each age. To begin with an infant's play centers on his own body. He discovers his hands, nose, ears, and toes, much to the delightful coaxing of parents. He likes to suck, to be petted and stroked. By repetition the child explores sensual perceptions, kinesthetic sensations, and vocalizations. He is busy learning the processes of life by which he will relate to self and society. In a sense the child virtually learns his first lessons of life in his *playpen*. These learning processes discovered through play prepare him for the future.

The kitten plays with a ball and will later chase a mouse in much the same way. So the child who in touching, tasting, and testing, is learning ways of relating to his body, his environment, and his family setting from the earliest moments of self-consciousness. He learns that his coo is more positively appreciated than his cry, though he soon perceives that the cry brings a faster—and ofttimes a frantic—response. He learns that his toes hurt when pinched, that certain behavior patterns almost automatically bring on an adult frown of disapproval. These learning experiences are largely a result of his play activity.

Erik Erikson has suggested that in play the adult steps sideward into another reality, whereas the playing child advances forward to new stages of mastery.[1] He learns to master new things; first his body, next toys, then people, his own fears and feelings, the world about him, et cetera. He learns new skills; in playing with sand, picking up rocks, and wading in water he has the opportunity to explore, to imagine, to learn. With each passing year the horizons broaden as new skills are mastered. This sense of mastery contributes to his total growth in an emotional, physical, intellectual, and spiritual sense.

Since studies of childhood play reveal that children derive their greatest satisfaction from experiences of mastery and control, it would seem that Reuel Denney makes a good point when he contends that adults might well take a leaf from the notebook of childhood play. Our dissatisfactions with contemporary leisure in the typical responses of anxiety, boredom, conformity, and dilettantism might be considerably relieved if we would face squarely the problem of sheer competence—"if we enabled people to become more workmanlike and at the same time more imaginative players." [2] As with children, it would do well for adults to have a sense of mastery over some one thing—however small—from which they could derive sheer joy and satisfaction.

For the growing child, the development of physical control and mastery of the body is a very important element in achieving a spirit of self-reliance and personal competence. A child learning to walk on wobbly legs is constantly in danger of

[1] *Childhood and Society* (New York: W. W. Norton & Company, Inc., 1950), pp. 195-96. In this extremely helpful book Erikson also suggests there are eight stages in the life of a growing child: Trust vs. Basic Mistrust, Autonomy vs. Shame and Doubt, Initiative vs. Guilt, Industry vs. Inferiority, Identity vs. Role Diffusion, Intimacy vs. Isolation, Generativity vs. Stagnation, and Ego Integrity vs. Despair. The play element is significant in each of these developmental stages.

[2] *The Astonished Muse* (Chicago: University of Chicago Press, 1957), p. 16.

falling until he masters the task of standing upright. Later he finds great glee in circus clowns who obligingly fall all over the place and remind him that there are big people who are even wobblier.

The importance of play in the *physical* growth of the child would seem to be obvious. In order to insure this growth, he must have freedom to run and climb and pound; he must be free to develop his muscles and to release his pent-up energy, which every healthy child has in such superabundance. Today, however, especially in the restricted and congested living quarters so common to crowded city centers, conscious provision for physically active play must be made. Thus where parks and recreational centers are not available, city streets are frequently closed to traffic and designated as "play streets."

There is, of course, a close relationship between the meeting of the child's needs for motor activity and his emotional health. Parents and teachers have observed children's moods changing drastically with opportunity for play, whereby states of tension and fatigue were relieved, anxiety and depression were diminished, and violent emotions such as hatred and anger were reduced.[3]

Through play the child can learn to handle emotional drives which are acted out or channeled rather than repressed. An example of this safety valve function of play is the feeling of aggression, which hopefully may be later channeled toward the solution of problems, rather than in attacks upon persons. Aggression can be channeled into doll play or hammering and sewing, while hostile feelings can be dispelled through pounding on clay, a punching bag, or father and mother dolls. Thus play may serve the purpose of draining off aggression and hostility and keeping them within manageable proportions.

The significance of childhood play is in the learning process that grows out of it. Through play a child learns by creating

[3] Cf. Mary O'Neil Hawkins, "Exercise and Emotional Stability," *Child Study* (Spring, 1955), pp. 7-10.

model situations to deal with his experiences.[4] Learning is the concomitant of play and leisure for the growing child. In the midst of his play the child is shaping his ideas of reality and learning how to cope with his ever enlarging relationships and responsibilities. By doing, achieving, trying, failing, succeeding, he is learning and growing through play.

Play as Relating Self to World

Play is a means whereby the child apprehends reality and comes to know the world. In the process of achieving a measure of autonomy the young child learns to know himself and his own abilities. He begins to relate to the world around him, and play is important in enhancing this process.

Through play the child is engaged, not only in self-expression, but also in self-discovery. He explores and experiments with sensations, movements, and relationships through which he develops self-understanding and forms his own concepts of the world.[5] A profound sense of mastery and adequacy is gained when the child is able to say, "I can feed myself. I can dress myself. I can jump off the curb. I know where Mommy keeps the coffee pot."

Play enables the child to make emotional and social adjustments. When he achieves some degree of autonomy the child is ready for and eager to have playmates. He should not be forced to share before he has had a chance to feel secure in his ownership, but he should have the opportunity to discover that many play enterprises require the co-operation of two or more. Besides he will soon discover that it is more fun to play house or store, or Mommy and Daddy with play companions.

The child needs the experience of working out in play the clashing of wills among his peers and the real encounter of playful mutuality. He can only learn the meaning of giving

---

[4] Erikson, *op. cit.*, p. 195.

[5] Ruth E. Hartley, Lawrence K. Frank, Robert M. Godlenson, *Understanding Children's Play* (New York: Columbia University Press, 1952), p. ix.

and sharing as he acts it out in his play. When his peers recognize his leadership and share with him, his own feelings of well-being are heightened. His own right of possession should be acknowledged as well as the need for sharing on a mutual basis. At perhaps no other time does play have a greater contribution to make to the enlargement of the child's world and to his growing ability to deal with himself in his world.

In relating the self to the world, play serves as a vehicle of communication. Play offers the child direct, nonverbal communicative possibilities. It provides a middle ground between inarticulate impressions and the structured language of adult conversation. Through play the child may express his self-concept and his appreciation or rejection of the world outside himself. There is an idiomatic quality in children's play which is often overlooked by adults. The child assigns reality to his play objects and may regard them in an animistic fashion. Play objects and situations often stand in for the real world of his sensory and emotional experiences. In dramatic play, for instance, the child is given an opportunity:

to imitate adults and other children;
to play out real life roles in an intensive and (to the child) real manner;
to reflect relationships and experiences as these are comfortable or threatening to him;
to express pressing desires, motivations, and needs;
to release unacceptable impulses through acceptable channels;
to reverse roles usually taken and to experiment with possible projected roles;
to mirror growth and to provide means for growth—physical, emotional, individual, and social;
to work out problems, experimenting with new, unique, and personal solutions.[6]

[6] *Ibid.*, pp. 27-28.

97

A great deal of reality, as the child confronts it, is not only meaningless, but also may be threatening and forbidding. In play the child scales the world around him down to simpler patterns. He reduces the bewildering complexities of the world to dimensions that he can readily grasp. As he grows and is able to cope more adequately with this world, his play activities gradually fuse with the adult's world of reality. Much of his play is an imitation or adaptation of events in his own life— his home, his father's work, dressing up, cooking, Sunday school, Christmas celebrations, birthday parties, the circus, et cetera. In playmaking the child tries on the roles of others. He rehearses his possible future roles as he becomes the cowboy, milkman, fireman, doctor, storekeeper, father. He is thus recreating and striving to clarify for himself the world of grown-up people.

Of course there are many bruises in the process of growing up—not only from physical falls, but also from fears and insecurity in encounter with his parents and others in his expanding world. Much of the child's play is quite naturally self-therapeutic. Erik Erikson said the child uses play, especially solitary play, "to make up for defeats, sufferings, and frustrations, especially those resulting from a technically and culturally limited use of language." [7] Much of this adjustment the child makes quite naturally if given a certain amount of freedom in his play. However, understanding adults can assist him in working out his feelings through the play process. Observing parents, teachers, and therapists are finding in children's play the language through which the child is communicating his inmost feelings and needs. This enables them to help the child work out his conflicts while they are still in process.

In his book *Psychotherapy with Children,* Clark E. Moustakas of the Merrill-Palmer School in Detroit details many verbatim case records of play therapy with both "normal" and disturbed

[7] "Studies in the Interpretation of Play," *Genetic Psychology Monographs* (1940), 22, 561.

children.[8] Play therapy provides an opportunity for a child to enter into a personal relationship with the adult therapist in a playroom situation where the child is absolutely free to express himself. Knowing that the therapist will accept him, the child does exactly what he wants, gives free reign to his imagination and dreams, and explores his innermost feelings about himself and others in the context of play.

The child is free to project his feelings and attitudes, his aggressions and hostilities onto the numerous toys and play equipment scattered about the play room.[9] Dorothy Baruch described a playroom as a place where fantasies that had brought dread and confusion can be looked at and whittled down to manageable size, where events that have been distorted by disappointment or by misapprehension, fear, and fantasy can be depicted and dramatized.[10]

Children reveal themselves as they play out their feelings. We may find that a "well-behaved, clean, quiet" child, when given his choice, plays with a box of soldiers armed for bloodshed with bayonets, machine guns, and canons. Through play he reveals his inner thoughts and suppressed emotions of hostility and fighting, resentment and anger. Children are helped by playing out their feelings in the same way that adults "feel better" in talking out their frustrations and anxieties.

In the therapeutic setting of the playroom normal children tend to express themselves more freely and spontaneously, whereas the disturbed child is more apt to be devious, indirect, and suspicious. The normal child is happy in his play, finding numerous attractive objects in the playroom from which to choose. He too may find the play-therapy setting a vehicle for playing out the minor tensions and frustrations that accumulate in the course of daily living.

[8] New York: Harper & Brothers, 1959, p. 41.
[9] The discovery that toys are conducive to learning has been one of the principal reasons for the spectacular boom in U. S. toy sales, which now amounts to $1,500,000,000 a year, as compared to $30,000,000 fifty years ago.
[10] One Little Boy (New York: Julian Press, Inc., 1952), p. 10.

A frequent, though temporary, crisis in the life of many families is the arrival of a new baby. Although an occasion for joy, and despite much advance preparation, the older child or children may feel displaced or rejected and show signs of hostility or begin to regress. Through a series of play interviews the aggrieved child is enabled to express his negative feelings, channel his hostilities, and work out (or better, play out) his temporary conflicts. Hence the possibility that these feelings will be repressed, distorted, or eventually cause serious damage to the child's sense of self is removed. Play therapy becomes a means of self-discovery and of relating the self to the realities of the world.

Another experience not uncommon in family living is hospital confinement. Many children have difficulty mastering the anxieties brought on by hospitalization. In addition to separation from parents and familiar home surroundings, the child must face the strange, brisk, uniformed, mechanized world of the hospital.

A study conducted by Florence Erickson provides some insights into understanding these anxieties.[11] She held play interviews with twenty-two four-year-old children who had been hospitalized in an attempt to learn the meaning which intrusive procedures had for them and their methods for coping with these feelings. Several interviews were conducted with each child, both in the hospital and after they returned home. Part of the procedure was to give them a choice of toys to play with, including medical instruments such as thermometers and hypodermic needles which had been used in their hospital care. They were also provided with dolls which represented doctors, nurses, patients, parents, and children.

At first these children showed a readiness, almost a compulsion, to repeat over and over those procedures to which they

[11] *Play Interviews for Four-Year-Old Hospitalized Children* (Lafayette, Ind.: Child Development Publications, Society for Research in Child Development, Inc., Purdue University, 1958).

had been subjected in the hospital. The actions of the children toward the adult dolls showed clearly that they considered the intrusive procedures as being hostile or harmful in intent. Within the context of a warm positive relationship with the nurse who was holding the interviews, the children were able to communicate to her their feelings about what had happened to them in playing with the materials at hand. Through such play they were able to master their feelings against hospital treatment. After several interviews their play became less compulsive, for they were able to be active rather than helplessly passive. The children could verbalize their feelings in their play and thus were better able to relate to life crises.

The child who has both physical and emotional health has developed spiritually as well and has the foundation upon which future spiritual development may take place. In his own way he is asking the basic questions of human existence: Who am I? What am I like? Am I loved? Who are you? How do I relate to you? Can I trust you? What is the world like? Where do I fit in?

In the child's early developmental tasks he is finding answers, albeit gropingly, to questions his world poses for him. If he finds reason for a basic trust in life, he is laying the basis for satisfactory interpersonal relationships, both with others and with God. He has discovered that he is loved, that he has worth, and that he can trust and love others in turn. He continues to feel basic trust or distrust as he lives in the world of play, as he is loved for what he is and must accomplish in his developmental tasks, and as his needs for broadening contacts with his world are met. Through play a child comes to know his expanding world and how better to relate to it.

Freedom and Play

To develop initiative and physical and mental growth the child needs the stimulus of free creative play. Playing freely in a setting of security and acceptance, he may deal better with his own frustrations, may express his developing personhood, and may try on various roles that will guide his further socialization. Not only is play a means of self-discovery and discovery of the world, but it is also supremely the free activity that brings him psychic equilibrium in the early years.

Children should be given much freedom to play, but adults may have a helping hand in contributing to the optimum growth of the child through play. The mother who said of her five-year-old, "William is just so busy with his trucking business that he scarcely has time for anything else," showed a sympathetic understanding of the meaning of this play enterprise for her son.

Adults may help children by seeing that they have adequate materials which are designed to stimulate a variety of play—dramatic play, social play, creative play, manipulative and constructive play, and active physical play. Paints, clays, dolls, blocks, tools, wood, games, toys, and books do not constitute play itself, but they are the materials which children may use for play purposes. Common materials of water, sand, dirt, space, and time must not be overlooked. Perhaps most important is the atmosphere in which a child plays. Adults should show an understanding of children at play, respect the anger which may be expressed through play, as in dashing a bridge in the middle of construction, and appreciate the joy felt by a child in completely covering a piece of paper with red paint—without exclaiming, "And you think you can paint!"

Playing with children is a means of teaching and communicating that spans the age gap. A child's play may greatly aid the adult in understanding his needs and possibilities. Play is an important avenue by which adults can increase their insight into what children are feeling and how they are interpreting the situations they meet in life. Thus it is not surprising to hear the theologian Emil Brunner say that "play is the oil which makes the wheel of life turn less feverishly, and of all play the best is play with children; they are our best teachers in this respect." [12]

There is always an element of adult guidance in play. The child may play during certain hours, for instance. Adult guidance reached a high point in the recreation movement during the first half of this century, and many influences of this spirit are still with us. Yet we must remember that play does not submit fully to being institutionalized. Play must not be captured by adults for the utilitarian end of child rearing, for play functions most effectively in the moments of release from adult guidance.

Controlled and restrictive guidance of all children's play by adults may so channelize the activities of the growing child that he never faces the decision of what to do by himself. This may encourage a lack of interest in self-discovery or experimentation and lead to a strengthening of the passivity which leaves the child ill-equipped to meet the challenges and demands of life.

The free, spontaneous romping and joy, the noisy delights that one hears in a schoolyard filled with children during recess perhaps best symbolize children at play. Romano Guardini has captured the beauty and spirit of the child's play in his assertion that the significance of play lies:

. . . in the unchecked revelation of this youthful life in thought and words and movements and actions, in the capture and expression of its nature, and in the fact of its existence. . . . And because it does not aim at anything in particular, because it streams unbroken and spontaneously forth, its utterance will be harmonious, its form clear and fine; its expression will of itself become picture and dance, rhyme, melody and song. That is what play means: it is life pouring itself forth without an aim, seizing upon riches from its own abundant store, significant through the fact of its existence. It will be beautiful, too, if it is left to itself, and if no futile advice and

---

[12] Emil Brunner, *The Divine Imperative*, translated by Olive Wyon (Philadelphia: The Westminster Press, 1947), p. 390.

pedagogic attempts at enlightenment foist upon it a host of aims and purposes, thus denaturising it.[13]

Failure to encourage the freedom and unchanneled gaity of play may result in loss of creativity in the later years. If the child is not free to apply in his own unique and personal play life the principles that he learns, we can hardly expect him to work out independently complex ethical and religious principles when he passes beyond the childhood stage. The teen-ager who has become accustomed to having someone constantly tell him what he may or may not do in the classroom, on the sports field, at the pool, and in the crafts class will look only a bit more confused if he is left alone to make ethical decisions for himself.

Regimenting a youngster's play by keeping him busy doing something not only hampers personal decision making, but also renders him incapable of being left alone. Hence a child who finds himself alone in a room will first turn on the radio loud, for this detracts from his feeling of being alone. When left on their own children who have been under constant surveillance tend to fall into indolent idleness. Too much regimentation kills the spirit of play. Freedom to play enhances the development of *self-regulated* persons in later life. As plays the child, so lives the adult!

If we as a people are able to instill into our children the attitudes that lead to full and creative uses of leisure time our concern must be less with scheduling and timing than with providing the impetus for free, imaginative, and creative uses of this time. Childhood play is a means of attaining and expressing growth and maturity. It is a time when the creative impulses of the child must be reinforced and given primary value.

Failure to do this, and instead to elect the easier function of rigid scheduling and patterning of play to the standards of the group because it is more convenient to work with, may lead us rather quickly into the play nursery of Aldous Huxley's

---

[13] *The Spirit of the Liturgy*, pp. 179-80.

Brave New World. Here aseptic nurses roll in dumbwaiters each with four tiers of wire-netted shelves containing eight-month-old babies. The children are placed on the floor between rows of roses and brightly colored books. When they approach these, sirens blow, alarms ring, and they receive a sharp electrical shock from the floor. The second time they are exposed to the flowers and books they retreat and recoil screaming. "They'll be safe from books and botany all their lives," comments the educator-director. After all, "a love of nature keeps no factories busy."

At a time when it seems in vogue to turn to early childhood experiences for a clue to problems that crop up in later life, it is appropriate to ask whether our capacity for leisure or play has been helped or hindered by our own childhood experiences. Do we look upon children at play as so much silly business? Or can parents view the play of their progeny as an occasion for learning, for relating the growing self to the world, and for the expression of freedom and creativity?

Of course the growth that comes through play in childhood need not terminate with this period of life. It is never too late to acquire fresh knowledge and new skills and interests, to develop and deepen in new directions. The spirit of learning and of self-discovery is an open-ended, perennial process that provides renewal of the mind, body, and spirit. This is the essence of leisure, both for young and old alike.

6

Play and Delinquency:
The Tragic Use of Leisure

Juvenile delinquency is one of the tragic consequences frequently attributed to the new leisure society. Increased leisure time, so it is charged, is responsible for the alarming rise in juvenile delinquency rates. In earlier times young people commonly went to work as soon as they were physically mature, or even earlier.[1] Modern youth, however, have a lengthened period of education and enter later into the working force. In a sense, our economy of abundance no longer needs the labor of youth. This fact has given rise to the supposition that idle hands lead to temptation. As the children's song goes: "Busy hands are happy hands; hands that cannot go wrong."

Care must be taken not to correlate delinquency and leisure in any automatic or inevitable sense. Even an astute observer such as Frederic Thrasher commits this fallacy in his well-known book *The Gang,* when he contends that "The problem of dealing with the boy can be stated very largely in terms of his leisure hours. . . . The boy with time on his hands, especially in a crowded or slum environment, is almost predestined to the life of the gang." [2]

At the outset we must clarify what delinquency is: Taken in its legal sense a juvenile delinquent refers to a young person

[1] In 1900 one out of every five boys between the ages of 10 to 14 were in the labor force.

[2] Chicago: University of Chicago Press, 1927, p. 79.

106

who has violated a law *and* has been legally apprehended or tried in court. These violations run the gamut from harmless pranks of playful youngsters to gang violence that have all the trappings of armed warfare. Viewed strictly in the legal sense, delinquency affects only a small section of our youth—some 3 or 4 per cent. The problem cannot be minimized, however, and we cannot lightly dismiss the fact that this includes more than 500,000 young people who are wards of our juvenile courts and more than 1,750,000 who were arrested in 1962 by the police. Moreover, juvenile delinquency rates have steadily risen in these post-World War II years, not only in numbers but also in the gravity, violence, and brutality of the offenses. Indeed, the secretary of Health, Education, and Welfare estimates that if present trends continue 3-4,000,000 juvenile offenders will come before the courts in the next decade.

It may be true that some youngsters misuse their free time in tragic ways—gang rumbles, playing "chicken" in hot rods, or experimentation with narcotics. In an early study on *Delinquency and Spare Time,* Henry W. Thurston argues that 75 per cent of the delinquents studied developed their behavioral difficulties through the habitual misuse of leisure time.[3] In view of the dubious methods which informed this study, however, one must be cautious in accepting its conclusions uncritically.

To pin the blame for delinquency simply on leisure would be a gross oversimplification. Our concern in this chapter is not to search for causes.[4] Anyone acquainted with the field knows that the roots of delinquency are complex and multiple, that any simple or single causal explanation is likely to be misleading.

Granted the welter of reasons underlying delinquency causa-

[3] Cleveland: Cleveland Recreational Survey, 1918, pp. 105-18.

[4] For my own analysis of juvenile delinquency causation, see "Delinquent Youth in a Normless Time," *The Christian Century* (December 5, 1962), 1475-1478.

tion, we wish to deal with only one crucial factor that sets the problem in the context of idleness and the ensuing boredom that may lead to deviant behavior. Observers are prone to overlook boredom as a contributing source in their understandable attraction to the more obvious conditions that give rise to deviant behavior—slums, poverty, broken homes, lower class standing, rejection, comic books, lack of community resources, family, personality disturbances, et cetera.

As we noted earlier, boredom is one of the typical responses to the abundance of available free time. Boredom is associated with the sense of life's meaninglessness, emptiness, and pointlessness—too much time filled with nothingness. Delinquency may be viewed as a protest against this state of mindlessness, against the meaninglessness and emptiness of life. After spending several months roaming the streets with a delinquent gang, the perceptive playwright Arthur Miller came away with an overwhelming conviction "that the problem underneath is boredom." He wrote:

The boredom of the delinquent is remarkable mainly because it is so little compensated for, as it may be among the middle classes and the rich who can fly down to the Caribbean or to Europe, or refurnish the house, or have an affair, or at least go shopping. The delinquent is stuck with his boredom, stuck inside it, stuck to it, until for two or three minutes he "lives," he goes on a raid around the corner and feels the thrill of risking his skin or his life as he smashes a bottle filled with gasoline on some other kid's head. In a sense, it is his trip to Miami. It makes his day. It is his shopping tour. It gives him something to talk about for a week. It is *life*. Standing around with nothing coming up is as close to dying as you can get. Unless one grasps the power of boredom, the threat of it to one's existence, it is impossible to "place" the delinquent as a member of the human race.[5]

[5] Arthur Miller, "The Bored and the Violent," *Harper's Magazine* (November, 1962), p. 51.

The desire for "kicks," for the thrill and excitement that can break the aimless, endless, leadening monotony of life has in one fashion or another been given as the key explanation by many teen-agers after they were apprehended for wanton destruction and vandalism, senseless and brutal muggings and murders. It was boredom and a desire for "kicks" that prompted four Brooklyn youngsters to burn a vagrant old man alive and toss him into the East River. Children from upper middleclass suburban homes have increasingly been engaged in deviant and destructive behavior—from petty thievery and party crashing to violent beatings and brawls—"just for the fun of it," for the thrill and excitement it brings them.

When seventeen boys from well-to-do homes were arrested as a burglary ring in suburban Fair Haven, a shocked community responded as follows: One spokesman drew up a long list of places where boys could let off steam—including a half-dozen playgrounds, ball fields, and tennis courts; a swimming pool; and two church-directed community youth centers which held teenage dances and offered the free use of indoor swimming pools, gymnasiums, and an arts-and-crafts shop. A recreation director averred, "This town is stuffed full of parks and with the wheels and money these boys had they were free to roam the eastern half of the United States—including the Atlantic Ocean and Long Island Sound." Another community leader said,

It's a shame. Those boys had everything—cars, girls, money, everything. Now they're saying they had nothing to do. Why, there's schoolground on top of schoolground around here, playground after playground, P.A.L., Babe Ruth League, Boy Scouts, and I don't know what all. You know what they wanted? They wanted *more*. It takes something to beat the excitement these kids got.[6]

[6] Glenn White, "Why Did They Steal?" *Ladies Home Journal* (July, 1962), p. 116.

Shocked and bewildered parents of these privileged children throw up their hands in dismay in trying to understand "what went wrong"—after all, they had "given the children everything that money could buy." What they fail to understand is that their children are the victims of *boredom,* and no lessons were given on how to cope with this menace. They are drowning in boredom, and seemingly the only relief is an aggressive, antisocial act in some off-beat, attention-getting, deviant way.

Adolescence: Period of Adjustment

To understand the phenomenon of boredom and delinquency, we must turn first to a discussion of adolescence—a time of storm and stress. Adolescence is a period in one's development when suddenly he is not who he was and doesn't yet know who he will be. It is a "way station" in development.[7] However confusing this interim period may be for the adolescent, it is one of extreme importance. This is the time when his childhood is ending and he must discover his identity anew—now in relation to an adult world into which he is emerging. Some never find this identity and are lost in the bewilderment of their splintered personality in a fractured world.

Of course the process of self-discovery is a continuous one that can be enhanced by leisure, as noted earlier. This may be one of the realities an adolescent must accept. But in the conscious awakening of new awareness, of an extreme self-consciousness, the adolescent is increasingly pressured to form an identity. He "must learn to know a whole new body and its potentials for feeling and behavior, and fit it into his picture of himself. He must come to terms with the new constellation of meanings presented by the environment. He must define the place he will occupy in adult society." [8] He must deal with internal pressures, the urges so terribly frustrating, which lead

[7] Joseph Stone and Joseph Church, *Childhood and Adolescence* (New York: Random House, Inc., 1957), p. 268.

[8] *Ibid.*

him into perpetual restlessness. He must cope with external pressures from his parents, from his peer group, and from adults with whom he has contact.

The young adolescent wants to be part of a group or gang, to be like his peers, lest in his uniqueness he loses his sense of group identity. He wants to be an accepted part of his youth culture. In later adolescence he has a growing concern with the adult problems of independence, marriage, schooling, jobs; in other words, he is becoming more concerned with what to do about who he is.

Today the plight of the adolescent is compounded. Not only must he work out the conflicting pressures in his life, but he does so in an atmosphere charged with fear, frustration, and a sense of helplessness, in an age of world revolution and potential total destruction. Life is precarious, filled with anxieties and uncertainties. Most of today's youngsters have lived all their years not only with the ominous radioactive fallout in the physical environment, but also with the human fallout in the social environment—the fear of a known enemy and the fear of the massive powers of extinction both he and we possess and could touch off unwittingly. Has any other generation had to coexist with a threat of chaos on such a grand scale? Has any other generation had to live in such a gadget-filled paradise suspended in a hell of human insecurity?

In their quest for self-identity young people need to feel that certain things in the world are real and dependable. Especially now when the world remains so little the same from day to day, when the security of one day becomes the insecurity of the next, when, as one wit says, the future isn't what it used to be, it is difficult for the adolescent to find anything on which to hang his convictions. He is swept along by a vortex of unprecedented change.

What hope or idealism does the world offer to youth who are in the midst of what is usually thought of as the epitome of idealism? Idealism runs like an underground brook through

111

the adolescent's conflicting actions and emotions. Part of this idealism comes from the new sense of freedom and independence which he is unwilling to have fettered by the mundane responsibilities of everyday life. Freedom is a new-found treasure, a discovery which can open doors into a life that has hitherto been contained only in dreams. With this treasure one does not want to settle immediately into the routine of adult living. It is his own, this freedom. He is free and freedom is his—freedom to change the world, to assert his own power, to strike out even against people or property, to bring peace, to fly jets, perchance to live in another galaxy.

One manifestation of the adolescent's idealism is the search for meaning. Though he may suffer disappointment, he clings tenaciously to the conviction that there is a meaningfulness to human existence, however hidden. For some life has lost its savor, meaning and purpose are dead, and the only meaning comes in the fit of rage, after which one finds his moment of glory and recognition in an attention-getting front-page news-paper story of teen-age brutality, killing, or thievery.

Still another manifestation of idealism is the adolescent's rebellion, not just against his parents, but against authority in general and against the values of the adult world. Indeed, acute observers have noted that the rebellion of today's youth is unfocused. The adolescent has been largely deprived of things to rebel *for* as well as against. He is a "rebel without a cause." A healthy rebellion may be part of the process of growing up, but lacking any clearly defined target to rebel against may lead to a purely negative, destructive form of rebellion. Thus many of the antisocial acts of teen-agers—vandalism, rape, sadistic attacks—express a blind rebellion. Left blind and formless rebellion can easily sour into pervasive cynicism or explode into violence. This delinquency of rebellion has little regard for the articles stolen, the person beaten, or the property destroyed. The act itself is symbolically important to blot out the mood of boredom.

Throughout this period of adjustment, so fraught with either breakthroughs of the mind and spirit or self-surrender to aimless drifting, lurks the specter of boredom—time filled with nothingness and void of meaning, idleness which is the tragic death of the possibility of leisure. Thus the threat of leisure for the young is a double threat; it is time hanging heavy when the adolescent needs to feel that his time is for some purpose, and it is time empty of meaning, for the adolescent is having an increasingly hard time learning the meaning of work in a society that delays his entry into the labor force. Leisure cannot mean fulfillment if the youth can find little meaning in life around him, just as work can have no fulfillment if there is no opportunity for leisure.

The emptiness of life and its implications for delinquency have been discussed in a most provocative study by Paul Goodman in *Growing Up Absurd*.[9] Many of today's youth bear an attitude which Goodman characterizes as "chronic boredom." This malaise does not stem from the community's failure to communicate its values. The social message is clear enough; it is just that it's unacceptable. Worthwhile goals that could make growing up possible are simply deficient. Young people are faced with the reality that real opportunities to be useful are lacking. There are fewer jobs that are necessary, that require energy, that draw on one's best capacities.

Take the case of the automobile mechanic. He may feel that he is doing something very useful. Before long, however, he encounters the automobile manufacturer's built-in obsolescence intended to keep cars from being repaired after a few years. The realization that the manufacturers don't want the cars repaired leads to a sense of frustration and uselessness, which in turn leads to chronic boredom.

All the frustrations youth encounters in the perversions of national values prompt him to chronic boredom, apathy, and

---

[9] New York: Random House, Inc., 1956. See pp. 11 ff.

disinterest. Thoroughly disillusioned, he is reduced to simply "hanging around," and in his despair he does nothing at all.

Nowhere is this mood of the spirit of boredom that underlies delinquency better captured than in contemporary novels about adolescents. The issue of too much time and of aimless and mindless drifting is brought out pointedly as part of the difficulty of growing up in the twentieth century. Let us turn to a discussion of several of these novels.

Leisure and Adolescence in Contemporary Novels

In *The Young Manhood of Studs Lonigan* the title figure is an American boy growing up in Chicago's South Side. Studs' childhood prepared him well to be the aimless, deviant, and drifting young man he became, for he

stood in front of the poolroom at Fifty Eighth Street on the South Side of Chicago, associating with those older than himself, imitating them, thrilled when they permitted him to join with them in the perpetration of practical jokes, and viewing them as models for his own future conduct. He confidently told himself that soon he would be older, and then like them, he would really be "strong and tough and the real stuff."

During his adolescence, when the major question, "What'll we do?" comes up, Studs and the boys answer it by trying out the various experiences which they believe will lead to manhood: Getting drunk, visiting the "girlies," hanging around the poolroom, and, for lack of anything else, sitting in the park or going to the movies.

The most important characteristic in the physical environment of the boy is the lack of horizons. Small, narrow, parochial, the community afforded few opportunities for the children to stretch themselves. Baseball and prizefighting are the most absorbing topics of conversation, with the exception, of course, of sex. Other than this, life in the depersonalized asphalt jungle is empty of meaning.

Time, for Studs Lonigan, is a void, perhaps a vacuum, sucking him into its emptiness so that he is helpless to fill it. Trapped by empty time, he has no time either for work or for real leisure. He has no knowledge of the meaning of life and its rhythm of work and leisure; yet he seeks such a knowledge. Knowing that he should get a job, he finds it too big a step for him to take.

In such a way Studs drifts, getting his kicks where he can, managing for awhile to stall off getting a job. He knows, long before he takes any action, that his life is empty and devoid of deep meaning. With a depressing listlessness he pursues for brief periods the various roads he thinks might lead to life. He gets a job, goes on a health jag and gives up drinking and staying up late, but somehow, life takes on no real depth, and time still hangs heavy for Studs. Increasingly, he has delved into all areas of life, searching for excitement—he has been to the prostitutes, gotten stone drunk, escaped from the police, fought violently and, at times, unsuccessfully, and has gained a wide reputation for being "tough and the real stuff." Increasingly, he finds these former thrills now meaningless, with no near possibility of a substitute which might offer him fulfillment. Perhaps his greatest delinquency is the moral failure of abdication—a failure to realize his own potential manhood.

Emptiness and meaninglessness are not life characteristics confined to the "shook up generation" in depressed inner-city neighborhoods. Our second novel deals with a boy from upper middle-class surroundings. Holden Caulfield in J. D. Salinger's *The Catcher in the Rye* is perhaps one of the most tragic and yet poignant persons modern literature has created. An idealistic and at the same time a resentful adolescent, his search for meaning leads him beyond reality. His whole existence depends on the belief that somewhere he may find people who are real and authentic. So far in his life he has found many "phonies," and the shattering discoveries at so many points have left him bewildered in a pointless kind of living.

Having been given nothing but the best his parents could afford, Holden is caught going around and around on a carousel which whirls faster and faster; with each spin it becomes more difficult to grasp the solid, concrete brass ring that signifies the real and the meaningful in life.

Time has no special significance for him, because life is not what it should be. For the person who has given up life is just a series of unrelated moments. Unfilled moments hover, and Holden meets them as they come, sometimes in total apathy and self-resignation, at other times filling them with meaningless activity. It is a depressing way of living, to have time and no awareness of its potential fulfillment. Actually Holden Caulfield couldn't look forward to time of his own, for he had nothing of his own and even the search was beginning to elude him. One sometimes gives up the quest because he can see no alternative to his lostness.

In a period of forty-eight desperate hours young Caulfield wanders in a mental maze. He left school early to hole up in a cheap New York City hotel. During his entire stay he drifts aimlessly from one spot to another, unable to do the appropriate thing. Part of his problem is that he had no idea of what he wanted to do. Every venture attempted, therefore, became another fiasco ended.

Flunking out of his elite prep school is only part of his total confusion about life and the phonies that comprise it. Now the two touchstones with reality in this foggy semi-existence are his sister Phoebe, who is very much a part of the boy, and the question about the ducks in Central Park. With an urgency that characterizes his need for knowledge, for belief in something, Holden asks the cab drivers, "You know those ducks in that lagoon right near Central Park South? That little lake? By any chance, do you happen to know where they go, the ducks, when it gets all frozen over? Do you happen to know, by any chance?" [10] Holden doesn't find the answer, this time or next time. The question increases in significance as it remains unanswered, becoming somehow the young man's searching and unanswered question about himself. Suddenly there is no place for Holden Caulfield in a world frozen over, nowhere to go, "no exit," because life has no meaning.

When time is a blank, it stretches into the oblivion of unreality. So with Holden, who faces the uncertainty of all of his life crystallized in the brief span of forty-eight desperate hours on his own. Small wonder that he finds the knowledge of empty, meaningless time unbearable. While Studs Lonigan could drink his way into temporary oblivion, Holden Caulfield let his mind become the means of escape. Both youngsters are truants from life as well as truants from school.

A third, and radically different, perspective on leisure time and juvenile delinquency is encountered in a widely read novel which is all the more fascinating because its story is based on a set of brutal facts. *Compulsion* by Meyer Levin has its setting in a wealthy section of Chicago. Here, instead of one boy's taking the spotlight, as in the two previous books, there are two—Arthur Strauss and Judson Steiner, who commit a violent crime while still in their teens.

Both boys were extremely brilliant and had nearly completed a full course of studies at the University of Chicago. Education and ability to think brilliantly, however, do not automatically insure emotional stability or personal maturity. Intellectual growth can often far outstrip other aspects of a person's development, prompting people to forget that a brilliant teen-ager *is* still a teen-ager.

These two boys seemed to have nothing to do most of the time; even during classes they found it unnecessary to listen a great deal of the time—a luxury only the most brilliant can afford, or one that is taken by the poor victims of a bad lecturer!

[10] *The Catcher in the Rye* (New York: Signet Books, 1958), pp. 56-57.

Hence both Artie and Judd found themselves with ample time in which to scheme and plan for something more exciting—like committing the "crime of the century." Instead of poring over books in the library, like their less fortunately endowed peers, the two spent hours on end devising intricate plans, rode around in a car to look over the potential scene of their crime, or actually rehearsed the whole unfortunate incident.

Artie and Judd gradually evolved the idea of committing a perfect crime. From this they could derive a "thrill" as they watched the chaotic frenzy that would beset the parents of their victim, the police, and, yes, the entire city. Could they have guessed that it would be on the front pages of newspapers all across the nation? They did know that execution of this perfect crime would give them a terrific feeling of power. They would have accomplished something which few others have done and which no one could have thought was within their capabilities.

The thrill and challenge of it all drove the two boys relentlessly onward in their plot to kidnap and murder the son of a family that they knew well. Which family mattered little, just so they knew its members and could watch closely the reactions to their monstrous crime. An elaborate plot to collect ransom consumed hours of careful planning and discussion. Each step of the way every suggestion had to be weighed and gone over with a fine tooth comb. It was another form of play to them, and the author points out that "their game" had once gone on for a "whole evening." Indeed, they had become so engrossed in their game that they soon forgot it was play. Instead of a game, it became an obsession which was doomed to lead to tragic consequences.

To be sure, an infinite variety of psychological and sociological factors entered into the commission of this crime. Yet one can't help wondering if there would have been such a crime had the boys had more worthy objectives to fill their empty hours and to challenge their gifted minds. Their exceptional brilliance and a universal aimlessness coupled with excess time comprise part of the highly explosive and dangerous mixture that cannot be overlooked. In this book and in the reality it mirrors, then, it is possible to discern a compelling link between boredom and delinquency, prompting one to kill for a thrill.

The three examples we have cited from contemporary literature portray vividly the problem of boredom as it relates to delinquency—how to cope with spare time. They provide case studies of boredom, which has become such an important dimension in understanding the reactions of delinquent youth. Lacking anything better to do had brought each of the the young "heroes" in our novels to the point of a search for excitement and for kicks. Time for each was a void whose emptiness was filled with tragic consequences.

Play and the Gang

Perhaps the most obvious manifestation of "hanging around doing nothing" is the juvenile gang. Gang formation is, of course, natural, whether spontaneously or artificially created, for the purpose of play. In banding together natural leaders arise, and the gang members derive a sense of status, belongingness, and even pride. Group solidarity is enhanced by any number of things which draw the members closer together to fend off opposition—the existence of a rival or enemy gang about to invade its "turf," parental and neighborhood disapproval, or conflict with law enforcement officers.

Frederic Thrasher makes the connection between free time and gang activity clear in his contention that the "majority of gangs develop from the spontaneous play-group." [11] Not all gangs, however, grow out of play groups, though a large portion of their activities may be regarded as play of one kind or another. The gang's play life is usually undirected and uncontrolled by parents or adults, though some gangs are under direct

[11] *Op. cit.*, p. 29.

119

supervision and guidance of adult leaders who instill an extensive recreational program. These may take the form of athletic clubs or leagues.

Life in the gang consists of a variety of activities—playing roughhouse, traveling from place to place, aimless wandering, street games, gambling, predatory activities, attending commercial amusements, watching sports, reading dime novels or comic books, or just plain loafing. Often the ordinary routine activities of life are so boring that the quest for new and exciting experiences leads the gang members into trouble with the law.

Many of the serious acts of delinquency are committed in the framework of the antisocial gang. It should be clearly understood that the majority of teen-age gangs are not fighting gangs. Alone a youngster may hesitate before committing an act of violence, but under the stimulus and influence of the gang, discretion and caution may be thrown to the winds. Seemingly one would rather be caught dead than be a "chicken." Few members of "bopping" gangs know how to fight alone. Arthur Miller referred to them as dangerous pack hounds who are afraid of exposing themselves singly. Miller gave this example of gang activity even in playing baseball:

We started a baseball game, and everything proceeded smoothly until somebody hit a ball to the outfield. I turned to watch the play and saw ten or twelve kids running for the catch. It turned out that not one of them was willing to play the outfield by himself, insisting that the entire group hang around out there together. The reason was that a boy alone might drop a catch and would not be able to bear the humiliation. So they ran around out there in a drove all afternoon, creating a stampede every time a ball was hit.[12]

For the city gang the likeliest playground is the pavement of the block. It is to the street that youth turns, and it is to the

[12] *Op. cit.,* p. 52.

street that harassed mothers dispatch their turbulent flock when they seek a modicum of peace and quiet or the free use of limited and ofttimes dreary facilities. The street provides the dramatic, if somewhat dismal, setting for whiling away hours on end, for scheming gang forays and predatory activities, if only to break the binding chain of doing nothing. Where the only place for recreation and for passing the time is a public thoroughfare or a darkened street corner, it is little wonder that youngsters are goaded on to more perilous pastimes.

By way of contrast, small harm comes of gang activities in the open-country or rural communities. It is in the streets and squares and tenements of the city that the boisterous antics of gangs are a nuisance and are likely to be put down as a breach of the peace. Thus delinquency must be viewed from the perspective of what the community is willing to tolerate, for what is playfulness to one community may be threatening to another.

This point came vividly home in the remarks of a visitor to New York City from rural South Carolina. The Southern visitor was observing the activities of a group of boys who were "hanging out" on the steps of a brownstone building. Sometimes they sing, sometimes they play bongo drums, and on this particular occasion, they were doing both. "Just look at those guys," complained our friend, "they have nothing to do but hang around the streets. No wonder you have so much trouble with teen-age gangs up here." Apparently he had momentarily forgotten—but recalled after a little probing—that he himself not too long ago had nothing to do as a teen-ager, except "hang out" at the local filling station with his buddies during the afternoons and evenings. He would deny having been a "juvenile delinquent," but some of his "boyish pranks" would have gotten him into serious trouble were it not for a permissive and understanding local police force. In fact, "Halloween pranks" in which he and his gang were involved got so destructive that local merchants had to ask for protection from the state police. No arrests were made, but armed men guarded the stores that year.

Delinquency is often defined pragmatically in terms of what the community can afford; that is, a farm boy may steal watermelons from his neighbor's patch, but the neighbor seldom does anything about it. The worst that might happen to the boy is a peppering of buckshot designed to make an indelible impression! Think what might happen if a city boy stole apples from a fruit stand. All the mighty apparatus of law enforcement might be breathing down his neck—police, judges, courts, detention centers, probation officers, youth workers, et cetera.

One can seriously doubt that either the farm or the city boy is hungry enough to steal. Both do it primarily for the "thrill." Why then does one community permit a boy to have his "thrill" and another community sternly forbid it? It seems to be a "normal" teen-age desire to want to do things occasionally just for the "heck" of it. In this respect, *all* youngsters of both sexes are involved. The real difficulty comes in the mode of action and the community's reaction to it. Clearly, what is permissible in the country is not permissible in the city.

No one ever said to our Southern visitor: "You may ruin your life if you keep on destroying property at Halloween." He knew better; he might get caught, get a dressing down by parents and police, and even—at worst—have to pay a fine or compensation. No one ever viewed him as a case or said, "I wonder if he is a potential criminal." Of course, he did not become a criminal just because no one expected that of him. Rather, he felt no uncertainty about his future conduct. He knew perfectly well that one day he would cease to roam with the gang and play pranks. The community realized this and did not attempt to penalize him severely.

In an urban community it is quite a different story. There is no such realization. Instead a huge question mark hangs over the head of each teen-ager brought before a judge or an officer at police headquarters. They do not say, "Don't worry,

122

he'll outgrow it." There is no such community assurance. The teen-agers themselves are affected by this doubt. A group of boys on a street corner are joking and laughing. One of them playfully pokes another and there is a moment or two of jostling. It is not uncommon for a policeman coming upon such a scene to wade into the group with billy club swinging. At the very least he will gruffly admonish the youngsters, "O.K., Break it up. Move along now." He is alert for trouble; the boys feel guilty. Yet in a small town, the same incident would hardly draw any attention.

A teen-age girl from the South reported:

Once I went along with my "gang" in a new Buick out into the country to burn crosses. We had no particular reason for burning crosses. We didn't burn them in front of Negroes' homes or anything. We were just doing it for "kicks." If we had been caught there would have been a mild scandal. But we didn't care; the scandal would have been exciting anyway. We had the confidence that it would finally be crossed off as a "prank." It would never show up on our school records, keep us out of college, or from getting a job.

The community existing with doubts about its teen-agers will, statistically, have more delinquents. And the "delinquents" will have a harder time becoming anything but delinquents. Between the overindulgence of the country and the stern rigidity of the city there must be a more viable alternative.

It surely won't be found in the usual answers—better housing, supervised recreation, more social workers, reading clinics, and the like. Crucial as these measures are, they are inadequate to penetrate the pervasive sense of boredom. Boredom is essentially a condition of the spirit, and idleness is the despair from weakness which Kierkegaard analyzed as the "despairing refusal to be oneself." Arthur Miller set us in the right direction when he wrote:

I do not know how we ought to reach for the spirit again but it seems to me we must flounder without it. . . . The spirit has to be that of those people who know that delinquents are a living expression of our universal ignorance of what life ought to be, even of what it is, and of what it truly means to live. . . . Who from his own life, from his personal thought has come up with the good teaching, the way of life that is joy?[13]

It would seem, then, that leisure time can be potentially dangerous, but of course, is not necessarily so. When the person who finds himself with excess time on his hands does nothing with it but rather drifts aimlessly looking for "kicks" and for "thrills" to break the spell of boredom, either alone or in a gang, then delinquency is apt to be an invited guest.

However, when direction and aim are given to his use of time, a sense of purpose and meaningfulness to life, there is a good chance that youth will put leisure time, not to tragic, but to triumphant uses. At the end of the day the burden of proof seems to fall on the elders. Have they failed or succeeded in communicating to their progeny the reality and the meaning that is life? What do they know of joy? Leisure time is here and destined to stay. But must the same be said about its tragic use in the alarming amount of juvenile delinquency?

Our analysis of the depth dimension of leisure has been largely confined to a positive treatment of play in the growing child's life and to its negative consequences for some youth caught up in the tragedy of delinquency. Now it is quite possible to continue this discussion by considering other age groups in the life cycle. Indeed, later on we will comment on the agony that leisure has come to mean for some of the aged in our society. Lest we be too engrossed with contemporary issues, however, we must hasten to our third dimension—that of *length,* and deal with some historical roots of leisure.

[13] *Ibid.,* p. 56.

PART THREE

Length: Some Historical Roots of Leisure

7

From Holy Days to Holidays

Although religion often has been guilty of putting a damper on the enjoyment of leisure, this by no means has been its exclusive role. In considering the dimension of length we will see something of the major, positive influence which religion has had on the historical development of leisure through the observances of holidays and festivals. The roots of these celebrations can be traced to primitive times when men first set aside certain "holy days" as special occasions for ritualistic festivity. In the pre-industrial period these holy days constituted a chief source of leisure, and the transition from "holy days" to "holidays" reflects a major element in the evolution of leisure.

The importance of considering this historical source of leisure is evident from George Stewart's description of holidays in contemporary America.

Perhaps the most discouraging feature about American holidays is their tendency toward leveling. By a kind of erosion they all seem to be becoming the same thing. What people do on the Fourth of July is likely to be just what they do also on Decoration Day and Labor Day. . . . A holiday has simply become, for most Americans, a day when one is free from work.[1]

We might add to Stewart's description that our holidays are often celebrated with the same kind of active franticity or passive

[1] From *American Ways of Life* by George R. Stewart. Copyright 1954 by George R. Stewart. Reprinted by permission of Doubleday & Company, Inc. P. 274.

boredom which characterizes a good deal of what we call leisure time.

Of course we cannot return to a primitive or even a pre-industrial view of holidays, but we can benefit greatly from an understanding of both the original impulse to designate holy days and the historical origin of our holidays and festivals. Providing a conscious link for us with our past heritage, these days can be occasions for joy, self-awareness and wholeness of life; reminding us of happenings in our natural, social, and spiritual life, they can be times for re-affirmation of meanings and re-dedication to future actions and motivations. In short, if we blow a fresh breath of life into our holidays and festivals, the historical tap root of leisure, they can become for us sources of true leisure.

An analysis of holidays can reveal much about ourselves and our leisure, for people celebrate what they deem to have worth. In contemporary American holidays and festivals—and the way they are celebrated—we can see the pervasive sense of uncertainty and vagueness about what has value. Both leisure and holiday observances occupy a very ambiguous place in the thinking of most Americans. What factors have brought about this situation and what possibilities may be open to us will be the concern of this chapter.

Holy Days and Holidays

There is common agreement that holy days originated in primitive times as days set aside to worship and/or placate the gods or divine spirits. These gods manifested themselves in many ways—through the forces of nature, in birth and death, through the success or failure of the tribe in war and hunting, and so on. Because fear and superstition dominated man in this early period, a major response to the gods took the form of observing various "taboos" and restrictions on the holy days. The cessation of work at these taboo periods seems to have stemmed largely from the belief that the evil spirits would enter life through the labor done and bring disastrous results; therefore, the safest thing was to desist and do nothing.

On occasions of good fortune, however—a successful hunt, for instance—man at this early stage made a second important response to the "holy" which took the form of a festival celebration. At these times the normal work activity gave way to feasting and a general good time. This urge to celebrate the meaningful through feasts and festivals stems from a very basic inclination of the human spirit to express collective joy, which Huizinga locates alongside the impulse to play. In our day, when the fear response of "taboos" has nearly disappeared, this play spirit in feast and festival persists with great force. From the spontaneous celebration of such playful events as winning a football game or such serious matters as winning a war, to the planned celebration of national holidays and regional observances—Frontier Days, Grape Festivals, Rose Parades, and so on—the willing participants far outnumber the Ebenezer Scrooges.

The feast and festival celebration in its earliest form, however, was not separated from religion and from a sense of worship. Rather, *both* responses, taboo and feast, originated in a sense of holy mystery. "From the beginning it would seem that man did not rely wholly upon his own initiative and ingenuity to ensure that all his needs were met." [2] In setting aside certain "holy days" he acknowledged his dependence on that which was transcendent to him. Whether as taboo restrictions or as feasting regulations, the origin of these rites and rituals rested in the sense of awe and wonder about why and how things happened as they did.

A second factor in the development of holy days and holidays concerns the formulation of the calendar. Since man in his early days worked very close to nature it was natural that he should observe a phenomenon on which he could hang a way of mark-

[2] E. O. James, *Seasonal Feasts and Festivals* (New York: Barnes and Noble, Inc., 1961), p. 11.

ing time—the changing seasons. Perhaps man's fascination with the rhythm of nature in the seasons and his celebration of the changes by festivals grew out of the fact that there he found the source of his food supply. Festivals marking the periodic changes in nature were thus the first holy days to be celebrated regularly, and since the rhythm was observed most obviously in the different phases of the moon, that change became the guide in setting the celebrations as well as the basis for the first calendar.[3]

The lunar year of 354 days eventually had to be reconciled to the solar year in order to have the seasons come at their proper times, and an accurate calendar was not finally accomplished until 1582 by Gregory XIII—and then not adopted in England until 1752.[4] A *workable* calendar year was realized quite early, however; it provided a basis for observing holy days and festivals. Since pastoral and agricultural conditions were conducive to recognizing the divine control of the rhythms in the natural world, these observances remained primarily as occasions for ritual activity relating to food supply and worship of the sacred powers around them.

Man, of course, did not only *respond* to the divine power and mystery in taboo restrictions, feast celebrations, and various forms of worship; at times he also sought to control and master that mystery. We can see this attempt to control in the development of ritual which was based in the belief that what was done on the human level (the microcosm) would directly influence what happened in the world of nature (the macrocosm). Here was the impetus for fertility rites which attempted to induce fertility in the natural realm through acts in the human realm;

---

[3] This was true, for instance, for the Jewish festivals: "The Israelites have probably from ancient times counted their days according to the periods of the moon: new and full moon." J. Van Goudoever, *Biblical Calendars* (Leiden: E. J. Brill, 1961), p. 4.

[4] See "Calendars," *The Oxford Dictionary of the Christian Church*, edited by F. L. Cross (London: Oxford University Press, 1957), p. 217.

here was the incentive for American Indians, as well as others, to enact their "rain dances" and various cosmic dramas. This activity also became part of holy day ritual.

Throughout all these early observances, however, there was an essential unity to life for the people. At times it was a narrow unity, as when fear and superstition made life terrifying and gave rise to the attempts to control the forces of nature. At other times it was a supportive unity with a healthy sense of reverence and mystery. Leisure (unknown as such) was part of the basic rhythm of life, and holy days were special days of worship within that rhythm—either festivals of joy or rest days for penance.

Then as civilization became more complex, a third factor in the development of holy days and festivals took shape. Empires arose, and with them the sense of national ties and mutual dependence for self-preservation. This gregariousness prompted the setting of festivals and feasts of gratitude for deliverance and military victories, and celebrations honoring the military and religious leaders. The calendar was stabilized for more effective social organization which meant that the celebration of holy days and festivals could also be structured in more detail.[5]

Under these urban conditions the agricultural seasons of the natural world lost much of their importance, and holy days as times to offer prayers for a good crop at planting or thanksgiving for a successful harvest became less relevant—except perhaps in periods of drought, famine, or other calamity. Cessation from work on holy days took on the character of relief from labor in which the play instinct was catered to, rather than rest days where play was contained in a larger context of worship and celebration. Under state control, festivals were established to honor particular gods and events quite apart from

[5] See Hutton Webster, *Rest Days* (New York: The Macmillan Company, 1916), p. 85: "As civilization develops, festivals tend to increase in number, to elaborate their ritual, and to fix more precisely the time and order of their celebration."

the seasons, and as the people believed that the gods were present among them it was thought that enforced idleness would be pleasing. Abstinence from work was a recognized way of expressing proper reverence for the divinity. This evaluation of the worth of work as a fitting sacrifice to the gods—in this case to refrain from work rather than to do it—foreshadowed the separation between work and leisure as well as between work and worship which finally came with the Industrial Revolution.

With urbanization and the structuring of the calendar, life became more efficient. Holy days with their fragmented, "natural-world" meanings were given universal meaning as symbols of the state—honoring its gods as well as its leaders—around which the people could organize and with which they could identify. Here was the divine force at work gathering together and preserving the people. Holy days become days of community dedication. But as urban life also brought a division of labor certain things became more complex and impersonal. Leisure on a large scale became the state of a few with the majority having rest from work only on the holy days—this in itself came to be cause for celebration quite apart from the religious meaning of the festival and tended to overshadow the primary intention.

Furthermore, with increased material means and sense of power, men were inclined to elaborate their celebrations and make each one bigger and better than the previous one. So the festivals grew far beyond their original impetus and were perverted. The Greeks had their gigantic feasts and the Romans had their circuses—all in the names of various gods and each more lavish than the one before. Greek celebrations finally reached the place where feast days outnumbered working days; Roman holidays with their games grew to 135 days a year in the second century and then to 175 in the fourth century. Rather than commemorating great past events in their history, the celebrations became involvement in present experiences of thrill—orgiastic and brutal. At this point the transition from holy day to holiday became complete.

As we turn now to a further stage in the development of festivals it might be helpful to summarize what would seem to be the main difference between holy day and holiday. In essence it might be described this way:

Holy Day: A special day centered primarily in the meaning of divine mystery and revelation as expressed in the event it commemorates. It is celebrated in worship, either by a joyous thanksgiving festival or as a solemn penitential quiet time.

Holiday: A day in which freedom from the requirements of work is the primary focus. It may also relate to the meaning of its origin and thus take on special preparation, but the intent is basically to have a good time in the celebration.

Christian Holy Days

Growing out of Judaism, early Christianity had its roots in the traditions observed in Jewish festivals and holy days. Therefore it is important that we review briefly what the major occasions were. The most important holy day was, of course, the sabbath, but we will save discussion of it for another chapter. The next most frequently observed holy day was a new moon festival at the beginning of each month, expressing the importance of the lunar changes as the basis for the liturgical calendar.

Of the yearly feasts the three primary ones were agricultural in origin—Unleavened Bread in the Spring, Weeks (Pentecost or First Fruits) in the Summer, and Ingathering (Tabernacles or Booths) in the Fall. The Passover (Pesach), a pastoral observance, was early associated with the first day of the Feast of Unleavened Bread—Passover being characterized by a speedy consumption of the sacrificial lamb before the full moon disappeared, and Unleavened Bread, a leisurely affair lasting a week. In time, however, each observance was re-interpreted in terms of national and social significance in the history of Israel.

Passover and Unleavened Bread came to commemorate the deliverance from Egypt; Weeks or Pentecost was celebrated as the occasion when Moses received the Law on Mount Sinai; and Ingathering or Booths became a remembrance of the pioneer days of the Jewish people when they wandered in the wilderness.

Two festivals, called "Days of Awe," carried a very serious and solemn atmosphere: Rosh Hashana (the New Year's celebration) and Yom Kippur (the Day of Atonement) —with the latter observed by fasting. The difference between these two festivals and the rest lies in the fact that "they bear no relation to nature nor to any historic event in the Jewish past. They are concerned only with the life of the individual, with his religious feelings and innermost probings." [6] Ten days of repentance were observed between Rosh Hashana and Yom Kippur.

Two other major festivals, Hanukkah and Purim, were added in the second century. Hanukkah commemorated the Maccabean revolt and, celebrated for eight days in December, became the first major winter festival. Purim, two days of great merrymaking, celebrated the story in the Book of Esther (although it may have been "an ancient festival for which the Book of Esther was created as an explanation" [7]). Both Hanukkah and Purim were observed as joyous festivals of deliverance and dedication in the history of Israel's salvation.

All these celebrations lasted from two to nine days, with periods of preparation often preceding them. Add to these times the various minor festivals and certain fast days, plus the new moon observances and the strict keeping of the sabbath, and it is apparent that the Jewish liturgical calendar of holy days was quite elaborate. This calendar of observances ensured times of rest for the people, which united them in shared meanings and reminded them periodically of their uniqueness as

[6] Hayyim Schauss, *Guide to Jewish Holy Days*, translated by Samuel Jaffe (New York: Schocken Books, Inc., 1961), p. 112.
[7] *Ibid.*, p. 250.

people called of the One God—distinct from the pagan religions where people were at the mercy of many gods. Perhaps as an unintended consequence, these festivals also gave experiences of variety and meaning to the present existence within the rhythm of work and leisure which characterized life in Israel.

However, the rules and ritual prescribing food preparation, cleansing procedure, gifts and sacrifices, times of prayer and worship, abstinence from work, and what could or could not be done on holy days grew in number and in strictness, and as the influence of Greek and Roman culture increased those rules became quite legalistic.

Out of this cultural and religious background Christianity grew—inheriting the institutions of Judaism but infusing them with new meaning. The early Christians gradually reduced the number of holy days, re-interpreting the ones they kept in terms of the fulfillment which their faith in Jesus Christ as the Messiah had given them. Only two of the Jewish festivals were retained finally in Christianity, Passover and Pentecost, and these were celebrated in the light of the significance they had for the Christian life.

Passover was important because of its association with the Last Supper, the Crucifixion, and the Resurrection. For a time there was controversy over whether Christians should celebrate the Jewish Passover (set according to the full moon of Nisan 14, which could make it any day of the week) or should observe the Friday before Easter (Easter Sunday being set by the moon, but Friday being a fixed day of the week in relation to Sunday, and the day on which the crucifixion actually occurred). Some did both, but finally the latter tradition prevailed. Eventually the limits of March 21 and April 25 were set for the Easter festival to insure that Easter would fall on or after the spring equinox. Jesus' resurrection had taken place just on the spring equinox, and the rejoicing over new life which characterized

135

the spring festival seemed an important link with the Easter celebration of joy.

Pentecost, the Jewish Festival of Weeks or First Fruits, celebrated the end of the seven weeks, or fifty days, of grain harvest following Passover. On the first of the fifty days the Jews had offered the first sheaf of newly cut barley as a sacrifice; when this became the day of Christ's resurrection, the Christians celebrated in joy the resurrection of Jesus Christ as "the first fruits of those who have fallen asleep." The fiftieth day itself, Pentecost, became the Christian celebration of the descent of the Holy Spirit as recorded in Acts 2.

These were the first Christian holy days. How they were observed we do not know, but probably in services of worship similar to the ones held on the first day of each week. No doubt the persecution of Christians during the first two centuries curtailed any large public celebration.

Gradually the Christian Church began to develop its own calendar of special holy days, and with the legalization of Christianity by Constantine, this activity surged ahead. Certain fixed celebrations were established; Epiphany, January 6, and Christmas, December 25, being the primary ones designated in the fourth century. Although both dates originated as observances of Christ's birth, Epiphany in the East and Christmas in the West, the December celebration became the accepted date for that celebration and the January one became the festival of Christ's baptism and finally the festival of the visit of the Magi.

It is interesting to note that before the fourth century many studies had been made to calculate Christ's birth, but none gave rise to a festival. On the other hand, January 6 had long been an important sacred time in pagan religion, and December 25 was the date of the Saturnalia celebration honoring the birthday of the sun by the sun cults and the designation of *Sol Invictus* as the deity of the Roman Empire. Some people have looked askance at Christianity's taking over pagan observances, but when one considers the difficulty in starting new holy days and the fact that such reinterpretation kept new converts from falling away into the old revelry, it seems that the Church Fathers might have been very wise!

The number of holy days increased. Feasts of the commemoration of the Virgin, apostles, circumcision, ascension, and so forth were inaugurated in the fifth century; saints' days honoring the martyrs, patron saints and saints whose names were given in baptism became more and more numerous. In the Middle Ages, "Since the Church stipulated that all compulsory holy days be observed with attendance at mass and abstinence from unnecessary servile work, many communities were bidden to keep virtually two Sundays in the week." [8] Ida Craven cast this situation of holiday observance in terms of the leisure possibility:

throughout antiquity and the Middle Ages the normal number of holidays during the year was about 115. Except in periods of unusual economic stress even slaves enjoyed such holidays, although their means of utilization of such time were limited. But the grouping of work around numerous holidays probably resulted in more effective leisure than the one day of rest out of seven in industrial society.[9]

On this question of leisure, however, there has been much debate. Some writers have emphasized the opportunity for leisure and worship which the numerous holidays in the Middle Ages gave the people, while others have pointed out that forbidding people to work these days created economic impoverishment and idleness. Historical evidence seems to indicate that it did both. It is true, with the demands of long hours and hard work being great, that many laborers were free only on holy days, but as the number of days to be observed

[8] "Festivals and holy days, Christian," *An Encyclopedia of Religion*, edited by Vergilius Ferm (New York: The Philosophical Library, Inc., 1945), p. 276.
[9] "Leisure," *Encyclopaedia of the Social Sciences*, IX, 403.

grew it brought an economical burden of work not done as well as time "unfulfilled." Riotous and drunken behavior became characteristic of holy day celebration in the Middle Ages, with taverns and sporting events the loci of disorder and abandoned merrymaking. The more this happened the more the Church condemned these available forms of recreation and urged a pious morality.

Furthermore, as people consulted the ecclesiastical authorities as to what could and could not be done on holy days, a legalistic system again developed. Those in agricultural and laboring work were often hit hardest by work restrictions because their occupations seemed the most apparently "servile." In some areas the burden of holiday observance became so great that people could not get their necessary work done—yet other than attending mass there was nothing for them to do. As one writer noted: "In enjoining the observance of so many holy days the Church had obviously failed to take full account of the indigence of the populace, or their inability to put their leisure to profit." [10]

Objections to the number of holy days on the ground of economic necessity and of holiday misuse were raised as early as 1274, but nothing was done until the Reformation. "Men like Wyclif [argued] that multiplication lessened the value of these days and fostered indifference to them." [11] In 1520 Martin Luther proposed to the nobility of the German nation that all holy days except Sunday be abrogated (he would have included Sunday except for reasons which will be discussed under the Sabbath) and that any festivals be observed on Sunday. His action proved to be the culmination of many attempts to lessen the ecclesiastical laws on holy days. Thinking practically, and with their penchant for social order, the Reformers perceived that so much idleness on holy days was ill suited for people dependent on manual labor for their living.

[10] Edith C. Rodgers, *Discussion of Holidays in the Later Middle Ages* (New York: Columbia University Press, 1940), p. 93.
[11] *An Encyclopedia of Religion, op. cit.,* p. 276.

It would seem evident, then, that the subsequent Protestant "elevation" of work as a noble use of time was largely a relevant perception of the need in their age, a reaction against an enforced and legalistic idleness—which was not what we would now regard as leisure—and against a licentious kind of recreational pursuit which led the people into degrading behavior. The subsequent development of legalistic rules to enforce work, such as developed in Puritanism, is another subject.

American Holidays

Those who settled in America were heirs of the revolt against holy days which shook the seventeenth century. Thus the religious heritage of our country is marked by the belief that in austerity and hard work man makes his true response to God. It is quite possible that the Puritans punished ceremonies and liturgies as such for the sins committed by a church which happened to be ceremonial and liturgical. This distrust of religious formalism left the people bereft of holidays as well as ceremony and liturgy in worship; the free and informal characterized every major American religious movement, with the "ceremonial" branches of Christendom (Roman Catholicism, Episcopalian, Lutheran) being, for a time, a minority.

Another reason for the evident lack of holidays in the new country may be seen in the tie holidays have with their mother country, both in spirit and in whatever seasonal connection they might have had. For instance, "May Day in England was a festival to mark the opening of spring, when the blood first ran warm, and lad and lass thought of life. But in Carolina the spring came earlier, and by May 1 the land might already have been for a month under the blanket of sultry heat." [12] Then, too, there was much work to be done in the new land and paid holidays were unheard of. What got done depended on the energy and devotion of the people; time for the necessary tasks was precious.

[12] Stewart, *op. cit.*, p. 252.

The subsequent growth of holidays in America would seem to be an indication of the pervasiveness of the urge to celebrate and the need to have times set aside which mark significant events in one's history, as well as the growing recognition that there is need for leisure in life. Americans have developed a sizeable number of special days honoring various aspects of our religious and national life. Some of our holidays were revivals of days already observed in other places—Christmas, Easter, New Year's. A few were re-interpreted and adapted from similar occasions in other places—Washington's birthday replaced the celebration of King George's birthday; and others were created brand new—Thanksgiving, Independence Day, Labor Day.

The designation of special observances as times for "humiliation and rejoicing" is no longer applicable; nor can we speak of "taboo days and feast days" nor simply of "holy days and holidays." There are certain emphases in our present celebrations which can be described as patriotic, religious, seasonal, familial, et cetera, and an attempt will be made to organize our observances under these headings, but these themes themselves are somewhat ambiguous. Perhaps the most commonly accepted division which characterizes American celebrations is made in terms of money; that is, whether or not the employee is given the day off with pay.

Legal Holidays. This term will include those observances for which employees are given time off from work with pay. There are no national holidays in the United States; each state, by legislation or by gubernatorial proclamation, designates its own observances. When the President of the United States proclaims a certain holiday, such as Thanksgiving, his act applies only to the District of Columbia and to the territories and possessions of the United States. The individual states often make such a day their own, however, and there are six legal holidays in America which are observed by all states, the District of Columbia, and the territories. These six legal holidays reflect three major emphases or themes.

1. Patriotic: Washington's Birthday, Independence Day, Labor Day. (In origin Labor Day is not really a "patriotic" celebration, having been designated in honor of the laboring man in the U. S. at a time when his plight needed recognition, but more and more it is being observed as a day which honors the "American way of life." Then again, its significance as a day which marks the end of summer, the start of school, and the coming of fall might well mean it should be called a "seasonal" celebration!)

2. Seasonal: New Year's Day. The American version of this ancient festival recognizing the change in years is described by Sebastian de Grazia as a curious feast, "primitive in its celebrating a mythical death and birth, pagan in its Bacchanalian echoes, Christian in its commemorating the beginning of the Gregorian calendar year." [13]

3. Religious: Christmas Day, Thanksgiving Day. (In origin Thanksgiving might be considered a "patriotic" celebration, but the spirit of Thanksgiving is definitely of a religious nature.) No doubt Easter would be included in this area if it did not fall on a Sunday which is already a day off.

It is not possible to list all the legal holidays observed in each state, but the days observed in the greatest number include the following.

1. Patriotic: Lincoln's Birthday, Memorial Day (formerly Decoration Day), Columbus Day, Veteran's Day (formerly Armistice Day), Election Day, individual state's days, birthdays of leaders, anniversaries of battles.

2. Religious: Good Friday. This day is becoming a legal holiday in many states, and in 1958 the labor unions included it as a paid holiday in their demands.[14]

---

[13] *Of Time, Work, and Leisure,* p. 120.
[14] Francis M. Wistert, *Fringe Benefits* (New York: Reinhold Publishing Corporation, 1959), pp. 34, 35.

Special Days. This term includes all other occasions when something or someone special is remembered, but which is not a day when employees are given time off with pay. Those days listed above as legal holidays in certain individual states are often special days in other states, but will not be repeated here.

1. Patriotic: Flag Day, Constitution Day, United Nations Day, various birthdays, anniversaries of battles, and dates of discoveries or inventions.

2. Seasonal: April Fool's Day, May Day, Groundhog Day, Arbor Day, Valentine's Day. (Valentine's Day grows out of several ancient traditions, but essentially it retains the character of a spring festival to love.)

3. Religious: Most Christian holy days or special days now occur on Sundays (Martin Luther take note), and include the following observances:

A. Individual days such as Passion Sunday, Palm Sunday, Easter, Pentecost (Whitsunday), Trinity Sunday, Transfiguration Sunday, and the first Sundays in Lent and Advent.

B. The seasons of Advent, Epiphany, Lent, Easter, and Pentecost.

C. Special emphases such as Universal Bible Sunday, World Communion Sunday, Race Relations Sunday, Rural Life Sunday, Universal Week of Prayer, Youth Week, Brotherhood Week, Christian Education Week, and Family Week.

D. The Sundays near Thanksgiving, Memorial Day, Labor Day, Veteran's Day, Independence Day, and Reformation Day. Other days in the week which are often remembered include Reformation Day, All Saints' Day, All Souls' Day, Ash Wednesday, Maundy Thursday, Ascension Day, and the eves of certain special days—New Year's Eve, Christmas Eve, Epiphany Eve, Easter Eve. In the Roman Catholic Church, the Episcopal Church, and a few other Protestant churches certain saints' days are celebrated.

Two occasions which had religious significance at one time but are no longer observed in that light are Shrove Tuesday, the Tuesday before Ash Wednesday, and Halloween, the eve of All Saints' Day. The former started as a festival to consume all the food which could not be eaten during the Lenten fasting period; it has become a time of *Carnevale,* such as the New Orleans' Mardi Gras. The latter was both a preparation time for All Saints' Day and the date of an ancient autumn festival of the Druids; the ghosts and witches, superstitions from the Druid rite, evidently appealed to the imagination and became the dominant motif of the occasion.

4. Family: Mother's Day, Father's Day, birthdays, wedding anniversaries, graduations, et cetera.

5. Ethnic: Saint Patrick's Day for the Irish, Columbus Day for the Italians. (Columbus Day, a "patriotic" celebration as well, has a certain Roman Catholic background through its propogation by the Knights of Columbus.)

6. Organizational: the anniversaries of the founding of certain groups such as the Boy Scouts, Girl Scouts, Y.M.C.A., Y.W.C.A., fraternal orders, et cetera. Many institutions observe a Founder's Day.

Even yet this list does not include all the occasions which Americans remember in one way or another,[15] not to mention the growing number of weeks which call our attention to certain vocations and desirable traits—Secretaries' Week, Be Kind to Animals Week, Fire Prevention Week, Big Brother Week, et cetera, et cetera! It is apparent that the special days far outnumber the legal holidays in contemporary America, but there is an increasing tendency toward longer paid vacations, longer weekends, and longer holiday periods. For instance, Wistert notes that "being considered by unions as future holidays are: (a) Friday following Thanksgiving. (b) Employee's birthday. (c) Monday following Easter." [16] Legal holidays which fall on

---

[15] For a complete list of observances and dates see Mary E. Hazeltine, *Anniversaries and Holidays* (Chicago: American Library Association, 1944).

[16] Wistert, *op. cit.,* p. 35.

143

Sunday are almost always celebrated by giving the employee the following Monday off.

There are two major notes which must be made about American celebrations in relation to the leisure problem. In the first place, holidays are most often thought of strictly in terms of their existence as "fringe benefits"; that is, as days off work with pay—or days which pay "double time" if the employee has to work. This enhances the tendency to think of them as earned time off which should be spent in idleness, or in traveling, as a respite from work. Little attempt is made to tap the tradition of the occasion as a resource for the leisure which the day makes possible. As the number of legal holidays increases there will be more free time—but this time will not automatically be true leisure.

In the second place, the terrific commercial pressures exerted on holidays and special days make the values embodied in those occasions very ambiguous. Greeting cards, gifts, clothes, sports equipment, food, cars, et cetera—all goods and services are now slanted to the coming holiday or season. This process of commercialization is obvious in relation to Christmas, the high point in the retail year. The interesting thing to realize, however, is that some of our special days have been virtually created—in terms of widespread observance—by the commercial market! For example, George Stewart writes that "by trying to build up Valentine Day (February 14) as an occasion on which a husband buys his wife a present, stores are attempting to improve February, at present the lowest month." [17] Customs for observing special occasions are being set by the outside commercial world rather than growing out of the significance of the day itself. This increased secularization points to an endless circle which seems to be growing larger—more paid holidays, more money spent to celebrate those holidays.

In our more reflective moments, however, we know that the

[17] *Op. cit.*, p. 273.

enjoyment and the renewal, which sometimes breaks through on holidays and special days, has not been a result of money spent or miles traveled. In spite of their growing commercial nature holidays still give us a sense of anticipation and a feeling of the "extra-ordinary." It is from this persisting sense that holidays embody something special, and therefore should be significant times, that another reformation may arise. If we look to these times not in terms of freedom from work nor money to spend, but in the light of meanings to be rediscovered and reinterpreted, they may become resources for true leisure. We turn now to a consideration of that possibility.

Toward a New Reformation

In an age of anxiety and boredom the lack of meaning and purpose can be seen at the root of the leisure problem. It can also be seen at the root of the leveling process which is making of all holidays a general and vague time of celebration. Whether the activity surrounding the festivities increases because the original significance of the day has been lost or whether the original significance is gradually obscured in the growth of the accompanying activity is a question which remains with us— but in historical analysis we have seen that both happens, and are happening again. With each holiday there is an increased tendency to buy more, get more, eat more, drink more, see more. The speed, carelessness, and recklessness of our holiday traffic, which causes so many holiday deaths each year, appears somewhat as a modern equivalent of the Roman gladiatorial games. The commercialized nature of our celebrations seems to indicate that we have confused "special" with "expensive."

We stand in need of a new reformation. We need to re-form our purposes and be reformed in our concepts of what is valuable. The reformation, then, must be a spiritual one, a personal and individual change in attitude and a re-evaluation of experience. It is possible that such a new reformation can be given its strongest initial impetus in relation to holidays—to recasting these times in terms of their original significance as holy days which are sources of religious and historical meaning and occasions for expressing our deep feelings.

Of course this re-discovery of the sense of the holy day cannot and should not apply to all the occasions listed. The important thing is not quantity but quality. We must find in our legal holidays and special days those which are most important to remember in the light of our life together and under God. In considering the most significant days we must not overlook whatever unintended as well as intended purposes the occasions may have. Lloyd Warner, for instance, has noted this double-level purpose with respect to Memorial Day and its sacred symbols and ritual. "Memorial Day is a cult of the dead which organizes and integrates the various faiths and national and class groups into a sacred unity. . . . Its principal themes are those of the sacrifice of the soldier dead for the living and the obligation of the living to sacrifice their individual purposes for the good of the group." [18] Other patriotic holidays can give periodic senses of unity and oneness in the midst of what often seems to be fragmented and chaotic relationships. In the celebration of Christian holy days this intended and unintended significance is present also, for whenever a congregation comes together in worship the consciousness that one is part of the long line of confessing Christians throughout the ages is present —and serves both to reassure and to challenge each individual about his place in that company.

Some people have argued that there should be no Christian holy days, that every day for the Christian is a special day for repentance, giving thanks, and expressing joy. Martin Luther evidently felt this way, although his concern with the economic burden of holiday restrictions on work made the situation in

---

[18] Lloyd Warner, *American Life: Dream and Reality* (Chicago: University of Chicago Press, 1953), p.3.

his time very different from ours. We are in need of rediscovering the ground of meaning in a time when many people are being freed from *both* work and worry over the economic means for life's necessities. There can be too many dates to remember, so that all blur together, but there is need to elevate certain times, seasons, and memorials to keep us mindful of our place together under God's care.

As far as the more secular holidays with popular appeal are concerned, it may be possible that within the context of the Christian faith they can be given new meaning—as the early Christians saw new significance in the Jewish festivals they kept and found a vital way to re-interpret some of the pagan festivals. On a few occasions something like this has been happening; for instance, New Year's Eve—long a time of wild revelry—is being observed often in the churches with a thoughtful and dedicatory Watch Night Service. Independence Day, Labor Day, Mother's Day, and other such occasions which originated apart from religious motivation are being included in the churches in a context of gratitude, recognition of common dependence, repentance for misuse of gifts, and rededication to living in the light of God's grace. Strangely enough, Halloween is taking on new meaning by those who now celebrate it as a time to collect money for UNICEF.

It is perhaps the attitude of thankfulness that is most lacking and most needed in regard to our rediscovery of holidays as holy days. In the sense of history which they encompass, telling of events and discoveries whose benefits we have reaped, we have been too little inclined to express gratitude. It is much more gratifying to feel filled with pride, an emotion which is generated in any number of patriotic celebrations, but in the last analysis it does not fulfill, satisfy, nor last in the "in between." Theodore A. Gill has suggested that probably for Christians Thanksgiving would be a more appropriate day to celebrate the birth of America than is the fourth of July.

That is because quiet thanksgiving is a more appropriate response to the facts of our history than is a drum-beating, breast-pounding, star-bursting pride. That special place in nature and in history which accounts so largely for our glory was *given*. The riches in our soil and streams, the space available to our restlessness and expansion, the distance set between us and international danger, the quiet time in history when we could tend to our own business and our own development—all this was *given*. . . . We were blessed—and not the least with men who knew what to do with the blessings.[19]

In our state of advanced scientific knowledge we have attained a staggering degree of control over the natural world and have pushed back the veil of fear and superstition which once held man. In pulling back that veil, however, we have eliminated the sense of mystery and wonder. In the long run we are finding that this is neither possible nor desirable, for no matter how much we know, there is still a basic mystery concerning who we are, where we came from, and where we are going. Trying to solve matters of the human spirit by rational processes has made us anxious; trying to live life without a sense of wonder has left us bored. A proper sense of these perceptions, however, is not to be blinded by fear, superstition, and ignorance—it is part of creation itself and completes our lives by allowing for the "extra-ordinary." Mystery and wonder is the soil in which celebration and leisure are nourished.

Every great discovery that man makes of his relation to God, to the universe, to his fellow humans, to himself, is so wonderful it calls for celebration. Religion marks it with a holiday. The state too has its holidays. A holiday is universal. It is celebrated not by the discoverers alone, but by all who share the wonders it reveals. . . . The holiday heals whatever rifts exist and reminds men that

[19] From an unpublished sermon by Theodore A. Gill, "Now Thank We All Our God." San Francisco Theological Seminary, San Anselmo, California.

they are bound together by the one equality with which they came into this world and with which they bow out. . . . the holiday is a day to celebrate the wonder of life.[20]

Both the impulse to worship God who comprehends the mystery, and the urge to celebrate the wonder of this life are present when leisure finds its fullest expression. It is for this reason that we may find again that holy days can be foci for leisure involvement which refreshes and renews our lives. These occasions are filled with meaning into which we can enter in joy as we become aware of who we are within our history, in humility as we acknowledge in worship and thanksgiving what has been done for us, and in assurance as we experience wholeness of life through the mystery and wonder of the celebrations. With discoveries to make, opportunities to share, and service to render, these holy days may become times of significant leisure.

How will such a reformation as we are suggesting, come about? Only through individuals, groups, perhaps communities and churches who have seen the possibility and have made it known. Also through the various mass media where concerned individuals make known their convictions in these ways. An "Editorial" in *The New York Times* called such attention to the origin of our holidays in a most illuminating way:

We call them the holidays, too seldom remembering that they are holy days, days of reverence for life and the spiritual meanings implicit in it. Root meanings that go back to pagan times relate the word "holy" to "whole" and even to "healthy," in the sense of completeness. Even in the earlier days of the Christian era, holiness and a degree of reverence extended to a host of everyday things and natural phenomena that we now have made commonplace, to our loss.

There were holy plants, among them the holy mallow. We still

[20] De Grazia, *Of Time, Work, and Leisure,* p. 435.

know it, still grow it in our country dooryards, but today we call it the hollyhock and forget its earlier significance. There were holy trees, each for a particular reason, among them one with thorny green leaves and bright red berries. We grant it holiday status today, but in the way we spell and pronounce its name, holly, we ignore the meaning it had.

There was a mystery and there was reverence for the whole of life, healthy mystery and holy reverence, before man began saying he knew all the answers. The basic mystery prevails, and on occasion man can even admit that he neither made the earth nor set the stars in their courses. The holidays we now celebrate are such an occasion.[21]

If we make the effort to be open to the significance of our holidays as holy days they may become vital forces for leisure and life, in our time even as they have been at other times in history. Nothing short of a new reformation will reverse the trend from holy days to holidays and restore the sense of holiness to our holidays.

[21] December 26, 1962. © 1962 by The New York Times Company. Reprinted by permission.

8

The Puritan Influence

As pointed out in the preceding chapter the settlers who immigrated to America were heirs of the revolt against holy days which characterized the Reformation. Of those early colonists, the group most criticized for its impact on present attitudes toward work and leisure has been the one which came from England to establish itself at Massachusetts Bay—the "Puritans." Exactly what the Puritan fathers believed and practiced is no longer really known; what exists in our day is the notion that anything which suggests strictness in morals, sobriety in conduct, piety in religion, thrift in business, diligence in work, or suspicion of pleasure can be attributed to the persisting influence of "Puritanism."

Illustrative of the view which traces the contemporary situation directly to the Puritan heritage is that expressed by George Soule:

A moral compulsion to work and to get ahead appears to be necessary in the mythos of a society if it is to operate an industrial system with the highest efficiency. The Puritans supplied this in England and a large section of North America. . . . The bitter essence of their conception of work lingers in our ethics—it is a duty, like most duties, unpleasant; and just because it is unpleasant it disciplines the soul. Any pleasurable pursuit they regarded for that very reason as vain or even wicked.[1]

[1] *Time for Living* (New York: The Viking Press, 1955), pp. 125-26.

Such an analysis seeks to locate America's preoccupation with work in the response which subsequent generations have made to the teaching of our New England ancestors that work is morally right while idleness and excessive merriment are a sinful waste of time. From this point of view it is then quite easy to infer that the Puritan fathers are also responsible for modern man's inability to accept and enjoy increased leisure.

It is a fact, however, that the extent of the Puritan influence on contemporary life is impossible to determine accurately. Any study of American history makes it abundantly clear that our complex makeup cannot be regarded as the result of any one political, religious, or social tradition. Puritanism influenced and was influenced by many other developments in the history of work and leisure in America, and it is important to include it in this study. The issues are too involved, however, to try to trace a straight line from original Puritanism to the present day with the thought of either condemning or defending the place of Puritanism in the development of leisure attitudes.

Furthermore, we cannot read present possibilities and alternatives into past history as though they could have been seen and considered at an earlier time. A leisure-oriented society in the terms we are coming to know it would never have occurred to the Puritans.

For one thing, the Puritans did not have a "leisure problem." They arrived in the New World hungry, ill, homesick, and generally miserable. They faced the task of carving out of the wilderness an existence for themselves—and for the first few years that existence meant just being able to survive. It was not suspicion of leisure or pleasure but stark necessity which made them say "the man who doesn't work doesn't eat."

In addition to this environmental factor there is the problem of what "leisure" actually meant to our Founding Fathers. Essentially, the word, when used, reflects an association with "idleness" or with luxury—at the expense of others—or with immorality—at the expense, they believed, of one's soul. No doubt these were characteristics of the leisure class in Europe and part of the way of life the Puritans sought to reform. They expressed attitudes concerning recreation and merriment, but how the New England Puritans felt or would feel about what this study has called leisure will have to be inferred from other material.

The first step in understanding the Puritan influence on the development of leisure involves looking at the Puritan frame of reference.

A Useful and Responsible Life Under God

Puritanism in England waged its war on two fronts—against persisting evidences of Roman Catholic influence in the Church of England, and against evils in personal conduct. As a religious phenomenon it sought to complete the Protestant reformation, to restore the English Church to its basis in and on Scripture and to foster behavior which would be pleasing to God. But Puritanism could not remain only a religious phenomenon, for "It involved a struggle for power—the power to exist, or the power to control. Puritanism found itself in the position of defying authority and was thus identified with the party of the revolution." [2] Affirming that religion should pervade life, the Puritans believed the state should support the church, suppress heresy, and legislate on the ground of Scripture. When, at the beginning of the seventeenth century, it seemed that governmental opposition was too great to surmount, the Puritans looked to the New World as the place for God to carry out his purposes.

The Puritans who formed the Massachusetts Bay Colony did not intend to separate from the Church of England as the Pilgrims had done earlier, but to separate from its impurities. What they actually established, however, was an autonomous church organization of congregational polity which stressed a

[2] Ralph Barton Perry, *Puritanism and Democracy* (New York: The Vanguard Press, 1944), p. 70.

simple, unadorned service of worship and a strict, disciplined way of life. Each congregation was a convenanted community whose members (persons eligible to partake of the sacraments and determine policy) were Christians who gave satisfactory evidence of conversion and regeneration.

The New England Puritans did not disavow allegiance to the King of England, coming as an English colony with a charter granted by the King. However, in Massachusetts they developed an autonomous form of government and were able to suppress at least one later attempt to bring over a British governor. Although the government was not theocratic in the sense that civil authority came from the clergy, leadership was given only by lay members of the church (regenerate Christians) who were pledged to do God's will. When a system of elected officials was introduced voting was restricted to members of the church for this same reason.

Calvin's theology, as modified by the English dissenters, provided the basis for Puritan faith. They affirmed the absolute sovereignty of God and the absolute authority of the Scriptures as a guide for all activities of life. They believed in the doctrine of justification by faith through Jesus Christ and in the doctrine of sanctification by God's grace—hence in the visible evidence of regeneration in the lives of Christians. Each Puritan felt it his responsibility and obligation to try to live in perfect obedience to God's will as a sign of his election.

But to remain faithful in this world proved no easy task, for since Adam's fall, sin abounded on every side, and at each step of the way a Christian could be tempted from devotion to God into evil. For the New England Puritans, life in all its aspects—work, worship, personal conduct, family life, government—was a constant battle toward "doing right in a world that does wrong." [3] Only by ceaseless activity and struggle could one

[3] Edmund S. Morgan, *The Puritan Dilemma: The Story of John Winthrop* (Boston: Little, Brown and Company, 1958), p. 203.

know if he were still on the path. Through self-examination and interpretation of natural and social forces one could discover certain "signs" of God's approval or disapproval. Economic failure, personal losses, and natural calamities were taken as signs of God's disfavor, while good fortune was presumably a sign of favor. Such a Deuteronomic philosophy of history, that the righteous are rewarded and the unrighteous are punished, continues to perplex Christians. It is interesting, however, that though the Puritans believed it they neither relaxed in times of plenty nor despaired in times of hardship.

For the Puritan, to do right meant to lead a useful and responsible life in this world that he might be eligible for election into his real home in the next world. As we consider their view of a useful and responsible life it is important to remember that the Puritans were not ignorant, fanatic, nor prudish. The men who initiated the Puritan move to America were intelligent, rational, educated men who found in Reformation Christianity a faith to live by. The lives they lived in New England reflect their "human background" as well as the doctrines in which they believed.

A useful and responsible life meant, for one thing, a life of devotion to a sovereign and almighty God, centered in a diligent study of the Holy Scriptures. Although they believed in the Bible as an absolute authority, they did not hold to a literal interpretation; Scripture was a practical guide to the daily activities of life and must be reasonable. Education was essential to the life of devotion and study, because each child must be taught to read the Bible for himself as preparation for his conversion. As the spiritual teachers, the ministers took the lead in interpreting Scripture, but theology was an important concern of every Puritan. Discussion of the Sunday sermon often provided the topic of conversation—even in courting!

Writing was also used to express the devotional life. In addition to the sermons, which the clergy carefully prepared in a simple and rational form, theological essays were written—by laymen as well as ministers—to explain an issue, defend a position, or attack a budding heresy. Through the writing of history the Puritans sought to make known God's will and providence. The general thrust of the histories was one of fulfillment, but since nothing happened without significance they included the bad as well as the good. Perhaps the most widely known expression of Puritan writing, however, was the diary. There, as a kind of confessional, he poured out to God his doubts and desires and took stock of his vices and virtues. Poetry, primers for children, catechisms, biographies, and autobiographies were still other ways the Puritans expressed their faith and hope.

The Puritan concern for education is illustrated in the fact that money toward founding a college was voted by the General Court of Massachusetts only six years after the colony led by John Winthrop arrived, and in 1642, twelve years later, the first class graduated from Harvard College! Schools to teach children to read, supported by public funds, were required by the end of 1650. The spirit of the first New England college was definitely religious, but the curriculum was rooted in the classical learning which the Puritans had known in England. "The humanist tradition, one of the noblest inheritances of the English race, went hand in hand with conquering puritanism into the clearings of the New England wilderness." [4] The Greek classics, Elizabethan and Cavalier poetry, and what was known in the fields of science and mathematics were taught along with theology. Contrary to much thought, the Puritans did not forbid the teaching of science. Being educated and curious about God's world, they stimulated scientific investigation, but all in the context of a God who was sovereign over nature.

Secondly, a useful and responsible life was rooted in work.

[4] Samuel Eliot Morison, *The Intellectual Life of Colonial New England* (New York: New York University Press, 1956; published as *The Puritan Pronaos*, 1935) , p. 55.

The breakthrough made by the reformers concerning the sacredness of vocation became one of the major tenets of the Puritan faith. Through his work the Christian makes his response to God, for as Richard Steele wrote in *The Tradesman's Calling*, published in 1684:

God doth call every man and woman ... to serve him in some peculiar employment in this world, both for their own and the common good. . . . The Great Governour of the world hath appointed to every man his proper post and province, and let him be never so active out of his sphere, he will be at a great loss, if he do not keep his own vineyard and mind his own business.[5]

Thus for the Puritan the choosing of a vocation meant trying to discern what work God was calling him to, and two rules guided his choice: The occupation must serve society and the public good in a useful way and the individual must have certain talents and inclination for the vocation.[6]

One can gather many quotations from Puritan folklore and literature which express grave admonitions against idleness and exalt work as a defense against wasting time. The story is told of an old elder who had passed away. While waiting in the darkened room for the funeral service to begin, his wife whispered to her daughter, "Pass me my knitting. I might knit a few bouts while the folks are gathering." Another story has it that New England Puritans drank a pint of yeast before going to bed at night to make them rise early in the morning.

It is true that because the Puritan felt responsible for using the talents which God had given him in the work to which he was called, such qualities as contributed to that end were emphasized—sobriety, honesty, thrift, industry, punctuality. Idleness and debilitating forms of recreation, activities which

[5] Quoted in Perry, *op. cit.*, p. 307.
[6] Edmund S. Morgan, *The Puritan Family* (Boston: Trustees of the Public Library, 1944), p. 32.

would hinder one's life as a working member of society, were frowned upon. Such a responsible view of work could not help leading eventually to economic success—a fact which has led Weber and Tawney to their conclusions about Puritan ethics and the rise of capitalism. However, two things kept the Puritan from amassing wealth for his own sake. He was to serve society in a useful way by his vocation and, as with all things of this world, he was not to care too much about his work and its rewards.

Finally, a useful and responsible life meant for the Puritan a fruitful and blessed marriage. In its emphasis on involvement in the world, Puritanism held neither with monastic retreat nor with celibacy but regarded the married state as a command of God and the family as the basic unit of society. The parents were responsible for educating the children, in both their theological and practical calling. Apprenticeshp seems to have been a common custom in New England, boys going to learn a trade if they did not go on to college and girls to learn how to keep a home. All servants and apprentices were under authority of the head of the family, and records indicate that courts sometimes turned offenders over to the head of a family for punishment.

Both love of partner and love of children were regarded as paramount necessities in the family relationship. But even these affections were to be subordinate to love of God. Earthly attachments were not ultimate, and often a widowed person who loved his partner deeply would remarry within a few months. In the early days of New England this theological principle was perhaps a kind of protection against the constant loss of loved ones in death.

The Puritan was a realist. He knew the meaning of the time in between the times and felt a responsibility to waste as little of it as possible. Though he believed that God's will was predestined to be done, his enthusiasm never waned as he sought to found a society and make his place in obedience. He loved and enjoyed God's gifts in this life, but viewed neither the accomplishments nor disappointments he encountered as ultimate.

> The Christian, knowing that he is only a stranger and eager to be at home, takes no delight in his journey. He enjoys the world only like a passer-by, having other and better business of his own elsewhere: "hee useth other mens goods for a night, but he setteth not his heart on them . . . because he knoweth he must leave them next morning, and may take none with him." [7]

"Seasonable Merriment"

Apparently the Puritans were essentially somber in nature. Assured that the Christian's true home is in another world, they felt that pleasurable experiences and enjoyment of earthly things were of little importance in themselves; insofar as such attachments could make one forget God altogether they felt called to overcome them. Furthermore, both the early New England environment and the Puritan theology emphasized the seriousness and difficulty of life—leisure was a luxury they could not afford. Thus Miller and Johnson noted that "There was almost always an element of narrowness, harshness, and literal-mindedness associated with Puritanism, enough to justify some of the criticisms of the bishops and some of the condemnations that have been made on the Puritan spirit in more recent times." [8] It must be remembered, however, that the original Puritans did not impose their code on people who did not accept the Puritan frame of reference, and narrowness and harshness did not constitute their total spirit.

As has been noted, the Puritans were realists, and the place of recreation and diversion in their view of a useful and responsible life reflects that realism. The need for recreation was

[7] William Haller, *The Rise of Puritanism* (New York: Columbia University Press, 1938), p. 149. His quote is from Taylor, *Three Treatises*, p, 123.

[8] Perry Miller and Thomas H. Johnson, *The Puritans* (New York: American Book Company, 1938), p. 59.

recognized as a basic part of man's makeup and was taken into account in the day's activities. Illustrative of this attitude is Benjamin Colman as he wrote from Boston in 1707 concerning *The Government and Improvement of Mirth:*

We daily need some respite & diversion, without which we dull our Powers; a little intermission sharpens 'em again. It spoils the *Bow* to keep it always bent, and the *Viol* if always strain'd up. Mirth is some loose or relaxation to the labouring Mind or Body, it lifts up the hands that hang down in weariness, and strengthens the feeble knees that cou'd stand no longer to work; it renews our strength, and we resume our labours again with vigour. 'Tis design'd by nature to chear and revive us thro' all the toils and troubles of life. . . .[9]

Such diversion was encouraged as healthful and helpful, but to keep it so the activity must be done in moderation. "Seasonable merriment" was the phrase the Puritans often used to describe the kind of recreation that was approved—merriment governed by the appropriate season.

The biggest criticism the Puritans had of immoderate, unseasonable diversion was based on its being "a waste of time." A man should gain refreshment from his recreation, and if, instead, he found the activity made him more tired and disgruntled it was wrong to do. Furthermore, if the activity required time and energy it should yield results which made it worth the effort. Edmund Morgan gives a delightful description of John Winthrop's argument for giving up shooting. It was against the law, exhausting, time-consuming, dangerous, expensive, and—the final point—he never hit anything anyway.

To Winthrop there was nothing incongruous or hypocritical about this reasoning. Shooting was not a legitimate recreation for a Puritan unless he got a satisfaction from it proportionate to the

[9] Quoted in Miller and Johnson, *ibid.,* p. 392.

time and effort it cost. No Puritan objected to recreation as such; indeed it was necessary for a man to indulge in frivolous pleasures from time to time, in order that he might return to his work refreshed. But to serve the purpose, recreation had to be fun and not exhaust a man physically or bore him or frustrate him.[10]

Instead of divorcing work and pleasure, this admonition not to waste time gave the Puritans a unity to their lives and the necessary activities. Barn raisings, quilting parties, weddings, cornhuskings, and all such elements of daily life became occasions for merrymaking as well as time spent in co-operative effort toward a useful end.

The Puritans were also aware of the excesses to which men became enslaved through pleasure. Such intemperance was an abuse of God's creation, serving only to gratify the senses and sidetrack man from his service to God. What they condemned and sought to regulate in these excesses, therefore, was not the practices as such but what they saw as the immoral consequences of the activities. Thus drunkenness was condemned, but not drinking. Indeed, one writer suggests that the label of "Puritan" which was attached to the twentieth-century prohibitionists would have surprised the New England Fathers no end! Eating for its own sake and ruling for the sense of power were condemned as excesses of the flesh along with adultery, gambling, and licentious behavior. Gambling—lotteries, cards, and dice— was objected to on the grounds that it tempted God's providence for frivolous ends. Often, however, dancing, drinking, and card playing took place in the privacy of homes as entertainment without comment, whereas the same activities in the public taverns were regarded as immoral because of the excess displayed there.

Dancing provided occasion for much controversy among the New England Puritans. In 1625 John Cotton wrote to a friend that "Dancing (yea though mixt) I would not simply con-

---

[10] *The Puritan Dilemma,* pp. 9, 10.

demn . . . Only lascivious dancing to wanton ditties." [11] By 1684 the state of things had evidently reached the place where the clergy thought a stricter tone was needed, and Cotton Mather published an essay called *An Arrow against Profane and Promiscuous Dancing. Drawn out of a Quiver of the Scriptures.*

. . . *Dancing* or *Leaping,* is a natural expression of joy: So that is no more Sin in it, than in laughter, or any outward expression of inward Rejoycing.

But our question is concerning *Gynecandrical Dancing,* or that which is commonly called *Mixt* or *Promiscuous Dancing, viz.* of Men and Women (be they elder or younger persons) together: Now this we affirm to be utterly unlawful, and that it cannot be tollerated in such a place as *New-England,* without great Sin.[12]

The fact that the dancing of men with men or women with women was not disapproved of no doubt indicates that mixed dancing was thought to be a temptation toward sexual promiscuity.

In regard to the arts as a proper diversion the Puritans showed greatest caution. While it is wrong to say the Puritans had no aesthetic perception, it is true that their distrust of the creative arts as glorifying the flesh retarded artistic development for some time. In poetry only those subjects which were of a moral nature or which fixed attention on God were thought worthy of consideration. So-called secular music was not objected to by the Puritan, but music in the worship service—as also any ornamentation—was thought to come between the worshiper and his attention on God. The theater and drama were anathema. Not only did such activity lack basis in scripture, it had been denounced by the early Christian fathers and

[11] Quoted in Miller and Johnson, *op. cit.,* p. 411.
[12] *Ibid.* pp. 411, 412.

in England was associated with the luxury and pomp of a court against which the Puritans objected.

To the Puritan the simple and orderly was beautiful because it did not interfere with the beauty of God as perceived through reason. Insofar as the arts often stimulate rather than relax, they were not regarded as appropriate forms of recreation. Since the arts frequently focus attention on man's life in the world, the immoral and sensuous expressions of that life as well as the good and noble, the Puritans did not consider them proper materials to study.

There is evidence enough to indicate that the Puritans were not opposed to diversion and recreation, provided it was truly refreshing, was not a waste of time, was not done in excess, and was not immoral or sensual. This seasonable merriment must contribute, along with all other activities, to the main business of living—acting in obedience to God. At no time were the lesser joys of earthly pleasure to get in the way of the highest joy, which was devotion to a sovereign God.

But leisure as we are seeking to understand it today is not to be equated with diversion; therefore, a further word must be said concerning Puritan activities which were not entertainment but which suggest elements of what might be called a "creative use of leisure."

For instance, men participated in government affairs for little or no financial remuneration because of talents or inclination for organization. The making of a home and family life provided another dominant interest which was more than just a duty. Attendance at worship and other religious meetings was looked forward to, not only as the central focus of the spiritual life, but also as occasion for social meeting. Entertaining guests, general visiting, and courting were activities in which all participated. Study of scripture and the continual process of education through intellectual pursuits of various kinds constituted an abundant source of "leisure" involvement. Even the rigid self-examination which the Puritan required of himself through

163

writing diaries and recording daily events and thoughts could be called a major leisure activity. "Indeed, it might be agreed that Puritan restrictions on purely physical enjoyment tended to stimulate intellectual life." [13] These concerns are also part of the historical development of leisure and provide a fruitful source of leisure involvement in the present day.

Finally, the very nature of the work which occupied the early Puritan settlers no doubt carried with it certain satisfactions and thrills which today often can be found only in leisure. The work they did was original and personal, whether planting crops, hunting, or making shoes. Perhaps the man who built a new barn or the woman who made a new dress, out of necessity, felt as much pleasure as the "do-it-yourself" enthusiast does in our time over a project he didn't have to do. Since the Industrial Revolution men have known a work-leisure division which did not always exist. In early New England each day brought its own round of necessary activities, but their work and diversion seem to have contained, at least in part, what we are seeking for in leisure.

The Fragmentation of Puritanism

A "last puritanism" will be a blend of puritanism and lastness— of the doctrinal peculiarities of puritanism with the mentality characteristic of any cult in its phase of decadence. Thus Santayana's famous book is an account not of the living puritan creed, but of its death; and its death resembles the death of any creed when its subordinations have become negations, its convictions rigidities, and its surviving zealots monstrosities.[14]

Before the end of a century the disintegration of original Puritanism had begun. Although the above quotation may seem harsh, it points out that the rigid morality and harsh piety which today are associated with the first Puritans were really the fruits

[13] Morison, *op. cit.,* p. 24.
[14] Perry, *op. cit.,* p. 64.

of the later puritanism which ushered in the 1700's. The degeneration of the pioneer thrust of the Founding Fathers took two major forms—a loss of religious fervor for the majority when luxury, comfort, and security came to New England and a defensive attempt to preserve and protect the uniqueness of Puritanism by the leaders.

In a way it is true that Puritanism carried within it the seeds of its own destruction. Started as a movement to reform and purify, it did not allow for its own reformation and purification. Coming from a country in which only one faith was allowed to exist as a state church, it did not perceive the possibility that a country could be based on diversity both in religious conviction and political conscience. In subordinating all activity to the middle-class virtues of hard work and industry, it did not anticipate that those virtues might carry their own consequences of idolatry, disobedience, and pride.

It was this very narrow, ingrown nature of Puritanism which enabled it to survive in the first place and to lay the groundwork for some of our most important American institutions—education, the church, free enterprise, family responsibility, individual integrity, et cetera. Had the leaders of the New England settlement not been bound in a common faith and been devoted to a common cause—the establishment of a holy commonwealth—it is doubtful if Massachusetts Bay would ever have survived, let alone have left a lasting influence. The Puritan dedication to the truth of their faith in a sovereign, transcendent God later became an intolerance of religious testimonies which claimed special inner revelation. Their belief that a government in which the leaders would legislate according to God's will could be established later became a denial of the right of non-Christians to vote or hold office. In original Puritanism, however, these were positive, unifying forces, not negative, suppressing ones.

The effect of this defensiveness on attitudes toward leisure, diversion, and recreation was also felt in two directions—rebellion by the non-Puritans, and by the younger generation of Puritans, and a greater prohibition by the leaders expressed from the pulpit and through restraining laws.

The cause for this defensiveness can be found in a variety of factors. For one thing the hardships and rigorous demands of the frontier were rapidly disappearing. In the eyes of the younger generation there was little need for such strict moral discipline; their fathers' theology of dependence on the providence of a sovereign God seemed irrelevant since worldly goods were clearly the product of human effort. The determined and enthusiastic faith in God which enabled the Puritans to leave their homes and fortunes in England to found a New England was a faith for times of persecution, crisis, and hardship. It lost its dynamic when attempts were made to communicate it to people who were more interested in bigger businesses and in the comforts of a settled life.

There was also a loss of control by the church over the lives of the people. Church membership declined, both because of slow population growth and as the children of church members defected under the strict requirement for conversion and visible regeneration. Puritanism was originally organized around the agricultural village with the land being farmed surrounding that center. As more land was absorbed, or as sons inherited portions, the families moved out from the population centers and established independent, isolated farms. These people, out from under the watchful eye of the clergy in daily affairs, often were unable to even travel into town for the Sunday sermon. Many people went into other fields of work, such as commerce and fishing. The equality enjoyed by the first Puritans in terms of a balance of wealth was upset, and influential groups who did not stand on Puritan principles arose to challenge that authority. In time the Puritans became a minority.

Furthermore, the New England settlement had been cut off from various currents of thought and fell behind in intellectual pursuits. As the Puritans were establishing their community in the wilderness and teaching their young people what they had learned of philosophy, science, culture, theology, et cetera, new strides were being made in these areas on the continent. Even the idea of religious toleration was making inroads in the Old World. When these changes reached American shores they encountered a Puritanism which was clinging to its old ideals and conceptions, believing that change would bring its total destruction. The Puritan leaders, once a liberalizing influence, became in essence the conservative faction of New England.

The Puritans lost their political control. By making voting rights and political leadership dependent on church membership, and by maintaining church membership on the basis of visible regeneration, they ran into a complex of problems. Not all the people were regenerate, yet all the people lived in the community; the nonchurch members began to demand a voice in the government. Even before the end of the seventeenth century the charter of Massachusetts was changed to make voting for the assembly dependent on property ownership rather than church membership.

Finally, a number of catastrophes took place—plague, drought, war, fires—in which the Puritans believed God was calling for the people to be restored to spiritual fidelity. In their terms this meant stronger discipline.

Thus Puritan leaders sought to stem the tide of change by reminding the people of the conduct of their fathers in matters of work and morality. "The early standards were accordingly preached to the youth and upheld as inherently worthy of obedience; their original practical value being less conspicuous, they were enforced by religious sanctions." [15] Not that there was no basis for stern preaching as the seventeenth century neared its end, but the emphasis was on the outward forms of behavior justified by the past code. The early Puritans had believed the

[15] Herbert Wallace Schneider, *The Puritan Mind* (Ann Arbor: University of Michigan Press, 1958; Henry Holt and Company, 1930), p. 82.

sovereign God could and would send destruction, but they did not dwell on it in their preaching. Their sermons were generally positive, appealing to the mind and instructing the believers on their journey home. The later preachers tended more and more to center their concern in the pronouncement of God's judgment on the evil of the times. Perry Miller notes with clarity that the second generation found its primary literary expression in terms of the "jeremiad." [16]

In the eighteenth century, prior to the Revolutionary War, there came a major split in the concern which had united the Puritan founders—the inter-relatedness of the individual spiritual life with its outer forms of work and conduct. On one side was Jonathan Edwards, the New England clergyman who spearheaded the Great Awakening. Edwards focused attention on the individual soul before an almighty and all-powerful God. Man's inner spiritual life—his sense of sin and his feeling of total dependence on God's grace—became all important; while man can do nothing to win election, he must—out of fear for his immortal soul and the hope of possible election—live a godly and sober life.

On the other side was Benjamin Franklin, American patriot, inventor, and patron saint of the industrious. Franklin found the Puritan virtues of work and thrift valuable for everyone apart from the faith which had contained them. Instead of seeing these virtues as part of the way to live a responsible life under a sovereign God, he gave them practical wisdom and intrinsic justification as the way to a successful life in this world. While Franklin himself used every opportunity to pursue in leisure his many interests, *Poor Richard's Almanak* gave a boost to the work-thrift morality as the way to health, wealth, and happiness.

Fragments of Puritanism are scattered throughout American life. The Congregationalists, Presbyterians, Unitarians, Meth-

[16] *The New England Mind: From Colony to Province* (Cambridge, Mass.: Harvard University Press, 1953) , p. 29.

odists, Baptists, and the various splinters from these denominations, bear in different degrees the marks of Puritan polity, Calvinistic theology, intellectual emphasis, and devotion to spiritual regeneration. In national life the virtues of Puritanism, especially as elevated by Franklin, have become an indigenous part of what is traditionally American—hard work with appropriate recreation and a seriousness about the business of life.

The churches have generally continued their suspicion of leisure on the grounds that it is a luxury, caters to the sensual enjoyment of man, and leads to an immoral use of time. Also, the renunciation of society's common pleasures—card playing, dancing, drinking, the theater—has continued to be regarded as an evidence of "true Christian living." The conventional wisdom of the nation, through business and political concern, has also been suspicious of leisure on the grounds that work is the way to progress, prosperity, and a greater nation. Only since the economic potential of leisure was discovered—the leisure industry of goods and services and the value of the person's consuming power during leisure—have secular walks of life given approval. This fact would lend credence to the conclusion of writers who have located present attitudes toward work and leisure in a utilitarian philosophy rather than in Puritanism.[17]

Both the wholesale denunciation of the pleasure of leisure and the pervasive thought that each person should work to amass as much wealth for himself as possible are foreign to original Puritanism. For this reason it is possible that we may find in authentic Puritanism some clues to help us in our present plight.

[17] See, for instance, Walter Kerr, *The Decline of Pleasure* (New York: Simon and Schuster, Inc., 1962), p. 46: "An ancient Puritanism returned to haunt us? Hardly. All of the other tensions engendered by Puritanism have long since been sprung, deliberately and with some abandon; why should the fear of pleasure alone have lasted?" And p. 51: "The philosophy that won the twentieth century without seeming to have fired a single shot was called 'utilitarianism.'"

Puritanism and a Leisure Society

As has been stressed before, the Puritans did not foresee the possibility of a leisure society; therefore, we cannot infer that they rejected it as an alternative. They had reservations about leisure when there was work to be done, yet they contributed to our increased leisure by emphasizing the building of a responsible society via responsible individuals.

Furthermore, a disciplined life of self-control and self-evaluation is still an honorable pursuit. To take the opposite side of the Puritan virtues merely because those virtues became narrow and rigid would make a peculiar stand: We should be lax in morals, drunken in conduct, impious in religion, unthrifty in business, a goof-off at work, and should indulge in all forms of pleasure readily offered by an affluent society! Ralph Barton Perry pointed to this danger in commenting that the activities the Puritans attacked were, in a sense, a "historical accident." But, he went on to say, such laxity and loose living has always existed and " 'Self-indulgence' is a term of reproach under any code, since it implies an indifference or resistance to that code as such, whatever code it be. Therefore he who takes arms against puritanism must consider that by so doing he gives aid and comfort to the puritans' enemy, who is in some sense also his own." [18] In questioning Puritan strictness we must not merely swing to the other extreme of antinomianism and license in leisure.

How then are we to evaluate our new state of leisure? Is it possible that Puritanism may provide help?

For one thing, Puritanism was rooted in a view of life as a unified whole under the sovereignty of God. Because work was their dominant necessity they did not see the other dimensions of life as "separate" within the total scheme of purpose and meaning. Attempts to speak to the leisure situation today have sometimes contributed to further fragmentation by divorcing

[18] *Op. cit.,* p. 267.

leisure from the rest of life: We are free in leisure, unfree in work; leisure is unobligated time, the rest (work, family, sleep, eating, et cetera) is obligated. The implication clearly is that leisure is the most desirable part of life because it is free and unobligated; the rest must be endured. No matter how much leisure time increases, however, it will have to be integrated with the rest of life if it is to be creative and meaningful. Often the person with a leisure problem, whether too much free time or too little, is the person who is just dissatisfied with his life as it is. To live abundantly requires a context in which all time and activities of life are contained and given significance—a perspective we shall elaborate in the final chapter.

In terms of the Christian faith we are called to wrestle with our lives under God and find our response in terms of our own situation. "To have leisure to the glory of God" is perhaps our possibility and task, and one can only find what that means by returning to the New Testament faith. It may well be that the Puritan concern for "a useful and responsible life" and for "seasonable merriment" will be part of the new leisure ethics. The idea of Christian stewardship—namely, a responsible use of time, talents, and possessions—applies to leisure as well as work. The Puritans failed to see that the successful practice of virtue in business might carry its own temptation to excess; let us learn from them and anticipate such problems in a leisure-oriented society.

A second area in which the Puritans may help us concerns acting in this world. It is interesting to note that though they affirmed this life only as a step to the next life, they nevertheless acted in it realistically and deeply. With worship and study at the center of activities, their faith then radiated out and pervaded participation in government, business, family, and social occasions. How much more could we, with lives free from the dangers, hardships, and demands which the Puritans faced, participate in the pressing concerns of society if we took advantage of our leisure to that end?

171

Perhaps the central place where we will depart from the Puritan view is in their attitude toward life in the world. The Puritans were urged to love the world with "weaned affections." So real was the evil on all sides that they felt the beauty of nature and the wonder of human relationships to be a snare to trap them in evil. So transitory was this life—death of loved ones was a constant fact, and there was little fulfillment of God's promises of peace in their experience—that to become a slave to affections or optimism would have brought despair. Their home was with God in another world.

A faith relevant to our "world come of age" must be based on the understanding that God created the world good, and to love it and its wonders is to love his work. In our surroundings of impersonal machines, phony commercials, and superficial relationships our greatest task is to penetrate those externals and love the world with "deepened affections." Material possessions are as relative and transitory for us as they were for the Puritans; but fellowship with others and involvement in the human family are joys to which we are summoned. For this reason the arts, as expressions of meaning, will be important for us; rather than "glorifying the flesh" they can make articulate the nature of our common experiences and feelings and enable us to push through the surface realities. Only by living deeply can we be prepared to understand the possibilities and utilize the potentialities of the leisure which is ours.

Finally, in the Puritan faith the church provided a supportive and a directing influence in human conduct. Perhaps it can now give aid in understanding and utilize increased leisure in the context of faith. Rather than leaving people to find their leisure standards through siren-voiced television commercials which urge them to buy their pleasure, we can give support to the view of leisure as a creative use of talent and responsibility in a variety of ways. Rather than letting the work motive "to get ahead" transfer to leisure, guidance can be given concerning the need to let go and rest in nonactivity. Self-improvement as personal growth is one thing, but allowing social pressures to turn leisure into more work is another.

The significance of church membership and participation for individuals and families as a leisure activity is another focus. To do this the churches will have to study the leisure needs and possibilities of its people. For instance, one study of the summer activities of children in relation to the church program revealed several important facts: The church cut its program in the summer because so many people went out of town, when really very few families were gone more than two weeks out of the summer; the church geared its activities toward the children, but evidence suggested that families liked to do things together; summer activities for children of low-income, nonchurch families was the greatest need, but few churches ministered to any but their own regular attendants.[19]

Amos Wilder suggests that in the Puritan heritage we may find "a common cultural and spiritual rebirth," for it is the tradition which brought to America the positive core of the Protestant Reformation—the reality of an autonomous and responsible personality which is rooted in neither subjectivism nor collectivism. Later Puritanism erred toward a rugged individualism; studies like *The Organization Man* suggest that today we err toward a subordination to the social group. Original Puritanism held both together in terms of faith in a sovereign, personal God and was enabled to shape a society which, though work-oriented, had meaning and purpose. By returning to the source of that spiritual power perhaps we can shape a society which, though leisure-oriented, also is pregnant with meaning and purpose. After all, "this is the rock from which we were hewn and the pit from which we were digged."

[19] Lauris B. Whitman, Helen F. Spaulding, and Alice Dimock, *A Study of the Summertime Activities of Children in Relation to the Summer Program of the Churches* (The Committee on Children's Work, National Council of the Churches of Christ in the U.S.A., 1959).

9

The Sabbath Tradition

Final consideration must be given now to the part played by the sabbath tradition as one of the historical roots of leisure. Of the three factors discussed in this "length" dimension, the sabbath practice of resting one day in every seven has contributed most consistently to man's opportunity for leisure. As a holy day/holiday the sabbath has been by far the most important—as George Stewart quipped, "fifty-two times as important as any other holiday." [1] In Puritanism the sabbath was regarded as the high point of the week and was protected as a day for worship and rest.

Originally, of course, the sabbath referred to Saturday—the Jewish weekly holy day. The importance of this observance is evident from its inclusion in the Law of Moses as the Fourth Commandment and in the fact that the Genesis story of creation culminates in God's resting on the seventh day. In Christianity Sunday became the weekly holy day. Though there have been, at times, attempts to transfer the sabbath commandment and the Genesis context to the first day of the week, it was not until the end of the sixteenth century that the Puritans actually began calling Sunday "sabbath."

The motivation for instituting the sabbath was apparently twofold: Humanitarian in its provision of rest for both men and animals, and religious in its positive designation as a day of worship and joy. There is little doubt, however, that it was the religious impulse which was primary and which enabled

[1] *American Ways of Life,* p. 247.

174

the faithful to secure the day as one free from work. This sabbath tradition, Alan Richardson noted, throughout Hebrew and Christian history, "gave to working people the only regular rest from labour they ever enjoyed." [2]

In recent times there has been a great deal of discussion concerning sabbath/Sunday rest and the constitutionality of Sunday "blue laws"—that is, state laws governing the conduct of business on Sunday.[3] Part of the controversy arises from a sense of justice: Should people who close their businesses and observe a religious day of rest other than Sunday be made to close on Sunday as well? Part of the controversy also involves the question of whether it is now necessary to keep Sunday as a strict, so-called day of rest. As leisure time continues to increase with longer weekends, and as the demand for goods and services mounts, the traditional role of Sunday will be called into question even more.

Concerned primarily with the historical dimension of leisure and its growth through the sabbath tradition, this chapter does not propose to deal with the contemporary problem of Sunday legislation. However, an analysis of the historical development of the sabbath and Sunday observances and of the theology which supports them may suggest a direction for the future. Therefore, the concluding remarks of this chapter will touch on the contemporary situation.

In the light of the present problem it is important to remember that the sabbath/Sunday observance was meant to be a blessing, not a burden. Discussing the rhythm of work and

[2] *The Biblical Doctrine of Work* (London: Student Christian Movement Press, Ltd., 1952), p. 54.

[3] Hiley H. Ward, *Space-Age Sunday* (New York: The Macmillan Company, 1960), gives an interesting footnote on the description "blue laws": "The term 'blue law' was originated by a Tory, Samuel Peters, who, after being driven out of New Haven, Conn., in 1781, fled to London. In retaliation, he wrote a satire, *General History of Connecticut,* one chapter of which contained the Sabbath laws of Connecticut as he recalled them. . . . Peters, however, did not select the term 'blue laws' because of its derisive nature, but because the lawbooks of Connecticut were bound in blue." (p. 7, footnote 4).

175

leisure in life, Emil Brunner noted that in the Sabbath commandment we see

a sign that work is not an end in itself, that labour must serve man and life, but that it must not dominate it. It is not that—"unfortunately"—we *are obliged* to rest, but that—and not at all "unfortunately!"—we *ought* to rest. Only in repose does the human quality in a human being become evident, just as inhuman qualities are revealed in those who cannot rest.[4]

In its provision for rest from labor and refreshment for the spirit the sabbath tradition has proclaimed that work is not the chief end of man, hence it has supported the opportunity for leisure. But the major problem has been, and still is, what is to be done in that leisure.

Seventh Day of the Week

How the Jewish sabbath originated remains a mystery. The practice may have grown out of certain "moon" observances. For instance, several passages in the Old Testament mention the Sabbath in juxtaposition with "new moon" feasts, as though it might have been a "full moon" festival.[5] Also, the Hebrew word—from the verb *shabath,* meaning "to cease working, to desist"—bears a close resemblance to the Babylonian word *shapattu.* This latter word was used to designate the middle day of the month as a boundary dividing the waxing and waning phases of the moon—hence a full moon day.

Some scholars suggest that the sabbath was a Canaanite institution which the Israelites assimilated when they entered Canaan and adapted to the new environment and culture. There is evidence that a civil code containing injunctions to cease work on the seventh day and to keep certain agricultural fes-

---

[4] *The Divine Imperative,* p. 389.
[5] See II Kings 4:23; Amos 8:5; Hos. 2:11; Isa. 1:13*b.*

tivals was in existence when the Hebrews invaded Canaan. Furthermore, the observance of a sabbath has been traced to a settled, agricultural way of life. As long as the Israelites were a nomadic people with pastoral duties they could not keep a day free from work. Only after they settled down to an agricultural life could they institute such a practice.

Other scholars trace the origin of the Hebrew sabbath to a combination of Mesopotamian and Assyrian practices which the Israelites accepted at about the same time (Mesopotamian new-month day restrictions and the Assyrian custom of seven-day restrictions). All these days were thought of as sabbaths by the Jews because all were the same kind of observances—days of restriction and rest. Then during the Exile the Hebrews took over the Babylonian custom of observing only the seventh day for rest and restriction, hence as sabbaths (*shabbath*). In this context Norman Snaith suggests that the connection between *shabbath* and *shapattu* (or *shabattu*) lies in the fact that "both words are used to mark the end of a period of time." [6] In our consideration, however, the exact origin of the sabbath is not the important thing. Regardless of how it began—whether as a moon observance or as a practice adopted from another culture—the important and interesting thing is that in the hands of the Hebrews the sabbath took on a character and religious significance which was very different from any of its predecessors or neighbors. Whatever connection it might have had with a "taboo," unlucky, or evil day, the sabbath for the Jews did not continue in that spirit.

Ultimately it became a day of positive worship of the Diety, characterized not only by complete abstention from all ordinary occupations and activities but also by assemblage in temple or synagogue and sacrifice or prayer and ritual observance there. In this, its major

[6] *The Jewish New Year Festival* (London: Society for Promoting Christian Knowledge, 1947), p. 123.

and only persistent aspect, the sabbath is essentially of Jewish origin.[7]

The characteristics of the sabbath as it developed in Hebrew history all revolve around the fact that it was believed to be a special day set apart from other days as a sign of the covenant between God and Israel. Thus labor was to be set aside; travel and business transactions were prohibited; even the preparation of food was to be done on the preceding day. Two of the sabbath injunctions in Exodus reflect this provosion for rest and renewal of strength. The older account speaks only of agricultural work (Exod. 34:21), but the other applies more generally and includes servants, animals and strangers: "Six days you shall do your work, but on the seventh day you shall rest; that your ox and your ass may have rest, and the son of your bondmaid, and the alien, may be refreshed" (Exod. 23:12).

In the Deuteronomic edition of the Ten Commandments, emphasis was put on the sabbath as a day to remember the deliverance of Israel from Egypt (Deut. 5:12-15). There is no evidence that the sabbath was observed by the Jews while they were in bondage in Egypt. As God's act of deliverance through Moses was regarded as the renewal of the Covenant with Israel, the Deuteronomists saw in the renewal of sabbath observance a visible sign of that continuing relationship. The cessation of work was here rooted in the motivation of gratitude and thanksgiving rather than in purely humanitarian reasons.

Finally, however, expression was given to the deeper and most significant of the motives for sabbath rest in Exod. 20:11 and in Gen. 2:2-3. God worked six days to make the heavens and earth and then he rested. In his rest God made his covenant with Israel and the seventh day was hallowed as a sign. Johannes Pedersen called our attention to this understanding: "It is not

[7] J. Morgenstern, "Sabbath," *The Interpreter's Dictionary of the Bible* (Nashville: Abingdon Press, 1962), 4, 135.

the welfare of this worker or the other which is the decisive factor. On the sabbath and other feast days work ceases because these days are holy. From the force gathered around them the rest of the time derives its strength, therefore all life is dependent on the maintenance of their holiness." [8] Thus the sabbath is set apart as the pivotal day of the week which gives meaning and purpose to the rest of the days. The holiness of this day of rest is a special reminder of the wholeness or integrity that characterizes all of life.

This holiness of the sabbath is the positive spirit of the observance. While the injunctions not to work, travel, cook, et cetera, are negative in character, the primary attitude of the Jews to the sabbath has been one of positive joy and pleasure. "Observe the sabbath day, to keep it holy," was an affirmation of Israel's faith in God as her creator and sustainer. In celebrating the sabbath the Hebrew people were strengthened and renewed.

From the time of the Babylonian exile the sabbath observance changed. On the one hand, it became the most important institution in Judaism for the communal expression of the people. "After the destruction of the Temple, and during the Exile, the other feasts could no longer be observed; hence the sabbath acquired a new importance, for it then became the distinctive sign of the Covenant." [9] Also, with the destruction of the Temple the synagogues grew in significance as the centers for worship and religious instruction. The sabbath, already a day of leisure, became the natural occasion for the assemblies in the synagogue. Ritual became established and then expanded as the weekly worship was regularized, marking an even greater distinction between the seventh day and the rest of the week. Although such sabbath worship was not enjoined by scripture,

---

[8] *Israel: Its Life and Culture* (London: Geoffrey Cumberlege, Oxford University Press, 1926), III-IV, 290.

[9] Roland de Vaux, O.P., *Ancient Israel: Its Life and Institutions* translated by John McHugh (New York: McGraw-Hill Book Company, Inc., 1961), p. 482.

it seemed more and more to be the proper way to spend the day.

On the other hand, however, prohibitions concerning the sabbath increased. Perhaps they started in the Exile when it was important to preserve the day as a distinguishing mark for the Jewish community in diaspora. Since the temptation to break the observance of the day would be greater in a foreign place, the rules had to be more strict. Perhaps the regulations grew as the spontaneous sense of the holiness of the day began to fade. Pedersen notes that the Deuteronomic version of the sabbath commandment as linked with Israel's deliverance from Egypt would point to this need—what once had been a simple recognition of the meaning of the day had to be spelled out and enforced. Then again, perhaps the need for regulations came after the Exile as the nation was being reunited.

In any case, the negative element grew, and anxiety over infringing on the sabbath law called for more elaborate injunctions. A list of thirty-nine kinds of work forbidden on the sabbath was in effect at the time of Jesus, with all work reducible to those basic categories. For instance, in picking and eating grain on the sabbath Jesus' disciples were guilty of reaping—by picking—and threshing—by rubbing the ears to get the grain. Such interpretations were to Jesus both narrow-minded and a violation of human need and value.

The unique contribution of Judaism to the sabbath tradition lay in its securing of one day in every seven as a day of rest, joy, and positive thanksgiving to God. This seventh day may be regarded as a "tithe of time," a holy day which points to the holiness of all time, a hallowed day which in turn reveals the consecration of all life. Thus in the sabbath observance man is assured that he is not only a laborer bearing the burden of work—he is a creature made in God's image and called to participate in God's rest. This leisure was not only grounded in a religious belief which said "do not work," but also it was filled with re-creative power for those who waited upon the Lord and found their strength renewed. It lost this value when adherence to legalistic codes became the primary focus.

First Day of the Week

The origin of Sunday as the weekly day of worship for Christians is somewhat clearer than the origin of the Jewish sabbath. Sunday, the first day of the week, was first of all the day of Christ's resurrection. "The Day of the Lord" or "the Lord's Day" it was called by the early Christians. As some of Jesus' followers went to the tomb on the first day of the week to find him risen in triumph over sin and death, so followers in subsequent generations found the day an appropriate occasion for gathering together in the worship of God and the living Christ. Sunday was given an additional significance as the day of Pentecost on which the disciples received the Holy Spirit and went forth to call men together in the name of Jesus Christ.

For some time, however, the first Christians continued to observe the Jewish sabbath as well as their own Lord's Day and even daily gathering. The actual designation of Sunday as a day of rest and worship developed only gradually. The New Testament in no way provided any authority for such a designation, nor is there any indication that either Jesus or the early Christian leaders thought of Sunday as a continuation of the Jewish sabbath simply transferred to another day.

Jesus himself seems to have kept the sabbath by visiting the synagogue, although he openly rejected the legalistic rules which had come to surround the day's activities. "The sabbath was made for man, not man for the sabbath; so the Son of man is lord even of the sabbath" he said (Mark 2:27-28), thereby setting love and mercy over all restrictions and regulations. To alleviate suffering, to satisfy hunger—these acts were regarded by Jesus as entirely consistent with the worship of the God of grace, on the sabbath as well as any other day. As "the lord of the sabbath" Jesus could and did bring an end to the Jewish sabbath, "for the New Covenant which he brought abrogated the Old Covenant, of which the sabbath was the sign." [10]

Paul saw the sabbath observance as part of the old Law which Jesus supplanted. "Therefore let no one pass judgment on you in questions of food and drink or with regard to a festival or a new moon or a sabbath. These are only a shadow of what is to come; but the substance belongs to Christ" (Col. 2:16-17; cf. Rom. 14:15). In his view the keeping of the sabbath was not binding on Gentile Christians. When a man enters into the new life which is lived in the spirit of Jesus Christ, he is freed from the old law which required observances like the sabbath as a sign of faithfulness.

It was not possible, of course, for the early Christians as a minority sect to observe Sunday as a day of rest from work, but there also is no overt expression that they felt it should be. Henry Sloane Coffin suggests that, in the light of the minor position the early Christians occupied, "Paul was not concerned with giving advice to churches that could influence the state to enact a legal holiday; he was thinking of little communities made up of slaves and artisans, who must live their lives under an altogether indifferent imperial government." [11] Perhaps it is true that it never occurred to Paul and the early church Fathers that Sunday could ever be a day free from work; nevertheless, they in no way felt it had to be, nor did they see the Fourth Commandment or the seventh day of the Genesis creation story as applying in any way to the Lord's Day. They were, in fact, very zealous in their attempts to give the Christian gatherings an independent foundation.

From meeting daily and on Saturday, emphasis finally shifted for Christians to the first day as their day of worship, and it thereby replaced the Jewish sabbath. As Christianity began settling in and expanding as an institution it, no doubt, required

[10] De Vaux, *op. cit.*, p. 483.

[11] *The Ten Commandments* (New York: Hodder and Stoughton, George H. Doran Company, 1915), p. 79.

a stated day for worship, and Sunday as the day of the resurrection dominated.

The celebration of the Lord's Day by assembling for worship —most likely before dawn—became the essential core of the maintenance and expression of the central truths and beliefs of the Christian faith. "The gathering of the faithful, the exposition of the Scriptures, the witnessing to the Resurrection, the administering of the Sacrament—based as they are on the events of Easter Day, these become characteristic acts of the *ecclesia* on the Lord's Day down through the ages." [12] In this form the Christian church drew more from the Jewish pattern of worship, perhaps, than was thought. But the emphasis was different. The Jewish sabbath was a day of rest based on a commandment which commemorated the renewed covenant between God and Israel as expressed especially in the deliverance from Egypt, and which pointed to the eventual fulfillment of the covenant at the end; the Christian Lord's Day became the proclamation of the new covenant in Christ in whom the promise had been fulfilled. Some of the early church Fathers even called Sunday the "eighth day," meaning the perpetual first day of the new age. "Like all the other promises of the Old Testament, these promises too are realized not in an institution, but in the person of Christ: it is he who fulfils the entire Law. Sunday is the 'Lord's Day,' the day of him who lightens our burdens (Mt 11:28), through whom, with whom and in whom we enter into God's own rest (He 4:1-11)." [13]

Ignatius, the author of the letter of Barnabas, and Justin Martyr all spoke of Sunday as supplanting the Jewish sabbath. In the middle of the second century Justin Martyr also related God's creation of light on the first day to the dispelling of darkness in the resurrection of Christ. This view may account for Justin's favorable association of the sun with the first day of

[12] H. B. Porter, *The Day of Light: The Biblical and Liturgical Meaning of Sunday* (Greenwich, Conn.: The Seabury Press, 1960), pp. 45, 46.

[13] de Vaux, *op. cit.*, p. 483.

the week in one of the earliest such references. It was Tertullian at the beginning of the third century who gave the first explicit reference to the need for Christians to abstain from work on Sunday, though he made a clear distinction between the Christian celebration and either Jewish or heathen observances.

Thus the duty of complete Sunday rest developed only gradually in the course of the history of the Church, as the solemn aspect of the Lord's Day was increasingly emphasized. Finally, in the early part of the fourth century Constantine legislated the first Sunday laws. This act was not so much an elevation of Christianity as the official religion of the Roman Empire, but an act of deference whereby the Christian day of worship was accorded the same civic honors traditionally given to pagan feasts. The law applied to all "Sun day" worshipers—of Hercules, Apollo, and Mithras, as well as Christ. Constantine did, however, require his soldiers to memorize a Christian prayer which they recited, no doubt mechanically and with empty formalism, on Sundays.

Subsequent emperors carried the Sunday legislation in favor of Christianity farther and farther, eventually giving the Church authority to force people to worship as well as refrain from labor on Sunday. Legalism grew up around Sunday as it had around the sabbath. Also, the sanction given to other holy days of the church tended to obscure the significance of the Lord's Day, and the problem of the middle ages, which was discussed in the chapter on holy days, arose.

In general the Reformers returned to Paul's view of the weekly sabbath—that in Christ such a requirement had been abolished. Having seen the legalized Sunday bear fruits in hypocrisy, slackness, idleness, and superstition, they emphasized free observance in the right spirit, the sanctity of all days as holy, and the fact that the righteous need no special reminders. But Luther also recognized the frailty of human nature along with the needs of public worship, so he wrote, "although . . . all days are free and alike, it is yet useful and good, yea, necessary, to keep holy one day, whether it be sabbath or Sunday or any other day; for God will govern the world orderly and peacefully; hence he gave six days for work, and the seventh for rest, that men should refresh themselves by rest, and hear the word of God." [14]

While some attempts had been made in the Middle Ages to justify the Christian Sunday on the basis of the Fourth Commandment, it was the Puritan movement of the sixteenth century which succeeded in ascribing to the Lord's Day the term sabbath and provided regulations for its observance as a day of strict rest and quiet. It is true, as noted in the preceding chapter, that the Puritans did much to maintain a moral standard in a time of laxity, and by securing Sunday as a day free from work they once again provided a source of leisure for the laboring man as well as a focus for his religious worship. However, their sense of proper Sunday activities brought, once more, a legalism and an austerity which later generations felt made Sunday staid and joyless.

The Evangelicals in England in the eighteenth and nineteenth centuries used Sunday as a time for education and religious instruction. William Hodgkins notes that "The greatest single contribution towards Sunday observance came during the latter part of the eighteenth century with the establishment of Sunday Schools." [15] Children and youth found in these schools an opportunity for friendship, education, relief from labor or idleness, and a moral standard which later undergirded some of the great reforms in the country. Rather than a dreaded time, Hodgkins observes that the Victorian Sunday with its rest, peace, worship, and social meetings was anticipated and remembered throughout the week. In a sense, the development of Sunday observance in the United States parallels this develop-

[14] Quoted by Philip Schaff, *History of the Christian Church* (Grand Rapids, Michigan: Wm. B. Eerdmans Publishing Company, 1949; originally published by Charles Scribner's Sons, 1910), VII, 493.

[15] *Sunday: Christian and Social Significance* (London: The Independent Press, Ltd., 1960), p. 81.

ment in England. Puritanism inculcated a strong regard for Sunday rest and worship, and the rise of the Sunday schools enhanced the use of Sunday time.

The contribution of the Hebrew sabbath to leisure was clear —it was a day of rest and worship. The contribution of the Christian Sunday is somewhat ambiguous—it has insured a day of rest, but did not originate as such and legislation to make it so has led to legalism. In what sense, then, has this first day of the week contributed to leisure, beyond its providing a holiday?

"Sunday We Give to Joy"

Somewhere near the end of the second century or the beginning of the third Tertullian wrote this moving and very significant statement concerning Christian worship: "Sunday we give to joy." In this affirmation the essence of the spirit of the new covenant which Jesus inaugurated was picked up, contained, and applied to the celebration of the Lord's Day by Christians. While the attitude of joy was, and is, characteristic of the Hebrew sabbath also, that day is grounded *primarily* in the commandment to cease work and rest. The Christian first day in its inception was a day *primarily* of joy over the resurrection and continuing presence of Christ—only later did it become an actual rest day.

It is in this sense of joy that the Christian Sunday makes its most significant contribution to the sabbath tradition and hence to the historical perspective of leisure. To be sure, the history of the Christian Church reveals that it has not always allowed this joy to exist on Sunday, but it also indicates that whenever it has, the sabbath tradition has borne its most lasting fruits in the enhancement of life. Only this abiding sense of joy could have enabled the early Christians to meet together in spite of persecution; only a return to that spirit here and there throughout history has enabled subsequent generations of Christians to find in the Lord's Day a source of strength and fulfillment. One indication of this experience can be seen in the description Vicesimus Knox gave in 1778 of the way working people in an English parish spent Sunday.

To them it is a joyful festival. They, for the most part, are constant attendants at church; and the decency of their habits and appearance, the cleanliness which they display, the opportunity they enjoy of meeting their neighbours in the same regular and decent situation with themselves, renders Sunday highly advantageous to them, exclusive of its religious advantages.[16]

Wherever such joy is present, the sabbath observance becomes a leisure resource of profound depth.

To reduce Sunday merely to "do's" and "don't's" will only succeed in undermining the potential joy of the day because attention is diverted from the meaning to the form. The fulfillment of the Christian Sunday rests ultimately on free involvement. No divine law can tell us how to spend it. The only norm we can be sure of as a guide for our Sunday activities is that which comes from a life lived in and with Jesus Christ. Our faith in him frees us from concern with laws and regulations and allows us to live his day in joy.

How can we lay hold again of this living faith wherein Sunday is a peculiar source of joy? One suggestion is that we might look to the sabbath tradition as an indication of the rhythm between rest and labor which is needed in our lives. Work and the things it buys can all too easily dominate us; in setting apart a time to remember where we find our true strength we may be saved from enslavement to continuous activity. Helmut Thielicke described the meaning of "subdue the earth": " 'When you put your stamp upon creation, see to it that your human life and your culture do not become a sign of your eternal restlessness and your blind titanism, but rather a thanksgiving and a response to him who gave you this earth.' " [17]

---

[16] Quoted in Hodgkins, p. 77.

[17] *How the World Began,* translated with an Introduction by John W. Doberstein (Philadelphia, Muhlenberg Press, 1961) , p. 110.

Sabbath rest calls forth this response and enables us to gain perspective on the meaning of our lives.

At least three meanings of Sunday which existed in the early Church need to be recovered in our day. For one thing, Sunday was regarded as the day of light. As God created light on the first day, so Christ—the light of the world—arose on the first day revealing the love and glory of God. Secondly, Sunday was the day of resurrection. As the Jews find in the sabbath the sign of the old covenant, Christians see in the Lord's Day a sign of the new covenant in the risen Christ. Finally, Sunday was the day of the spirit, the day when the gift of the Holy Spirit was bestowed on the Church as the community gathered for worship and mutual strength. These three emphases might well serve as resources for a renewed understanding of the significance of Sunday.

One of the most creative and suggestive interpretations of Sunday as the Christian day of rest and worship is presented by Karl Barth in his *Church Dogmatics*. When we read the creation story in Genesis, he pointed out, we read that man was created on the sixth day; therefore, God's seventh day was man's first day. This understanding sees the sabbath as a gift of grace prior to man's work, not as a reward for work done. Or, as Barth wrote:

From this point of view man after this day was not set on the way to a Sabbath still to be sanctified, but on the way from a Sabbath already sanctified; from rest to work; from freedom to service; from joy to "seriousness" of life. Rest, freedom and joy were not just before him. He had no need to "enter" into them. He could already proceed from them, or commence with them. They had already taken place. He had already sat at the divine wedding-feast, and having eaten and drunk could now proceed to his daily work.[18]

[18] Vol. III/1, translated by J. W. Edwards, O. Bussey, Harold Knight (Edinburgh: T. T. Clark, Ltd., 1958), p. 228. See also Vol. III/2, pp. 457-58; Vol. III/4, pp. 50 and 71-72; and Vol. IV /2, p. 226.

He goes on to suggest that this ought always to have been the chronology, the week gaining meaning from man's first day as rest with God. Furthermore, if it is true that in the resurrection of Christ we see the promise of God—as symbolized by the blessing of the seventh day—fulfilled, then the fact that Christ rose on the first day of the week supports the interpretation that God's seventh day was man's first day. Thus the celebration of Sunday as the sabbath was not a new innovation, but a revelation of what was already implied in the Genesis story.

Whether this interpretation is inherent in the story of creation or not, what Barth presents for our consideration is a new way of looking at the sabbath tradition as a source for understanding leisure in our time which reflects the truth experienced by the early Christians. The Lord's Day was the festival of joy which spread out into the whole week, even though it was not a day of rest in early times. In our time we have the opportunity to truly start the week with a holiday, a joyous celebration; the leisure of this occasion, and all leisure, is then seen as a gift and opportunity rather than a reward which has been earned and can therefore be horded or thrown away as a possession. For the Christian who finds Sunday a day of rest, joy, and renewal the other six days will follow in the same context and bear fruit accordingly.

Finally, the significance of Sunday as a day of rest and joy points us to the consummation of life as ultimate rest with God. In the resurrection we have been assured that our lives and labor are not in vain, nor our struggle and toil without end. We began, as Barth suggested, by participating with God in his rest, and we shall also end there. On Sunday we share the reality of God's presence among us and go into the week knowing that life and work, as part of God's creation, are good; in rest and joy we participate in the basic theme of life's crowning fulfillment. It is not always possible for the two to come together—as it was not for the early Christians—and we have no law which says they have to. When they do come together, when the Lord's Day is a day free from work, we have a greater opportunity to be aware of the source of our joy and should be grateful for the leisure to worship and perform service in his name. But if not, we can still pause in our work and be refreshed. As Augustine perceived, Sunday rest involves essentially a "rest of the heart":

God prescribes a Sabbath rest for us. What kind of rest? . . . It is internal. Our Sabbath is in the heart. There are many who idle, but their conscience is in turmoil. No sinful man can have Sabbath rest. Whoever has a good conscience is truly at peace; and it is this very tranquility in which consists the Sabbath of the heart.

Leisure and Contemporary Issues of Sabbath Observance

When Christianity became the major religion under Constantine it sought to free Sunday from work, and, as Henry Sloane Coffin noted: "Its motives were in part the identical motives that set apart the Jewish sabbath—the desire to obtain humane relief for the labouring classes; in part it wished to secure sufficient leisure for its religious services." [19] Doubtless such protection of Sunday by civil law had much to do with making the observance of Christian worship universal, as well as insuring that laboring men would not be overworked.

In the United States there are no national laws governing the conduct of business on Sunday—such laws are enacted in each state. To a large extent these so-called "blue laws" are not presently enforced unless the issue is pressed, and then they are broadly interpreted because of the archaic language in which they exist on the statute books. At the same time, there is no desire to bring the laws up to date because of even greater difficulty in interpretation. For instance, Hiley Ward notes, "if a new law actually speaks of grocery stores instead of 'cook shops and victualing houses,' who can say where a grocery store

[19] *Op. cit.*, p. 79.

begins and where it ends?" [20] The same can be said of drug stores, the big discount houses, and other businesses which include a wide variety of goods. To try to designate in detail what is and is not to be sold within each store would begin to sound like the legalistic hairsplitting which has plagued both Judaism and Christianity.

Amid much controversy the United States Supreme Court ruled in 1961 that the legislation of Sunday laws by the states *is* constitutional. In its decision the Court ruled eight to one that such laws do not constitute an establishment of religion, but support the purposes of health by creating " 'an atmosphere of entire community repose.' " [21] The fact that the day is the Christian weekly holy day is a matter of tradition only and is not important. No matter how illogical the laws may seem, it was maintained that the states do have the right to regulate commerce in this way. The justices further ruled (six to three) against making exceptions for those who observe, for religious reasons, a day other than Sunday as a day of rest. Granting that Sunday laws might make it difficult for people of minority faiths, the court felt that the difficulty is not a violation of religious freedom under the constitution. There might be specific laws which would be regarded as unconstitutional, but the majority of the Court agreed with Justice Warren that " 'people of all religions and people with no religion regard Sunday as a time for family activity, for visiting friends and relatives, for late-sleeping, for passive and active entertainments, for dining out, and the like.' " [22]

This ruling by the Supreme Court does not create Sunday laws, of course. What it does is leave the matter of Sunday legislation in the hands of the states, but acknowledges that the making of such laws is constitutional. The majority of the justices did, however, express a feeling that there is value in

[20] *Op. cit.,* p. 12.
[21] Quoted in "News," *Presbyterian Life* (July 1, 1961), p. 23.
[22] *Ibid.*

having a given day when the majority of people rest from business enterprises. Since tradition in the United States has made this rest day Sunday, it is the logical one to continue, as well as the most likely to be observed since the majority are already used to it. Many people, both in and out of the Christian Church feel that exception should be made for members of minority faiths, and it is possible that individual states will work out these provisions in their laws.

The issue of Sunday observance goes much deeper than whether it is supported by civil law, however. For one thing, in modern society it is impossible for *everyone* to rest on the same day as they could in the simpler agricultural life of ancient Israel. People in the area of public service, such as policeman, fireman, and doctors, must be available on Sunday, as well as those who supply such necessities as food, drugs, and gasoline and those who serve our recreational needs as lifeguards at the beach, ushers at the movies, and bearers of that great institution, the Sunday newspaper.

Furthermore, there is an increasing loss of the sense that Sunday is a religious holy day and a growing tendency to regard it as a regular day off to which working men are entitled. This feeling of Sunday as a secular holiday often results in two opposite attitudes: If employees have to work on Sunday they should be paid more, but for those who are free on Sunday there should be greater provision of goods and services (by someone!) for consumer use and enjoyment. This loss of the sense of "holiness" in regard to Sunday may well be part of the whole erosion of meaning which has taken place in American life. Interestingly enough, the rise of leisure seems to be at the root of the matter. When Sunday was the only day of leisure it was regarded as "special," and attention could not help being drawn to what made it special. As more leisure has become available Sunday has been absorbed into that broad category of "free time" which one has earned and can spend as he pleases.

It has been noted that the biblical injunction for a sabbath rest arose out of the humanitarian recognition that there are likely to be seven days of work if the sanctity of one day goes unpreserved. However, it is no longer possible to defend either Saturday or Sunday on the grounds of health, since work requirements are not nearly as stringent as in times past. Sabbatarian practices have been enforced at various points in history to insure that the day of rest be observed as intended—but it is doubtful that any such laws can ever again be enacted. The Supreme Court has upheld the right of states to regulate Sunday commerce, but the states may choose not to make such legislation.

The future of the sabbath tradition, however, is not as dark as this picture might make it look. New thinking is being called for in all areas of life in this time of rapid change—leisure and religious worship is no exception. What form the new ideas will take cannot be determined here, but there are at least two areas for consideration which should be mentioned.

In the first place, it is good that leisure is increasing, regardless of the complexity it causes. The biblical injunction to rest one day in every seven need not be considered necessarily as a sanction of six days of labor. The sabbath commandment, reflecting an agricultural economy in which work formed the basis of life, is not to be taken literally as a condemnation of the five- or four-day workweek. A leisure weekend is becoming the norm for most workers, freeing both Saturday and Sunday. Herein may lie our opportunity to enable the minority faiths who observe Saturday as their rest day to do so without economic disadvantages. As the Sunday leisure continues to extend backward into Saturday, and even Friday, for various industries, banks, and large businesses, it is possible that workers in smaller business, shops, and stores will desire the same advantage. Hiley Ward suggests that a three-day sabbath is not out of the question in the "space age." Such an arrangement would increase opportunities for participation in family, community, cultural, and church affairs.

A second area for discussion in the new age of leisure concerns the church's program for worship and study. When Sunday was the only day of leisure the church could center its activities on that day. The result has been to regard Sunday as the *only* day to go to church. Some churches are beginning to experiment with such new forms as retreats, breakfast meetings for businessmen, noon services in downtown areas, and week-night services. Classes for children after school during the week is another possibility for making religion more than a one-day-a-week affair. Sunday will no doubt remain the central focal point for public worship, because of tradition and because of the meaning which lies back of its celebration, but here too an early service for people going out of town or a late service for people who work during the day are potential areas for exploration.

No matter when we take time to worship God, the point is that "Sunday we give to joy." Whether or not this day is shifted to another, by finding that same sense of joy which the early Christians knew, perhaps the leisure which has been preserved by the sabbath tradition can reach its true fulfillment in our time. Luther noted that the righteous do not need a special day to remind them of God because all days are lived in that awareness. But he also acknowledged that human nature is weak and that a definite period for communal worship is good. So for us. We need the reminder and the opportunity for worship which Sunday gives. But the time is upon us when leisure for such activity is not preserved by law, but is an occasion in which each person must freely choose to participate.

Our increased leisure opens great opportunity for re-creation —for using our talents, resourcefulness, and imagination for the sake of inner satisfaction and community service. In our re-creative activity we can find a deeper relationship to the Creator of all things. Sunday has been, and can continue to be the reminder to the Christian of the source of his strength and the ground of his meaning. As each week speaks of the Creator's activity in the beginning, each Sunday is the assurance that this same God lives with us now and forever.

The sabbath tradition has directed our thinking to a "time" set aside for worship and renewal which illuminates the meaning and significance of all of time. In this category of "time" lies one of the most helpful theological resources for leisure, the discussion of which has been reserved for the last section. Thus we turn now to the consideration of time as the fourth dimension of our leisure study—a dimension which picks up and contains the other dimensions and which points to a new possibility for leisure in terms of a Christian understanding of time.

PART FOUR

Time: A Theological Resource for Leisure

10
Perspectives on Time

All studies of leisure must come to grips at some point with the fourth dimension of our inquiry—the question of time. We have called this fourth dimension a theological resource for understanding leisure. This should not imply that our formulation will provide pat answers to the problems raised by leisure or to the conditions which root in the human spirit. Nor does it presuppose that time as a theological category exhausts the possible or alternative theological approaches and resources. Our immediate task is to draw out the implications of only *one* theological resource—time—rather than to depict in a systematic theological fashion the full panoply of doctrines which bear on leisure. Perhaps these considerations, limited as they are, will stimulate further theological reflection in such areas as leisure in relation to the doctrine of Christ, vocation, sacraments, grace and law.

In viewing leisure in relation to time, let us note again that some observers conceive of leisure as synonymous with a certain segment of time, as essentially a block of time in which the feeling of compulsion is minimized.[1] Others have been adamant in maintaining an absolute difference between leisure and the segment of time we call "free," as is evident in the position taken by Sebastian de Grazia: "Leisure and free time live in two different worlds. . . . Free time refers to a special way of calculating a special kind of time. Leisure refers to a state of be-

[1] Charles K. Brightbill, *Man and Leisure* (Englewood Cliffs, N. J.: Prentice-Hall, Inc., 1961) , p. 21.

ing, a condition of man, which few desire and fewer achieve." [2]

These two viewpoints are not necessarily mutually exclusive. To the extent that all man's living is done in time, so is his leisure subject to that context; yet it is also true that a period of time free from compulsion will not necessarily yield leisure. Leisure, as we have earlier stated, is preeminently a condition of the spirit, a mental and spiritual attitude that is not the inevitable result of spare time.

There is, however, a deeper relationship between time and leisure, a relationship which is based on the fact that one's conscious or unconscious attitude toward time will affect how one chooses to use his time—including his choice of leisure activities. Moreover, one's attitude toward time will affect how one regards his life as a whole—including what part he sees leisure playing in that whole. Our discussion will now focus on time as a positive or negative influence on leisure.

The Problem of Time

At the outset it would be well to suggest the dimensions of the problem which time creates. Augustine described his own difficulty with this enigma:

For what is time? Who can easily and briefly explain it? Who even in thought can comprehend it, even to the pronouncing of a word concerning it? But what in speaking do we refer to more familiarly and knowingly than time? And certainly we understand when we speak of it; we understand also when we hear it spoken of by another. What, then, is time? If no one asks of me, I know; if I wish to explain it to him who asks, I know not. [3]

This elusive character of time is evident in our own experience, where time transcends the abstract theories about it. On the

---

[2] *Of Time, Work, and Leisure*, pp. 7-8.

[3] *Confessions*, Book XI, Chap. 14. Translated by J. G. Pilkington in *Basic Writings of St. Augustine*, edited by Whitney J. Oates (New York: Randon House, Inc. 1948), p. 191.

one hand, time is movement; "time marches on" regardless of whether we want it to or not. Whereas in the realm of space we might choose to go or not to go a distance on earth, it is impossible to grasp and hold constant even one moment in the flow of time. Of course, this perception of the ongoing nature of time and thus the transitoriness of life is the root of much anxiety. As James Muilenburg movingly expressed this sense of dread,

We are haunted again and again by the painful awareness that the shining moment passes, the day comes to an end, some silver cord of confidence is snapped, some dream dispelled, some faith shattered. The whirling of Time brings in its revenges. The present forever flees to the past, the future forever breaks in with relentless speed. We are forever confronted with the unexpected, the unanticipated, the new. . . . There is something profoundly disquieting and threatening in the temporality of existence.[4]

Furthermore, this time which is ever moving on, bringing the new and the unanticipated, is moving also toward an end which *is* known and anticipated—death.

> Our years come to an end like a sigh.
> The years of our life are threescore and ten,
>   or even by reason of strength fourscore;
> yet their span is but toil and trouble;
>   they are soon gone, and we fly away. (Ps. 90:9*b*-10.)

Thus in one of Henri Bergson's writings, life is likened to a clock which has been wound up and is ticking off the minutes, until it comes to its inevitable end—which is death.

"To be" is to be subject to all of the anxieties of what it means "not to be." To be conscious of the flow of time which leads to death is to be subject to the despair of seeing one's life as ultimately meaningless and time as empty. The extreme

---

[4] "The Biblical View of Time," *The Harvard Theological Review* (October, 1961), LIV, 226.

nihilistic view of life and time has been most vividly described perhaps by Shakespeare's Macbeth:

> To-morrow, and to-morrow, and to-morrow,
> Creeps in this petty pace from day to day
> To the last syllable of recorded time,
> And all our yesterdays have lighted fools
> The way to dusty death. Out, out, brief candle!
> Life's but a walking shadow, a poor player
> That struts and frets his hour upon the stage
> And then is heard no more: it is a tale
> Told by an idiot, full of sound and fury,
> Signifying nothing. (Act V, scene 5.)

On the other hand, however, time is not *only* movement—a steady march toward death—time also has duration. Thus we perceive time as being long or short in various situations. An hour spent in sleeplessness at night or in the 5:00 p.m. traffic at the end of a hard day can seem endless, but an hour with a good book or a loved one can seem like only an instant. Whether time seems long or short depends on whether what is happening has any meaning for us. Who has not felt that some activity was a sheer "waste of time"? Or who has not experienced uneasiness while waiting for a bus, waiting for a friend, or just plain waiting for something to happen?

The fruits of the problem of time as movement and as duration have been varied, but perhaps the two most common are anxiety and boredom. Whether anxiety arises from the feeling of having too little time or boredom from too much time that is unfilled, the manner of dealing with both has tended to be alike; there has been an attempt to fill up the time with frenzied activities, with anything that will enable one to forget it. Emphasizing the *anxiety* response found in neurotic illness, Alexander Reid Martin concluded that three characteristics may be identified: 1. Disturbances of the recreative functions, as in sleeplessness or restlessness so that play is perverted into compulsive activity; 2. The patient has gross conflicts and misconceptions about relaxation and leisure and finds it impossible to relax, being a slave to routine and schedule; 3. There is serious disturbance in his creative activity.[5]

Our second response—boredom—is no new thing in the annals of man. It is reported that some Melanesian tribes died out solely because of boredom. Modern man's boredom in which he is "distracted from distraction by distraction" arises from the fact that his time is without content; it is unfulfilled time. Brightbill puts the emphasis on boredom in suggesting that,

Free time is boredom's most potent fertilizer. . . . We can see this boredom all around us. It is written on the faces of people milling aimlessly up and down Main Street and visible in the habits of thousands of people who frequent the taverns in what appears to be a race to see who can soak up the most alcohol before bed time. It is also evident in our efforts to substitute motion and speed for emotion and solitude.[6]

As we discovered earlier in the case of play and delinquency, tragic consequences are associated with boredom. No less tragic are the consequences of too much time for the aged. With longer life expectancy and earlier retirements, many of our senior citizens face their later years with utter boredom and agonizing loneliness.[7] This sense of lossness is pictured poignantly in two passages. The first is from the Gospel of John: "When you were young, you . . . walked whence you would;

[5] "Leisure and the Creative Process," *The Hanover Forum* (April 9, 1959) VI, p. 8.

[6] *Op. cit.,* p. 60.

[7] At the founding of our nation, life expectancy was around 35. Now it is close to 70 years. The average number of years spent in retirement by men has doubled during the past 50 years from 3 to 6 years. It is forecast that the average years of retirement for men will be 9 years by the 1980's.

203

but when you are old, you will stretch out your hands, and another will gird you and carry you where you do not wish to go" (21:18). The second is from Thomas Wolfe's *Look Homeward, Angel,* a description of one of the members of the Gant family: "He was fifty; he had a tragic consciousness of time—he saw the passionate fullness of his life upon the wane and he cast about him like a senseless and infuriated beast."

There is irony and tragedy in the fact that many people who retire with the anticipation of spending their time in leisure pursuits ("enjoying life") so frequently become disillusioned and find their days of retirement a terrible burden to bear. So absolute is the identification of work with life that frequently when work ceases life too comes to a halt. Unable to work, many oldsters feel that they no longer have a part in life; faced with time in which they might pursue other interests, they feel only that they are useless and their time is empty. Along with this, of course, is the very real fact that work provides avenues of social contact, but if only the social factor were involved it would seem that clubs and other social activities would fill the need. Instead, as De Grazia underscored, "Work is still the way to a virtuous life and a great and prosperous country. It is good for you, a remedy for pain, loneliness, the death of a dear one, a disappointment in love or doubts about the purpose of life. The man without a job is a misfit." [8]

One's free-floating anxieties caused by lack of knowing what to do with too much spare time, resentment toward society for not permitting him to work any longer, càn very easily turn into hostility toward community issues, such as school bonds, water floridation, censorship of library books, religious and political liberalism. This displacement of anxiety may be carried over into a powerful political voting bloc as political action groups enlist the free energies of the "emotionally underemployed."

[8] "The Uses of Time," *Aging and Leisure, op. cit.,* p. 129.

When leisure is devoid of meaning countless older people live their retirement with a sense of dread, waiting—not only with time on their hands, but time which hangs heavily, veritably killing time until time kills them. No wonder the authors of *Crestwood Heights* wrote, "Retirement, more than menopause, is a sociological death." [9]

Safeguards are needed by the aged against boredom and the sense of uselessness. The later years can be a period in life filled with adventure and personal growth, or it can be a period of torment, of aimless drifting. It will hardly be sufficient merely to fill this void with frenzied activities. Such compulsive activism may also be the undoing of the older person—leaving him in a state of fatigue or exhaustion. What is needed is not the means for whiling away the excess time, but rather a perspective which gives meaning to the time, an outlook which redeems the time.

Many studies are being made on the increase in leisure time now available due to increased productivity and automation. What these studies indicate, however, is that more free time does not seem to be leading to a more abundant life. With free time more available, the greater problem of the significance of time itself is now raised. The conscious or unconscious perception of time as meaningless and fleeting exhibits itself in social behavior, especially in how a person chooses to spend his leisure time. Students of leisure have noted that the bored or the anxious person will often act in ways which have far-reaching social implications. But just as a negative view of time can pose problems for leisure, it is possible also that a dynamic view of time can exert a creative influence on the understanding of leisure and its uses. On this subject, especially, does the theological understanding of the importance of time offer a valuable resource for our thinking. It is along these lines that our discussion will now proceed.

[9] J. R. Seeley, R. A. Sim, and E. W. Loosley (New York: Basic Books, Inc., 1956), p. 72.

Ways of Looking at Time

Many and varied have been the ways of looking at time. Some of these views have lasted only as long as the age or culture which gave birth to them, while others still persist in similar or modified form. In all the views, however, there has been an attempt to give unity and meaning to time by finding a way to measure it. Since man's own subjective experience of time tends to be misleading (as suggested earlier, time can seem long or short depending on how the person feels), it has been desirable to find an objective criterion for measuring time. This objective criterion has been located basically in the realm of nature.

Starting at this base, we may examine some of the major directions the views of time have taken, particularly as these have affected our view today.

1. *Recurrence.* From the beginning of creation the observable phenomena of nature have provided a basic means of measuring time—the nearest and most familiar being the constant succession of night and day. Thus the groundwork was laid for the development of the view of time as eternal recurrence. Experiencing the cycles of life and death, growth and decay, the coming to be and the passing away of things, classical culture came to regard time in terms of this circle. This cyclical pattern in nature was also applied to the affairs of man, as Marcus Aurelius expressed it in the Stoic view:

The rational soul wanders round the whole world and through the encompassing void and gazes on infinite time and considers the periodic destructions and rebirths of the universe and reflects that our posterity will see nothing new and that our ancestors saw nothing that we have not seen.[10]

[10] *Meditations,* XI, i. Quoted by Reinhold Niebuhr, *Faith and History* (New York: Charles Scribner's Sons, 1949), p. 41.

Attempts to understand the time dimension of man through changing cycles have found expression in various religions of the East, the Stoics, and in such men as Schopenhauer, Nietzche, Spengler, and Toynbee, though the latter sees the cycles as having a direction more like spirals because of the challenge and response factor. But whereas the classical conception of recurrence as expressed by Plato and Aristotle[11] explained time by reference to a changeless, objective, eternal model, later interpretations have come to regard the law of cycles itself as a timeless dimension outside time since it is not affected by its own temporal manifestations.

Hans Meyerhoff makes an interesting observation concerning the cyclical view of time in relation to myths. In the development of the Greek myths, and in the present return to mythical forms in literature, he sees an attempt to come to terms with the problem of time from the humanistic point of view. "Myths are chosen as literary symbols for two purposes: to suggest, within a secular setting, a timeless perspective of looking upon the human situation: and to convey a sense of continuity and identification with mankind in general." [12] In the myth a kind of "timeless prototype of human existence" is caught which is repeated in other times and places; by participating in this same situation we acknowledge our common membership in the family of man.

The cyclical view of time basically excludes novelty in the world, or if a certain amount of "newness" is observed in the affairs of men its subsequent decay—as in the fall of civilization —tends to reaffirm the idea of eternal recurrence. In classical culture there was no knowledge of the emergence of novelty in nature.

[11] See John F. Callahan, *Four Views of Time in Ancient Philosophy* (Cambridge, Mass.: Harvard University Press, 1948), Chap. 1 (Plato) and Chap. 2 (Aristotle).

[12] *Time in Literature* (Berkeley, Cal.: University of California Press, 1955), p. 80.

2. *Progression.* With the Renaissance and its subsequent revolutions in the fields of science, economics, art, et cetera, there came an increasing recognition of growth, progress, and the evolving of new forms in nature and history out of old forms. No longer just a repeating of itself, time now could be seen as bringing about the emergence of the new and novel. As Henri Bergson expressed it in the early part of this century: "The more we study the nature of time, the more we shall comprehend that duration means invention, the creation of forms, the continual elaboration of the absolutely new." [13] Furthermore, the temporal process could now be regarded as self-explanatory since the new phenomena could be explained by their "natural causes."

In the classical view there is little room for mystery because the world—including time—is regarded as the imitation of an eternal model. In the modern view there is no sense of mystery either, because the world and its time process contains its own meaning, which man can discover through his own rational powers.

Underlying the recognition that new forms emerge in both the natural and historical processes is the belief that the new forms are superior to the old—that the emergence has a progressive character which is good. In this view, then, time has direction; it doesn't just recur; it moves man toward something. What that "something" is has taken various forms—perfect democracy for the democrat, the absence of government for the anarchist, the classless society for the communist, or the discovery of truth for the scientist. Whatever the goal, time and history in this sense unfold the meaning of life, and there is no need for an "eternal" dimension to existence.

But as the cyclical view of time has often brought despair because its repetition excluded newness, the progressive view

[13] *Creative Evolution,* translated by Arthur Mitchell (New York: Henry Holt and Company, 1911), p. 11.

of time has often brought cynicism because the new forms have not necessarily been better. In the moral and spiritual realms the evidence that man has greatly improved is not convincing. The progressive view held that reason would eliminate evil, not by conquering time in the contemplation of the eternal, but by participating in the growth process inherent in time. But time, valued as good because the course of history developed in time, has revealed itself as a medium for both good *and* evil, indeed as an almost indifferent medium for man's efforts. Wars, crimes, and abuses go on, and time continues to perplex us, for time documents the mounting record of man's inhumanity to man.

With the thwarting of the possibility of reaching the goals toward which it was believed history and time were inevitably progressing and with the loss of belief in an eternal dimension to time, modern thought now finds itself with time which is ever in a state of transition and change and which is turned in upon itself. Endless change like endless cycles brings no fulfillment of purpose and provides no goals to which man may commit himself.

3. *Clock time.* Doubtless the primary way of regarding time in our culture is in terms of "clock time." It is difficult for twentieth-century Americans to imagine a life where time is not divided up in such a way as to enable a person to know the exact hour, minute, and even second, of the day. In fact, so conscious of the clock have we become, it is not surprising that, should the earth suddenly rotate in half its present time, man would continue to live his twenty-four clock-hours, even though the clock is a mechanism designed to imitate the rotation of the earth. It now seems almost as if the rotation of the earth imitates our clocks! How inconceivable to imagine Western man in an environment not dominated by clock consciousness. We get up, work, eat, sleep, play, visit, and, in short, live by what time the clock tells us it is. We are encased by the time and tempo demands of our mechanical creation.

Sebastian de Grazia expressed his interest in *why* precision in time became so important to Western man. He pointed out the fact that the mechanical clock did not appear until the thirteenth century, and even then it was not until Cellini's time that it had any degree of reliability; then he wrote:

In the beginning, the clock exerted a strange, almost morbid attraction as though it were ticking off life itself. . . . But more and more they came to exercise the attraction of an ingenious mechanism. People felt as if they were carrying the brain of a genius in their pocket. Watches became the foibles of rich clients, kings and queens. . . .

Not until the nineteenth century did the clock begin to spread. The cheap watch appears in Switzerland in 1865 and in America a few years later, in 1880. . . . Why didn't the clock remain a toy? Why didn't it delight or fascinate a few people, and stop right there, to suffer the fate of the ingenious toys invented by the ancient Greeks and Moslems? Why were the nineteenth and twentieth centuries its day of diffusion? People don't buy a thing just because it is cheap, and in any case watches, though mass-produced, were not *that* cheap. Evidently they were needed.[14]

A need for precision seemed to express itself most vividly in the areas of work—as a rational and uniform way for men to start and stop work together. The more industrialized and commercialized culture became, the more precise it needed to be in timing. Appointments must be made, schedules kept, connections for transportation planned for, and certain work hours established.

As "work time" was thus defined, so the rest of the day or week came to be designated "free time." This free time, in turn, became more and more important because (1) as industry became more complex, jobs more specialized, and concentration on precision in routine more exacting, the need for free time increased; and (2) as industrial output rose and the num-

---

[14] *Of Time, Work, and Leisure,* pp. 304-5.

ber of working hours decreased, more free time became available. Thus the problem of free time is not just the fact that men suddenly found they were so used to working that they did not know what to do with themselves, but also this situation in which free time is defined in relation to work time, particularly in terms of the economic dimension. This brings us to one of two ways of looking at time which have grown out of the clock-time view.

4. *Time Is Money*. The man who first articulated what has become an accepted view of work in our technological age was a Scottish philosopher named Adam Smith. In essence Smith observed that work produces goods and goods produce wealth. The significance of this view for time is apparent. The more goods that can be produced, the more wealth will be created, and to produce the goods requires the time of the workers. Thus time took on great technological significance. Time is equated with money because the commodities produced in time mean money. From time basis it is but a short step to saying the more goods that can be produced in a period of time, the more valuable the time.

George Soule suggests that while this fourth dimension, time, has not generally been adopted formally by economic theorists into their systems, it is regarded as very important on the practical level. The changing value of capital and expectation about prices and profits are two areas in particular where the concept of time plays a part, but it is time as a "scarce resource" that Soule regards with most importance. While the economic concern with time has been in relation to how more goods could be produced in less time, the approaching problem is not enough time in which to consume the goods! [15] Whether it is used to make money or to spend money, man's time has economic importance. Small wonder then that "time is money" in our culture.

[15] *Time for Living*, pp. 89-90.

As earlier noted, the amount of money Americans spend on leisure time activities, goods (equipment), and services (use of facilities, lessons, et cetera), indicates that this industry is a big business. Lured by advertising which dangles all sorts of brightly colored trinkets in front of him, and goaded by siren voices which tell him he should enjoy himself after a hard day's work, the individual seeks to buy his leisure as he buys other commodities. People endure jobs in order to have money to spend as they please in their free time. They buy hula hoops, twist records, and new sports cars. And the thing that makes it possible seems to be the monetary rewards of work which are the equivalent of time. "Time is saved by saving money—to buy 'leisure.' " [16]

Alas, there is at least one thing money cannot buy—time. This is doubtless why time is one of our scarcest resources. On a national scale the recognition that money cannot buy everything is given poignant reality in a news item concerning our space race:

President Kennedy, after the Soviet "Twins in Space" feat, said the U.S. was "well behind" the USSR in the space race, but he did not ask for more money. An unusual scene occurred in Congress: space officials fought off efforts by Congress to vote them more money. Vital research needs *time* now more than money.[17]

So the view that time is money works in one direction—one earns money with his work time and spends it in his free time. But the equation does not work in the other direction—money is not time. Money cannot buy more time—except perhaps in a relative sense, as money for an operation might lengthen the life span of an individual—and money does not give time more value in the long run. After all, the most important question

[16] Seeley, *et al., op. cit.,* p. 64.
[17] *Christian Science Monitor* (August 27, 1962).

is not the cost of a certain leisure activity, but whether the time spent in that activity had any significance and meaning in his life.

5. *Time in the Social Sense.* Another way of looking at time that has grown out of the emphasis on "clock time" (the equation of time with money being the first) might be called "time as social organization." One of the most significant analyses of this understanding of time is discussed in the book *Crestwood Heights.* Studying a real suburban community under the fictitious name "Crestwood Heights," the authors conclude that,

In Crestwood Heights time seems almost the paramount dimension of existence, not only in the simple sense that all human events occur in sequence, and therefore in time, but rather because of the pervasiveness of time as a force in life and career patterns. There are constant demands for efficient work (that is to say, for the most economical use of time), for punctuality, for regularity, which call for an acute sense of timing. These are important factors in the estimation of success or failure.[18]

Thus the people in this suburban community—and, of course not only there—live a "schedule-dominated life." Work time, meal time, appointments, social activities—all require punctuality. Indeed "Being on time for school becomes more important than eating breakfast." [19]

In general, time viewed in the light of social organization revolves around the work requirements of the father (and/or mother). The interesting thing, however, is not so much that this is necessary, but that the work schedule exerts such an influence on the way the rest of the day is spent. Thus Crestwooders agree that "the man works to have 'time off,' and that when he leaves his male environment of harsh exacting deadlines to

18 Seeley, *et al., op. cit.,* p. 64.
19 *Ibid.,* p. 65.

return to his home and family, he expects and is expected to relax." [20]

While home life may allow for a greater degree of quiet and relaxation, the area of secondary relationships outside the home requires the same kind of scheduling and regularity that work does. No doubt it is the feeling that *producing* something gives time value that drives people to seek the secondary activities.

The *quantitative* units of time that were observed in the physical and natural spheres of life, and which reached such precision in measurement with the second hand of the clock, have now been taken over completely in the social dimension. The *qualitative* aspects of time have been generally submerged because of the pressures of scheduling in the social world, and because of the dominant view that time has value because of what is produced or consumed in time. Not only has the sense of the quality of time been lost for us, but so has any sense of continuity with the past—history is no longer important for us. It is the present and what we are doing now that counts—which means also that the future is of little concern.

Thus the Crestwood Heights dwellers show little interest in such historical matters as ancestry. The fragments of time merge together to form days, weeks, years, in which one seeks to be as happy and secure as possible in each present moment. Two of the most critical times facing Crestwooders are menopause for the women and retirement for the men—looked upon, perhaps, as indications that their "productive" times are ended.

Our consideration of the social meaning of time prompts us to discuss one more aspect of leisure time in relation to work. It is the thesis that our society is undergoing a loss of values in relation to work; the functions heretofore performed by the institutions of work in providing meaning and value to life are now being transferred to leisure institutions.

[20] *Ibid.*, p. 64.

Bennett Berger suggests two principal ways in which a person comes to terms with his sense of alienation in work: 1. By accepting work as something he must do in order to be able to do what he really wants to, thereby engaging in leisure activities that are completely unconnected with his work; 2. By developing a cynical attitude to work, characterizing it as a "rat race," et cetera. Either adaptation indicates that such attitudes are "proper" and reflect the feeling that " 'I am not what I do; do not judge me by what I do for a living.' " [21] Thus the Protestant idea of vocation, of work as a "calling," is losing ground, largely because there are so many jobs that seem to have little meaning, or may even be "degrading." But they are necessary in order to have the means to buy leisure. Yet Berger is correct in his judgment that we have not completely lost the expectation that we have some right to moral satisfaction in work: "The Protestant Ethic dies hard—values always do—and leaves in us a lingering sense of betrayal when work seems meaningless." [22]

If Berger's view seems inconsistent with opinions expressed earlier in this book, it only indicates the general ambiguity—if not, indeed, paradox—in thinking about these matters. Some observers argue that work, in modern society, has been infused with new meaning, that it has been upgraded and has become even more interesting in view of labor saving tools that eliminate many backbreaking jobs. Others are impressed by its lack of meaning and satisfaction, its psychic, rather than physical, demands, the loss of a sense of craftsmanship, and the feeling of unfulfillment that comes from very minute, partial involvement in a gigantic process.

On the one hand, work does not have value; yet, on the other, it does. We endure work while we have it and often feel like quitting; yet when we aren't working, or can't work, we seem

[21] "The Sociology of Leisure," p. 42.
[22] *Ibid.*, p. 39.

to lose a sense of status and personal identity. Work seems to eat up what little time we spend on earth, yet the difficulties of too much time in retirement point to the belief that work was what filled time and gave it meaning.

However work is appraised, at the end of the day, men are turning to leisure in their search for meaning and personal fulfillment. If men now look to leisure for values once found in work, then we must acknowledge our predicament that little sense of a leisure ethic or moral responsibility has been carried over into the leisure realm. Many think of leisure as the sheer pursuit of fun. Free time is fun time, and anything that smacks of responsibility or morality—family, community, politics, and religion—is regarded as other than free time activity. But time cannot always be filled with fun, and it has been shown over and over that to pursue *only* pleasure leads to ultimate meaninglessness.

When the amount of time available for volunteer activities is increasing there is need for a vision of leisure that includes free acceptance of obligation in the public sphere—in politics, social service projects, organized church activities, and support of artistic endeavors. There is a moral dimension to time which reflects itself in time; the choices a man makes in his use of leisure time will bear fruits, good or bad, in his own life and in his community life. In this sense leisure time is a social *possibility,* but only if the individual will recognize his responsibility for his actions.

To order one's life on the premise that man is the *master,* not the *slave,* of his time is to recognize that every single act requires a moral decision. . . . For not only is man himself unique, but every event in which he participates is unique, and in every one of these singular events, it is within his own human right to make a choice for better or for worse. This power of moral choice defines the place of the individual in the world, where he is not helpless, but can be a partner in the process of the continuous creation of the world he lives in.[23]

To take responsibility for one's choices, however, requires belief in someone or something which exercises a judgment on our actions; to see oneself as a "partner in the process of continuous creation" requires belief in a Creator. And this belief in a Creator is not an inherent part of the view of time as social organization. Next, then, we turn to a discussion of the theological perspective on time.

[23] *Problems and Challenges of the New Leisure,* Spiritual Statesmanship Conference Convened by the Jewish Theological Seminary of America (Boston, 1956), pp. 9-10.

11

Time as God's Creation

The preceding analysis of ways of looking at time brings us to a major insight regarding the relationship between time and leisure: The views which provide a positive means of understanding time have also created *problems* about finding the ultimate meaning and value of that time. Perhaps the reason for this is that time is explained by referring to something else—an eternal, changeless model; a continuously evolving form; an objective reference in the physical universe; the amount of goods that can be produced and wealth that can be earned; the pressures and demands of work and other social organization.

Problems have occurred when the reference was given ultimate value and then did not prove itself true in human experience, or did not fulfill the aspirations and needs of the human spirit, or did not provide a sufficiently sturdy point of reference when social change took place. Each of the references provides some truth about time. But that truth has been *partial*, and when men have sought to exalt a partial truth to universal application it has proved inadequate, as our critical summary of each perspective will indicate.

1. *An Eternal Changeless Model.* Thus the perception of *classical culture* that there is an eternal realm apart from the created world and its time gave man an objective frame of reference for understanding life. However, in assuming that the world was only an "imitation" of the eternal model, and in applying the cycles observed in nature to the realm of

human history as well, the possibility of any new act taking place was stifled and the idea that there may be a purpose in history moving it toward a goal was ruled out. Man's hope for fulfillment lies in the ability of his reason to emancipate him from the cycle of natural and historical recurrences; the essence of living is contemplation of the eternal. Ethics exist, so it seems, either in pure rational form to be comprehended apart from daily living or as inherent in the cyclical process of history and thus do not really possess any meaning for man's action. What about those who cannot spend their time in contemplation? Do their lives lack meaning? Work must be done and decisions made—but for no ultimate purpose? A man's aspirations to be or to do something new in his life doom him to despair and cynicism in this view of time as cyclical recurrence because human time has no significance in itself. Furthermore, both nature and history betray these observations of recurrence because new forms continually come into being.

2. *A Continuously Evolving Form.* The *scientific revolution* and the Renaissance in general brought an independent purpose and value to man's time. Time was seen as the arena where new forms evolve from old forms—mutation and change became the keys to understanding the meaning of life. Time did not just recur over and over; rather it stretched ahead with limitless opportunity for new development. It was assumed, however, that if higher forms of life developed in the world of nature, then it must be true that higher—and better —forms of life will evolve in the realm of human history if only the right conditions are provided. Evil was thus regarded as belonging to primitive or ignorant states of being which education and controlled environment could eliminate.

But once again the human spirit revealed itself to be more complex than the natural world in which men live. Some of the greatest horrors and atrocities of the last war were committed by highly trained and educated men. Higher forms of political and social life have created greater possibilities for good, but they have not always been used for good. In believing human history to contain its own meaning and fulfillment, man lost the belief in an eternal dimension beyond man, and thus any transcendent perspective on human affairs. Ethics became relative to the process, and time was viewed as progressive movement toward Utopia. Consequently this view has brought man no closer to seeing the meaning of life and history, for the value it ascribed to human time has been given a serious setback as time has brought quite the opposite of the results envisioned.

3. *An Objective Reference.* Precision in measuring time was a necessary development in the growth of a complex industrial society. Anyone who has known a person who has no regard for keeping appointments will agree that it is good to be able to make and keep an agreed meeting time. It is also nice not to have to wait all day to catch a bus because the driver comes when he feels like it! There is truth about measuring time so that people may live together with reasonable efficiency. But then when all time is thought of quantitatively, when each fragment is given equal weight because the clock gives them equal duration, there is a definite loss in perceiving the quality of events. Does the length of an activity give it its value? Does merely doing a lot of things in a short time give them added significance? We ignore the significance, the real meaning and depth of much activity by using a strictly quantitative assembly-line conception of time—time as a moving belt of equal units.[1]

4. *Amount of Goods Produced.* When men began to organize life on a scale larger than the one-to-one *exchange of goods and services* so that the opportunity for making goods available and distributing them could be expanded, it was necessary to develop a means to organize work and reimburse men for their labor. Moreover, the recognition that an individual is a unique soul with certain rights and privileges means recog-

[1] De Grazia, "The Uses of Time," *Aging and Leisure*, pp. 142-43.

nizing that his *time is valuable*. When a man works to produce goods for others, he should be paid for his time and effort so that he can buy what others have worked to produce.

The difficulty with this view comes when it is made the supreme value in one's life, so that making as much money as possible is the ultimate use of time. Furthermore, it frequently fosters the fiction that what a man makes is exclusively his because he earned it, and the fact that around the world there are still people who do not have the opportunity or ability to work has nothing to do with his own stockpile of wealth. The unconscious application of this view to leisure time is twofold: Leisure is time in which to "produce" leisure activities on the same pressure schedule that work demands, so that life is one big tension and anxiety about never enough time; leisure is time off that has been earned and in which one should just have a good time, with the result that the pure pursuit of pleasure in the long run ends in boredom, emptiness, and conformity.

5. *Demands of Social Organization.* Community life requires *social organization*. There are functions which man as a member of society must perform either because of a sense of need—such as sending the children to school, or because of a desire—such as going to parties. The present time is the most important social dimension because the pressures, demands, and hopes apply to the here and now or to the immediate future. So, for instance, advancing in one's career *now* is important, achieving security and happiness *now* for one's family is important.

To concentrate exclusively on the present, however, is to lose any sense of continuity with the past or thought about the end of one's life in the future. Moreover, no capacities for the contemplation of meanings nor of transcendent values are developed, so that no goals are shaped beyond the immediate ones of happiness and security. Thus if life is oriented only around career and family and the social activities related to these, then retirement, loss of family, or inability to participate socially on the same scale one is accustomed to means a disillusioned end to life and a wondering if it was all worth it.

It is always a tendency on man's part to make a partial view of truth the whole truth. To be able to keep these partial views of time in perspective is to find in them help and understanding, but to subscribe ultimate value and significance to any or all of them is to cause disillusionment when questions still persist about the meaning of time, the value of activities in time, and what happens to a man when his time is over. What is needed, then, is a dynamic frame of reference which contains these partial views of time, but is not subjected to them; a view of time that will contain the fragments of meaning and point to their fulfillment, that will give man perspective on his time but recognize his responsibility for it.

Toward a Christian Understanding of Time

Christian theology has always believed that time is important because its point of reference is God, the Creator and Sustainer of man and his time. There is, of course, no "theology of leisure" as such, but in theology there are basic affirmations that have important implications for leisure. And one of the most important affirmations is about time. If man's time has value and significance, then so does his leisure time; and how it is used is of utmost concern. It is possible that a Christian view of time may offer the kind of dynamic and creative resource for understanding time and leisure that men have been searching for. With this hope in mind we begin our discussion.

Rather than trying to define time by equating it with another phenomenon in human experience—recurrence, progress, clock measurements, money, social organization—let us simply state a basic definition which is implied in the views discussed earlier but which is both simpler and more inclusive: *Time is the medium of human existence* (medium in the sense of "material" or "vehicle," as the painter's medium is watercolor, oil, et cetera) . This may seem too obvious, but the truest thing we can say about time is that we live in time. In this way we most immediately apprehend time, and around this perception all definitions revolve. We want to understand time in relation to *us*—our experiences, purposes, needs. Time is the medium in which *our* lives are etched.

But merely this recognition of time as the dimension of human existence would give no clue as to the meaning and purpose of man in his time, nor his possible destiny beyond time. Christian theology affirms that time, the medium of human existence, was created by God—the God of the Hebrews who became incarnate in time in Jesus Christ—and its meaning, purpose, and possibility are found in him. The distinctive features of this view will be brought to light as the discussion proceeds.

1. *Natural Time and Historical Time.* The Judeo-Christian heritage recognizes two dimensions to man's existence in time: his existence in nature and his existence in history. Man is part of nature, but human affairs are not entirely subjected to the natural order. Reinhold Niebuhr expressed the relation of nature and history to time thus:

Time is both the stage and the stuff of history. Insofar as human agents have the freedom to stand above the flux of natural events and create forms and institutions not governed by natural necessity and not limited to the life spans of nature, time is the stage of history. Insofar as these human agents are themselves subject to natural flux and their historic achievements and institutions are also subject to decay and mortality . . . time is part of the stuff of history.[2]

Understood in this light, time in nature is observed to reoccur—day and night, summer and winter, life and death, are

[2] *Faith and History,* p. 35.

characterized by recurrence and repetition. Insofar as historical events come to be and pass away they exhibit a degree of recurrence, but the dominant motif in history is not circular. It is characterized by uniqueness and thus by a forward moving pattern. Historical events are unique even though they have some resemblance to each other. Thus there are parallels between the lives of Caesar and Napoleon, but each is unique, not only in character, but also in the circumstances of the epoch in which he lived and by the set of factors which determined his actions. Man seemingly never steps into the same river twice.

What makes uniqueness the prevalent character of history is the factor of human personality and its action which is unknown in the realm of nature—his capacity to make decisions. Though the decisions may vary as to the degree of their uniqueness, the fact remains that a man can and does make decisions that may alter the course of his life, of his nation's life, and even of mankind's life. Natural time is the arena of necessity; historical time is the arena of decision.

Another way theologians often characterize natural time and historical time is to say natural time is chronological time (the temporal duration of events as they follow each other in succession, in nature, and in history), whereas historical time is the time of opportunity and fulfillment. Both views of time are present in the Bible, but the one that is by far the most important is the latter. Time for the Hebrews was primarily thought of as the concrete events, the content which filled time, not as an abstract quantity. "The colourless idea of 'hour' measuring time in a purely quantitative way, is far from the old Israelitic conception." [3]

It should be noted here that some commentators have built this understanding of time as chronological and as fulfillment

---

[3] Pedersen, *Israel: Its Life and Culture*, p. 489.

on the two Greek words *chronos* and *kairos*.[4] In his book *Biblical Words for Time,* James Barr criticizes this method on the ground that the division is not always consistent; that is, there are instances where *chronos* is used when "opportunity" is clearly meant and where *kairos* is used when reference is to chronological time. It is Barr's conclusion that "A valid biblical theology can be built only upon the *statements* of the Bible, and not on the *words* of the Bible." [5]

Recognizing the validity of Barr's claim, we shall not try to press a definition of these two "times" by using the Greek words—though usage has now made it common to ascribe *kairos* to the time of opportunity and *chronos* to the temporal succession of time. The fact remains, however, that the Bible mentions these two kinds of time, and time as filled event or opportunity is the dominant concern. In general, it might be said that *chronological* time is represented by a date book filled with daily or hourly appointments, whereas *kairotic* time is made up of God's appointments. Furthermore, the dominant biblical view of time is characterized by its content or its eventfulness, the fulfillment of which is man's opportunity. As the content of time is endowed by God, man responds to God when he responds to the events of time.

A vivid awareness of the concreteness of time is found especially in the Old Testament. Nowhere is this eventfulness of time better depicted than by the writer of Ecclesiastes:

For everything there is a season, and a time for every matter under heaven:

[4] See especially John Marsh, *The Fullness of Time* (New York: Harper & Brothers, 1952) and "Time," *A Theological Word Book of the Bible,* edited by Alan Richardson (New York: The Macmillan Company, 1960). Oscar Cullmann's work, *Christ and Time* (Philadelphia: The Westminster Press, 1960) uses the words *aion* (duration of time) and *kairos* (moment in time), but his method of deriving the meanings through etymology is the same as Marsh's.

[5] Studies in Biblical Theology (Naperville, Ill.: Alec R. Allenson, Inc., 1962), p. 147.

a time to be born, and a time to die;
a time to plant, and a time to pluck up what is planted;
a time to kill, and a time to heal;
a time to break down, and a time to build up;
a time to weep, and a time to laugh;
a time to mourn, and a time to dance;
a time to cast away stones, and a time to gather stones together;
a time to embrace, and a time to refrain from embracing;
a time to seek, and a time to lose;
a time to keep, and a time to cast away;
a time to rend, and a time to sew;
a time to keep silence, and a time to speak;
a time to love, and a time to hate;
a time for war, and a time for peace. (3:1-8.)

With justification, for it is already implied, we could add to this catalogue "a time for work, and a time for leisure."

Whereas all religions have sensed the divine at work in the forces of nature, it was a unique perception of Israel to see, very early, God at work in its *history*. God chose the people of Israel to be his people that he might make his salvation known through them; he made a covenant with them in which he sustained them, fulfilled his promises, chastized them when they fell away, and delivered them out of the bondage of Egypt. In the Hebrew mind God was first and foremost the God of history, of human events and human experience. From the beginning God is an active and eager participant in the affairs of men, judging, demanding, and yet merciful.

Thus every event is charged with meaning, and time is alive with significance. Each day is lived in the awareness that "This is the day which the Lord has made" (Ps. 118:24), and the final affirmation is the trust that "My times are in thy hand" (Ps. 31:15).

Abraham Heschel, who suggests that Judaism is a religion of time—as opposed to space—which teaches the holiness of time, traced this observation to the Genesis story of creation:

"And God blessed the seventh *day* and made it *holy*." There is no reference in the record of creation to any object in space that would be endowed with the quality of holiness.

This is a radical departure from accustomed religious thinking. The mythical mind would expect that, after heaven and earth have been established, God would create a holy place—a holy mountain or a holy spring—whereupon a sanctuary is to be established. Yet it seems as if to the Bible it is *holiness in time*, the Sabbath, which comes first.[6]

This sanctity of time has been caught up into Christianity, so that the New Testament proclaims the coming of Christ "in the fullness of time," the entry of Christ upon the stage of history into time *and* space.

2. *The Event of Jesus Christ.* At the heart of the Christian faith is the belief that God, having revealed himself in the history of Israel and through its prophets, has revealed himself most completely and uniquely in Jesus Christ. "The Word became flesh and dwelt among us," the writer of the Gospel of John proclaims. God became man, in time and history; therefore in the life, work, suffering, and death of the man Jesus we see God acting decisively for man. The implication of this event for the Christian understanding of time is apparent. Though we may have doubted the meaning, importance, and even reality of human time, the event of Jesus Christ shows, in essence, God's "stamp of approval" on man's time—it has meaning, importance, reality, because God himself has shown us it is good by entering it. As Theodore Gill once said, "In the event of Christmas we see a huge sign on the world that says, 'God slept here.' " Or as Karl Barth wrote in his *Church Dogmatics*, ". . . the existence of the man Jesus in time is our guarantee that time as the form of human existence is in any case willed and created by God, is given by God to man, and is therefore real." [7] Because God revealed himself to us in this

---

[6] *The Sabbath* (New York: Farrar, Strauss and Young, Inc., 1951), p. 9.
[7] Vol. III/2 (Edinburgh: T & T Clark, Ltd., 1960), p. 520.

way, to kill time or to abuse it is to deny God and reject Christ. It is to express one's self-denial and self-alienation. The futility of it all is that man may kill time, but time will not die; at the end of the day, man himself is the victim. This is precisely the fate of the author-artist, Ralph Barton, the illustrator for *Gentlemen Prefer Blondes,* who left this suicide message: "I have run from wife to wife and from home to home in a ridiculous effort to escape from time. I'm fed up with the effort of living twenty-four hours a day."

With the entry of God into human life in Jesus Christ, man's time has been hallowed forever—it is good. This perception that God became incarnate in the person of Jesus is not apparent to everyone, just as the fact of the relative uniqueness of historic events does not elicit common agreement. The Jesus of History, the man, however, can be seen by all, but Jesus Christ, the Son of God and Savior can be seen only through the eyes of faith. Of course the secular historian or philosopher may regard this claim of Christianity as foolish or scandalous, but for the man who has taken the leap of faith, for the believer, it is the ultimate source of meaning and the possibility of creative living. Several things may happen, then, concerning his understanding of time.

For one thing, time takes on a dynamic and redemptive character. In Jesus Christ a "new age" has dawned in the history of mankind—an age in which the Messiah is no longer a hope but a reality, an age in which the suffering servant is seen to be the Savior and Victor, rather than the powerful hero of battle. In weakness there is strength, in losing oneself one finds himself, in repenting old sins there is given the possibility of new life. Paul wrote "if any one is in Christ, he is a new creation; the old has passed away, behold, the new has come" (II Cor. 5:17). Redemption takes place in time, enabling a man to live freely in time; in each moment there is opportunity to turn and be reconciled with God and men. We know this because the focal point of our redemptive history is Jesus Christ.

In the second place, time is seen as moving toward a goal. It neither recurs endlessly nor progresses on forever. Just as time had a beginning with the creation of the universe, so it will have an end which is *telos* and not *finis*—but both the beginning and the end are in God's hands. Of more immediate concern for the individual, of course, is the fact that his own time ends in death, just as his own time began in birth. Both these events are mysteries as far as how and why they occur. What the Christian affirms is that their meaning and purpose are comprehended by God, and that as we live in love and fellowship with him and with our fellowmen, we are living in that meaning and purpose. As Jesus died, so do we; as Jesus was raised to eternal life, so it is within the province of our hope and trust that we share this with him. It is not so difficult to believe that the God who created this life can create another beyond this one. Though death may be our frontier, Karl Barth has said, our God is the frontier even of our death. The goal toward which time and history are moving is the time when sin, death, and the ambiguities and contradictions of existence are ended and man lives in eternal fellowship with God.

The event of Jesus Christ has brought us the assurance that our time here and now is vastly important. God calls us to enter completely into human history and "get our hands dirty" in the making of decisions as well as to know the joy of human love and nature's beauties. But he has also brought us the reassurance that our time is not the ultimately important time; that we need not try to redeem mankind by ourselves, nor try to make our time perfect for him, for even now God is at work moving history toward its goal and fulfilling his purpose in each moment.

3. *Time and Eternity.* "Eternity," which is frequently re-

garded as the opposite of man's time, has long been a subject of thought and speculation. Most of these conceptions of eternity have centered around either the idea that eternity is "infinite time" or that it is "timelessness"—a state that is absolutely different from time. These two conceptions—the one a continuation forever of what we know, the other the imagined opposite of what we know—are perhaps the two most obvious notions that occur about eternity. But, as we have stated, Christianity affirms that time had a beginning and will have an end, so "infinite time" is an inadequate conception for eternity. Neither would "timelessness" seem adequate because man's time as created by God is important because of that creation and because God has entered time in Jesus Christ. Thus a sudden annihilation of this form of human existence does not follow. There must be a relation between God's eternity and man's time which upholds, enhances, and contains our time.

A basic direction for such an understanding is suggested in an analysis made by Johannes Pedersen of the Hebrew word for "eternity." Pedersen contended that,

Eternity is not the sum of all the individual periods, nor even this sum with something added to it; it is *"time" without subdivision,* that which lies behind it, and which displays itself through all times. That the throne of David is to remain eternally, means that it must be raised above, or rather, pervade the changing periods, in that it has its foot in primeval time itself, the stock from which all time flows.[8]

Eternity for the Hebrew, as suggested here by Pedersen, is the fusion of past, present, and future into "time without subdivision." However, we may ask, who encompasses and views this in its entirety? The fact that the language of the Hebrews is lacking in verb tense designating past, present, and future,

[8] *Op. cit.,* pp. 490-91.

and the indications in their literature that their past events were still immediately with them in their present would indicate that they lived in the experience of this unity of world events or eternity. Insofar as this experience is grounded in the affirmation that God created and sustains time, there is the implication that God is the one who holds this unity together.

In a similar vein, Emil Brunner wrote:

God's Eternity is not present that is broken up into parts. It is an undivided present. When He reveals Himself to us, God enters into our time, into our temporal existence, but He does not become temporal Himself. He remains Eternal so that past, present, and future are one in Him. We human beings who are created after the image of God somehow share in this supratemporality, for whenever we perform meaningful acts, acts of synthesis, we somehow transcend the crumbling of time. On the other hand, we are creatures and all our thinking and understanding is embedded in "crumbling-time" and is impeded by it.[9]

Thus in God's eternity man's time and history is contained and fulfilled. This promise of consummation does not mean that there is no mystery about eternity; from our finite human view of things it is an infinite mystery. To perceive the relationship between time and eternity in this way is to affirm that our past, present, and future are now in God's hands, as they always have been and will continue to be.

Such a view of eternity may be of particular interest when related to an experience we have all shared, when it seemed as if time stood still or that we somehow stood outside time. Concerning this experience, Proust wrote: "A single minute released from the chronological order of time has recreated in us the human being similarly released." [10]

[9] "The Christian Understanding of Time," *Scottish Journal of Theology*, (March, 1951), pp. 10-11.
[10] Meyerhoff, *Time in Literature*, p. 54.

Perhaps in those moments when we feel we have transcended time, we have perceived that unity and simultaneous co-inherence of succession in time that is God's eternity—what Brunner refers to as "acts of synthesis." The fact that in the present we can remember a past that was once imagined as a future is an inadequate example of this experience, but it does suggest something of the dimension of what we have sought to depict. What we can sometimes perceive in part through our memory and our imagination, God holds simultaneously in his eternal present.

In any case, at the bottom of the relationship between time and eternity there is something which "the Christian experiences in time and which remains in Eternity, when everything else, even faith and hope, shall be done away: that is, *love*. Love, in the sense of *agape*, is of the character of eternal life, nay, it is the very essence of God. 'God is love, and he that dwelleth in love dwelleth in God, and God in him.' " [11] When we live in self-forgetting and disinterested love, love which has only the other person or God as its concern—the love which God shows for us—in those moments we live both in time and in the eternity which is our hope.

4. *Past, Present, and Future.* As we have noted, a Christian view of time sees temporality as the essence of humanity. To be human is to have an allotted span of time that contains past, present, and future. Sometimes the reality of any true present, however, has been denied because of the fact that, analytically perceived, the minute a thought which was future has become present it has already become past.

Philosophers who have thus emphasized this negative element "point to the movement of time from a past that is no more toward a future that is not yet through a present which is nothing more than the moving boundary line between past and

[11] Brunner, *op. cit.* pp. 9-10. Also Cf. Marsh, *op. cit.*, p. 154.

future." [12] In this case the present is illusion. Others have emphasized the positive character of the present, the fact that "it is only in the power of an experienced present that past and future and the movement from the one to the other can be measured." [13] Both of these emphases dwell on the transitoriness of the present moment, which in turn is the root of anxiety because it keeps moving men toward the fact of death—to what Tillich calls "nonbeing." Man does, however, have the courage to affirm his temporal existence. If it were not for this courage man would give in to the annihilating forces and cease to have any present at all. It is the reality of this courage, Tillich says, that leads one to ask the question about God—the "cosmological question."

The answer to the question of the search for this ultimate courage is found in God—the eternal God who conquers the anxiety of past and future by relating man to himself, the ultimate ground of all being. Thus even the unreality of the present time and the anxiety about death can be the possibility of finding and entering into relationship with God. In this relationship there is a real present, then, which moves from past to future without ceasing to be present.

Another dimension to the lack of any real present for man is suggested by Brunner: Man not only has a sense of anxiety about the future, but he also has a sense of guilt about the past. This fruitless concern with past and future, to the exclusion of having any real present is the state of sinful man—man too preoccupied with his own past and future to have regard for the other who is in his presence.[14]

In Jesus Christ man finds freedom to live in a real present, for there he experiences true forgiveness of past sins which frees him from his sense of guilt, and he experiences the assurance

[12] Paul Tillich, *Systematic Theology* (Chicago: University of Chicago Press, 1951), I, 193.
[13] *Ibid.*
[14] *Op. cit.*, p. 11.

of eternal communion with God which frees him from his anxiety and fear about the future.

Christian faith recognizes that man cannot liberate himself entirely from his anxiety and guilt about time, nor extricate himself from his sin. The more he tries to do this, the more enmeshed in himself he becomes. The past is real—a man is in the present what his past has brought him to; the future offers little new hope to him because his present leads into it just as the past led him to the present. In repentance and forgiveness, however, a new possibility is granted to him and to us. When we stop trying to make something of ourselves, stop boasting —in both obvious and subtle ways—in what we are, have done, or are doing, and when we surrender to the grace of God, then we enter into a real present where we are free from the past and are open to the future. Thus the Christian can never say that he has "arrived"—he lives in the faith and hope that the love he experiences in the present will continue, by the grace of God, in the future.

5. *The Christian and His Time.* For the Christian, then, time is important. It is the medium of his existence which has been created by God, and which has been forever hallowed and pronounced good through God's revelation in Jesus Christ. Man's time is part of the processes of nature which had a beginning and will end, but in his affairs with other men—the realm of history—there is a characteristic freedom and opportunity for decision that is unknown in nature.

Man experiences time as succession—past, present, and future —and often his fear of the end of his future keeps him from being able to live fully in the present. If, however, he can acknowledge his utter dependence on the grace of God, he may experience a forgiveness of his sins and an assurance of God's continued care; for it is in recognizing his dependence on God that the Christian becomes truly free to live, in the present fellowship of love with his fellow men which has freed him from bondage to the past, and in openness to the future and the

234

continuation of God's grace. This does not mean that the Christian is automatically free forever from doubts and anxieties, but it does mean that his doubts and anxieties are continued in a context of ultimate trust and confidence in God to which he returns again and again.

The fact that the Christian stands as a citizen of Augustine's "two cities"—the City of God as well as the city of man— does not make time and the world any less important. Indeed, the Christian is freed from the time panic of Western materialism because though he may live in time he has his base in eternity. "The Christian relation to time is neither that of panic nor that of indifference, but a paradoxical unity of freedom and intense concern in the time-process." [15] Or as Barth expressed it, the Christian "understands his life here and now as one which is affirmed by his beyond." [16]

For the Christian there is a sense of the reality of time—a real past which is redeemed by faith, a real present which is lived through the communion of love, a real future which is fulfilled through hope.

The implications of this perspective on time for leisure will be discussed in more detail in the following chapter, but let us here examine the direction that discussion will pursue.

1. All time is a gift—both work time and leisure time. An understanding of this point in the life of the Christian is needed. Neither work nor leisure are to be endured or wasted, but both are to be the sphere of man's action and reflection, giving and receiving.

2. Time is not an abstract measurement but consists of the content which fills it. We need to find a way to put the pressures of scheduling in their proper perspective and to open ourselves to the events of time which give meaning and purpose. In leisure time there is the possibility of reflection and contempla-

[15] *Ibid.,* p. 8.
[16] *Op. cit.,* p. 640.

tion of that which enhances life and the opportunity for physical restoration.

3. As God has acted in time, we are called to make decisions and act. Life together involves commitment and responsibility in community on all its levels—social, political, national, and international. Leisure offers an opportunity for the Christian to be engaged in these activities as never before. Only by thus acting does a man play out his vocation and exert the freedom that is often only a latent possibility in his life.

4. The true essence of life is joy. Blessed indeed is the man who has found this pervading sense of the joy of life which God intended in his creation. For the one who has found it, there is no power which can ultimately prevail against him. Though suffering and times of despair are never eliminated from human experience, they can become a means of deepening and making more vivid the sense of joy to which the person returns from the valley of the shadow. In leisure this true sense of joy can be nourished as the source of creative living and use of time.

12

Time, Life, and Leisure

What are the implications of a Christian view of time for leisure? The conclusions expressed in the preceding chapter are based on the belief that the biblical record points to an understanding of time as the medium of human existence created by God. Insofar as the Bible knew no "leisure problem," it has no direct word for us concerning a Christian view of leisure.

Alan Richardson stated the matter bluntly when he declared:

The Bible knows nothing of a "problem of leisure." No such problem had in fact arisen in the stage of social evolution which had been reached in biblical times. The hours of daylight were the hours of labour for all workers. . . . The general standpoint of the Bible is that it is "folly" (i.e., sinful) to be idle between daybreak and sunset. A six- or an eight-hour day was not envisaged. Hence we must not expect to derive from the Bible any explicit guidance upon the right use of leisure.[1]

Insofar as the men of the Bible perceived certain insights about the living of life in time, we can draw some implications that are relevant for our understanding of the contemporary problem of leisure. Moreover, we can point to theological resources which speak directly to the human conditions of our new leisure society—anxiety, boredom, conformity, meaninglessness, and "killing time."

[1] *The Biblical Doctrine of Work*, p. 53.

Time Is a Gift

In the beginning God created the heavens and the earth. (Gen. 1:1.)

Fear not, little flock, for it is your Father's good pleasure to give you the kingdom. (Luke 12:32.)

What have you that you did not receive? If then you received it, why do you boast as if it were not a gift? (I Cor. 4:7b.)

The first implication for leisure suggested by a Christian understanding of time concerns the recognition that all of time is a gift. When an individual perceives that all his "lifetime" has been given to him, it becomes necessary for him to view the work and leisure division in a new light. As noted earlier, leisure has always been associated with work, because the boundaries of leisure were first set in relation to the central focus of life—the working hours.

Thus leisure developed as "left-over" time, or as "earned" free time, and has been thought of primarily as time for having fun—no obligations, no requirements, save to enjoy oneself. Basically, then, there is an attitude that at work one "gives" (time, energy, "the best years of life"), whereas at leisure one "receives" (pleasure, enjoyment, renewal for more work, the benefits provided by work). Man, the owner of time, sells part of his time to make things and labels the rest "free time" which is his to dispense with as he pleases.

We have sought earlier to avoid equating true leisure with mere free time in suggesting that leisure is the fulfillment of free time. We have noted too De Grazia's redefinition of leisure as "freedom from the necessity of being occupied," and how he located the essence of Aristotle's meaning in the interpretation: "Leisure is a state of being in which activity is performed for its own sake or as its own end." [2]

---

[2] Of Time, Work, and Leisure, pp. 14-15.

By equating leisure with a "state of being," De Grazia has succeeded in separating leisure from free time. He has left the idea of *work* where the Greeks put it however—as a necessity to make leisure possible, as the life of slaves, as a state of being unfree. Now this idea of work, as we have seen, is shared by many today and the notion of work as a necessity to earn leisure is part of today's leisure problem. For the most part men have ceased regarding work as vocation, a "calling from God," but they have not entirely lost the expectation that their work should provide some sense of fulfillment. Furthermore, the increased amount of time free for leisure has left many people with only a sense of "empty" time—time which should be filled with things that are meaningful, but which turns out to be time without any lasting significance.

On the other hand, almost all studies have revealed that there are some people for whom the work/leisure distinction simply does not apply—research scientists, statesmen, doctors, professors, creative artists, clergymen, et cetera. For them, work and leisure come together as a "way of life"; time is not divided up and equated with money, it is opportunity for discovery, creation, and service. Obviously many jobs by no stretch of the imagination could be regarded in these terms, but many others could be thought of at least as "service." Perhaps the mingling of work and leisure found in the vocations just mentioned can be a sort of guide in other areas.

From this analysis, and in the light of the Judaeo-Christian affirmation that all time is a created medium given to man by God, we should like to suggest a new understanding of the work/leisure relationship: That work and leisure be viewed as a rhythm in life rather than as segments of time in which separate functions are performed. In this understanding, giving need not be limited to work and receiving to leisure, nor serious requirements to work and fun to leisure.

When we evaluate our own experience very few of us can say that we have *never* received anything from our work—

knowledge, vision, friendship, pleasure. And perhaps we will find that leisure has often been most rewarding when we have taken our actions and commitments to others seriously. This is not to say there should be no pure fun in life—even Einstein welcomed occasions of "distraction"—but it is to suggest that both in work and leisure man is called to exercise his freedom and to find his fulfillment. Perhaps some talents will be used and developed most in work and other talents in leisure, but the fruits of each will interact if the person sees his life as a whole containing these rhythms.

There has been a tendency to condense the working hours into the shortest amount of time so that the leisure period could all come together in a big chunk; thus the lunch break is now often only a half-hour, the work day is actually getting shorter, and "business and pleasure shouldn't mix" is a watchword. (Given the choice, some people would probably not prefer the coffee-break, choosing rather to finish work earlier.) This tendency has resulted in a life of fragmented meanings and too much pressure, in which we cram as much work into one period as we can and then cram as much leisure as possible into the other. *But,* thinking now of the work/leisure rhythms, what if businesses and industries would provide:

1. A longer lunch break in which encouragement would be given to such activities as discussion of various family, social, political, and life problems, as well as criticism of television, plays, et cetera; individual reading; artistic presentations; analysis of daily political issues, current events, and international news.

2. Information centers to provide resources for such leisure pursuits as gardening, reading, hobbies, cultural activities, do-it-yourself activities, and educational studies, including the field of theology.

3. A system of "sabbatic leave" for employers and employees, when they might study, relax, and work in a different setting for a year. This practice (which is traced to the ancient Hebrew

custom of leaving a field fallow every seventh year) exists at present chiefly among some universities and seminaries where professors are granted every seventh year for study, research, or teaching elsewhere, at full or partial salary. For men in areas of responsibility in business or labor such opportunity might be the resource needed for creative thinking as well as personal growth.

4. A program of graduated retirement, so that the working hours are decreased gradually in a "phasing out" procedure, rather than the current practice of an abrupt halt, which symbolizes a sharp end to one's usefulness in work and in life.

5. Encouragement of study centers, academy movements, and lay schools of religion where theological dialogue that relates faith to life in the world is stimulated.

It is *possible* that policies and programs such as these would exert an integrative force in life and restore to both work and leisure the meaning they should have.

Insofar as the nonworking hours are increasing and such directions in work as suggested above may be a long time coming, the leisure side of the rhythm will play a major part in providing creative possibilities for the individual. Here a good deal of education of the kind suggested by Mortimer Adler is needed; that is, liberal education in which opportunities for pursuing meanings in life are opened up rather than occupational training which only prepares one to work and which should be done on the job anyway. Adler rightly contended that liberal schooling prepares for a life of learning and for the leisure activities of a whole lifetime. "Adult liberal education is an indispensable part of the life of leisure, which is a life of learning." [3] This education relates definitely to work, but it provides a foundation which enhances life in all rhythms and which sustains a person with continuing opportunities for using his time when his working days come to an end.

[3] "Labor, Leisure, and Liberal Education," *Toward the Liberally Educated Executive* (New York: The Fund for Adult Education, 1959), p. 86.

241

What does all this have to do with a Christian understanding of time? Basically this: For the Christian there is the affirmation that God has given each person his life and his time, his work and his leisure. Furthermore, there is the assurance that God, as revealed in Jesus Christ, desires that we enjoy an abundant life—not solely in terms of wealth and things, but in terms of rich experiences, mutual help and sacrifice, and faithfulness to him and to our fellows.

By our work, then, we not only make a living, but we provide needed services for others. This is true whether we sell ink or shoes to others so they don't have to make their own, or provide heat or postal service for the comfort and joy of others. By the same token, as recipients of goods and services we are not to think that the man in the service station exists to serve us, but rather we are to be grateful that he has chosen to provide something we would otherwise not have. Finally, we are reminded that what we have is not ultimately our own and is to be shared with others who have less than we.

In our leisure we need not frantically pursue time and things as though we could store up relaxation and enjoyment for a rainy day, or as though we could buy the kingdom with boats and TV's and new cars. Jesus tells us that it is the Father's good pleasure to *give* us the kingdom. We must be willing to accept it as a gift, and that is often the hardest thing in the world to do. The novelist Charles Morgan perceived that "The greatest need of our age is to make itself accessible to grace by releasing itself from the pressures of its fears, its anxieties, its self-pity, and allowing itself to be renewed." [4] To make ourselves accessible to grace we will have to be quiet and listen and be at rest in the moment; in our times of leisure we can be aware of God's continuing presence.

It seems paradoxical that, though time is a gift, so many claim that they don't have time; life is one great whirl, filled

[4] "Time Out," *The Writer and His World* (London: Macmillan and Company, 1960) , p. 77.

with a ceaseless round of activities. Many people simply refuse to take the time for creative leisure. Against this sentiment, Michel Quoist wrote with sensitivity in "Lord, I Have Time":

I went out, Lord,
Men were coming and going,
Walking and running.

Everything was rushing: cars, trucks, the street, the whole town.
Men were rushing not to waste time.

They were rushing after time,
To catch up with time,
To gain time.

Good-bye, Sir, excuse me, I haven't time.
I'll come back, I can't wait, I haven't time.
I must end this letter—I haven't time.
I'd love to help you, but I haven't time.
I can't accept, having no time.
I can't think, I can't read, I'm swamped, I haven't time.
I'd like to pray, but I haven't time.

You understand, Lord, they simply haven't the time.

.   .   .   .

And so all men run after time, Lord.
They pass through life running—hurried, jostled, overburdened,
    frantic and they never get there.
    They haven't time.
In spite of all their efforts they're still short of time.
Of a great deal of time.
Lord, you must have made a mistake in your calculations.
There is a big mistake somewhere.
The hours are too short,
The days are too short,
Our lives are too short.

243

You who are beyond time, Lord, you smile to see us fighting it.
And you know what you are doing.
You make no mistakes in your distribution of time and men.
You give each one time to do what you want him to do.
But we must not lose time
  waste time,
  kill time,
For time is a gift that you give us,
But a perishable gift,
A gift that does not keep.

Lord, I have time,
I have plenty of time,
All the time that you give me,
The years of my life,
The days of my years,
The hours of my days,
They are all mine.
Mine to fill, quietly, calmly,
But to fill completely, up to the brim,
To offer them to you, that of their insipid water
  you may make a rich wine such as you made once in
  Cana of Galilee.
I am not asking you tonight, Lord,
  for time to do this and then that,
But your grace to do conscientiously, in the time
  that you give me, what you want me to do.[5]

How can we find our leisure rhythm in the midst of the many claims and pressures in our lives? Perhaps there can be no satisfactory answer to that question except to agree with Charles Morgan: "By desiring it, by imagining it, by not rebelling against it, by not hardening your heart." [6] For those who worry

[5] From *Prayers* by Michel Quoist, © Sheed & Ward, Inc., 1963.

that leisure will merely be idleness, we can say that there is a distinct difference between idleness and leisure. Idle time is time that neither refreshes nor fulfills us. But if we pause in our work or in our play and perceive a moment of freshness, of purpose, of dedication, of grace, then we have experienced leisure and our lives are richer for it.

It is not in laying up treasures on earth that we buy or save time. Rather we are called as Christians to accept time as a gift and live it for the glory of God—giving and receiving, in seriousness and joy, in our work and in our leisure, for

The heavens are the Lord's heavens,
but the earth he has given to the sons of men. (Ps. 115:16.)

Time, then, is one of God's ways with men. It is the garden in which we grow.

Time and the Quality of Events

Will the Lord be pleased with thousands of rams,
with ten thousands of rivers of oil?
. . . .
He has showed you, O man, what is good;
and what does the Lord require of you
but to do justice, and to love kindness,
and to walk humbly with your God? (Mic. 6:7a-8.)

For whoever would save his life will lose it, and whoever loses his life for my sake will find it. For what will it profit a man, if he gains the whole world and forfeits his life? Or what shall a man give in return for his life? (Matt. 16:25-26.)

The second implication for leisure concerns the quality of events in our experience, for throughout the Bible there is ex-

[6] Morgan, *op. cit.,* p. 74.

pressed the belief that time has significance because of the content that fills it—not the quantity, but the quality. Thus we find recorded there both triumphs and defeats, joy and suffering, because these are the experiences that heighten life and infuse it with special meaning. Curiously enough, to perceive time in terms of the significant events within it opens up a new perspective on what constitutes the duration of time. Instead of the sleepless hour seeming long and the hour with a loved one seeming short, an element is introduced which reverses this. As John Steinbeck perceptively wrote, in *East of Eden:*

Time interval is a strange and contradictory matter in the mind. It would be reasonable to suppose that a routine time or an eventless time would seem interminable. It should be so, but it is not. It is the dull eventless times that have no duration whatever. A time splashed with interest, wounded with tragedy, crevassed with joy—that's the time that seems long in the memory. And this is right when you think about it. Eventlessness has no posts to drape duration on. From nothing to nothing is no time at all.

The element Steinbeck introduces here is "memory," so that times of meaning and significance stay with us in the present. Earlier we reviewed how the Hebrews brought their past with them into their new experiences. Perhaps this gives us a clue to establishing a sense of history in our own lives, a link with the past that gives us a feeling of continuity as well as reference points to remind us of God's presence. In times of tribulation the Hebrews remembered God's deliverance of them from bondage, in times of disobedience and apostasy the prophets reminded them of the physical and spiritual famine such activities had precipitated. So, for us, remembrance of things past could be a steadying and redemptive influence for present crises.

But in order to remember events, to be part of a community of remembrance, we first must have experienced them—and this is where a concern with the *quantity* of time has stifled such perception. T. S. Eliot put his finger on this in *The Family Reunion* when he has Lord Monchensey say to his family:

> You are all people
> To whom nothing has happened, at most a continual impact
> Of external events.[7]

To give oneself to time and to let the events of life "happen" is to open oneself to the meaning contained there. Unless this openness is present nothing has any ultimate meaning, and we will eventually become bored with ourselves, our leisure, and our world. If this kind of awareness *is* present, however, we will not need to seek only distraction (as Paul Elmen says, "The noisiest and most gaudy entertainment"), but may find within our own experience a variety of exciting, interesting, and challenging activities that will fulfill our leisure time.

To experience events in depth requires courage and it requires a trust that life is basically good in spite of the experiences of suffering and pain that seem to be part of it. For the man who has truly placed his life in the hands of God, because he has seen God's love and care in Jesus Christ, there is present an enabling power of awareness and sensitivity. It is possible that this assurance may come from another source, but for the Christian it has happened because of Jesus Christ—whereas we felt alien in the world, we now begin to feel at home.

Of course this quality of events does not exclude difficult times or moments of loneliness. Indeed, in experiences of loneliness there can come this same sensitivity and awareness of new dimensions of self, new beauty, and new power for human compassion. We avoid loneliness as we avoid so many of life's real experiences. But there we may find a depth and maturity not possible elsewhere. "Let there be loneliness, for where there

---

[7] *The Complete Poems and Plays* (New York: Harcourt, Brace & World, Inc., 1952), p. 234.

is loneliness, there also is love, and where there is suffering, there also is joy." [8]

"Which of you by being anxious can add one cubit to his span of life?" Jesus asks; the only possible reply is "no one." Therefore let us not waste our time worrying about not having enough time, but let us drink deeply of what we experience— friendship, solitude, the sense of order, beauty, and wonder. Let us not kill time by filling it with small and unnecessary activities; such continuous distractions will, in time, desensitize us until we fall prey to the despair of boredom.

Time and the quality of events in their most dynamic sense were captured by the late Lewis J. Sherrill:

Time, then, is long uneventful flow; and time is the instant when some event lights up the whole landscape like a flash of lightning which reveals the shape of things that had lain hidden. . . .

. . . There is time which breaks in upon our dull routine and opens the door to life. There is time which frightens us because we cannot yet see its meaning, and then we cry out, My God, why! And there is time when it is as if we caught some glimpse, however fleeting, of the meaning of all things.[9]

It seems clear that a mere analytical and scientific description of time will not foster in us a greater sense of the quality of events in time. Rather, it is often through art and literature, in the life experiences recorded there, that we recognize our own experience or are made aware of things we ordinarily overlook. This same illumination of life fills the literature of the Bible.

Thus the world of literature, drama, and the various media of artistic expression beckon to us in our leisure for both enjoyment and illumination. To be aware of the significant events of our lives is to live time at its richest depth; also it provides leisure with an overflowing wealth of experiences for explora-

---

[8] Clark E. Moustakas, *Loneliness* (Englewood Cliffs, N.J.: Prentice-Hall, Inc., 1961), p. 103.

[9] "My Times," *Union Seminary Quarterly Review* (May, 1957), XII, 4, 7.

tion and reflection. Furthermore it enables us to see God acting in human history, creating and redeeming in and through our common experiences.

The Committed Life Is the Free Life

Commit your way to the Lord;
  trust in him, and he will act. (Ps. 37:5.)

Truly, truly, I say to you, unless a grain of wheat falls into the earth and dies, it remains alone; but if it dies, it bears much fruit. (John 12:24.)

"I know your works: you are neither cold nor hot. Would that you were cold or hot! So, because you are lukewarm, and neither cold nor hot, I will spew you out of my mouth." (Rev. 3:15-16.)

Times of refreshing [shall] come from the presence of the Lord. (Acts 3:19b.)

A third implication for leisure in a Christian understanding of time concerns commitment. As the medium of human existence created by God, time is also the arena of responsibility and decision making for men. The discussion thus far has revealed a tendency to regard leisure as time free of any sense of obligation; so politics, the church, social-service projects, and sometimes family life are often excluded as leisure activities because they hint of moral responsibility. However, it is this very lack of sense of goal or context for action in leisure that now calls for re-examination. For instance, discussing why people find politics so boring, Stimson Bullitt observed:

Our anxiety, which in America now seems to be endemic, is due more to the absence of appealing paths of aspiration than to the lack of a ceiling on some kinds of competitive effort. Our discontent is caused less from trying to scale a greasy pole of infinite height than from the absence from our sight of any poles which we think worth a climb. Universal leisure intensifies, and largely creates, the need for new ideals. Even guided leisure is not an adequate substitute for ideals since it provides artificial temporary goals but is aimless in the long run. The politician who assumes the role of the games director at a resort fails to fulfill the people's need for goals. Aimlessness, whether applied to leisure or to work, is a dull doctrine for a politician to expound.[10]

One of the important things to remember when discussing the need for goals in leisure is the fact that freedom of choice plays a vital part in leisure. Insofar as work requires a concentration on specific pursuits, the exercise of our freedom of choice in that area takes place within definite limits. (Perhaps the greatest use of free choice in work is the decision to take a particular job or not.) Leisure presents a wide-open realm of possible alternatives, however; our freedom is given full rein to choose on a broad scale. The growth and fulfillment which comes in the exercise of this freedom in leisure is one of the greatest possibilities for the individual to realize in his choice of leisure pursuits.

With the factor of freedom in leisure, however, is the possibility that it will be misused as well as used wisely. So, for instance, we puzzle over the fact that at a time when so many nations are struggling to win independence and so many people are fighting and dying to win a free voice in the election of government officials, we in America must urge, beg, and cajole to get people to exercise their right to vote. More and more Americans seem to be assuming a passive attitude toward their basic freedoms, and only a crisis of some kind—war, riot, or natural calamity—will rally the majority around a common concern.

Sebastian de Grazia cited two facts which bear upon this situation. One involves the increase in devices for projecting

<hr/>

[10] From *To Be a Politician* by Stimson Bullitt. Copyright © 1959 by Stimson Bullitt. Reprinted by permission of Doubleday & Company, Inc. P. 158.

sound and images which have "removed people from direct contact and thus lowered their critical attention to the point where they are almost in the state of the older cats and dogs." [11] Whereas the old kind of spectator free-time activity could be called passive, de Grazia indicated that this new kind of spectator activity might better be called "uncritical" or "unthinking" rather than merely passive. This attitude extends to the area of reading as well as TV.

The second fact involves the commercial and industrial world we live in, where "free time is spent generally in the company of commodities, sometimes called leisure equipment, facilities, products, or items—a TV set or a juke box.[12] Such a mass of luxuries so readily available seems to contribute to a closed-in, apathetical attitude. We have become so used to sitting and waiting for the good things in life to be discovered, manufactured, and shipped to our neighborhood store for us to purchase that we expect purpose and goals to come that way too. We have come to think of freedom as choosing or not choosing to buy what is advertised, and the free person as the one who is in no way biased by commitment or decision.

In the first place, however, the aimless or neutral man cannot be called a "free" man, for he is at the mercy of whim or chance or the decisions of others. Karl Barth has said that "freedom cannot be possessed otherwise than by being seized and won." [13] Commenting on Samuel Beckett's play *Waiting for Godot,* Paul Elmen described Vladimir and Estragon as they wait under the tree where Godot said he would meet them (though he didn't say when he would come), and then noted: 'What is implied is that it is impossible to do the one thing in the world worth doing—going in search for Godot—and therefore it does not matter what one does or says while waiting. It is

---

[11] *Of Time, Work, and Leisure,* p. 336.
[12] *Ibid.,* p. 338.
[13] *Church Dogmatics,* vol. III/2, p. 195.

necessary only to find diversions ('How time passes when one has fun!') ." [14]

Rather than waiting for his goal to come to him, man is called to use his freedom to search and explore and discover his goals and purposes. Here, it is true, the Christian finds himself in something of a paradox: He has searched for God until God found him; he has searched far and wide only to find that God has already come to him and has sustained him even as he searched. Nevertheless, unless he had gone to look he might never had found God waiting for him, and unless he continues to search, in that relationship, for courses of action in this world he will not live relevant to the times.

In the second place, freedom in its most profound sense demands commitment; anarchy is as much a misuse of freedom as is tyranny. Democracy is based on the assumption that freedom for everyone can exist only if each person will freely choose to limit his own freedom for the sake of others, and to do this requires commitment to a higher goal. In marriage it is only when husband and wife share a real commitment to each other that their relationship is free to develop in mutual love and trust. In friendship freedom of expression is greatest where the commitment is greatest. The Christian discovers that in committing himself to God in Jesus Christ he has become truly free, for in that relationship he is most himself. Whereas before he was in bondage to the past, to his guilt, to anxiety about the future, to his defensiveness—his commitment has made him free to live. Thus for the Christian the key is not so much Socrates' "the unexamined life is not worth living," but that the uncommitted life is the unlived life. When one stands on a basic foundation of trust and assurance, then he is free to live and to act in the light of that commitment.

This recognition is voiced in the words of an old hymn:

[14] From *The Restoration of Meaning to Contemporary Life,* by Paul Elmen. Copyright © 1958 by Paul Elmen. Reprinted by permission of Doubleday & Company, Inc. P. 192.

Make me a captive, Lord,
　And then I shall be free;
Force me to render up my sword,
　And I shall conqueror be.
I sink in life's alarms
　When by myself I stand;
Imprison me within Thine arms,
　And strong shall be my hand.

To give this kind of commitment is both simple and difficult—simple because it is possible for everyone, regardless of station in life; but difficult because it requires renunciation of pride and cowardice. To make a commitment is to be held responsible, but it is also to be freed for responsibility. Often we escape from freedom because it is a difficult burden to bear, but without it we live bored or anxious lives, or both.

God does not force us to commit ourselves to him—but he would evoke our responses, and he would enable us to respond. The Christian is called to responsible action in the community of which he is a part, to act in and with his fellow men in love and concern. Just because he has no blueprint for the future or precise program to follow, the Christian must be always discovering new duties. Freedom for the Christian involves both commitment to God and to his fellow men and requires that he act responsibly in his time.

This kind of action does not mean activity for the sake of activity, and thus does not mean that our leisure is to be filled with busyness. Rather it means that as all our time is the arena of decision making and participation in community life, so our leisure time is not to be thought of as only fun time. There is nothing wrong with fun and pleasure; it is an essential part of life, but it is not all there is to life or leisure. Let us therefore get rid of our ideas that leisure is time for irresponsibility and no obligations. Instead of detachment, leisure leads to deeper involvement and more responsible decision making. It

253

provides no excuse for indifference, for retreat into an inner world of the private self, or for removal from modern man's communal and social concerns.

Leisure offers a marvelous opportunity for freedom to be exercised, but where there is no commitment that freedom becomes aimlessness or apathy. To engage in politics, participate in the life of the church, visit the sick, work with needy children and troubled youth, crusade for peace—these and many other activities are also part of leisure, and unless they are recognized as such they may be lost and our community life seriously undermined.

Remember that in a world where misery and the threat of war persists the "leisure problem" is one that we are privileged to have. Our material benefits should have freed us to aid other countries to enjoy the same, but instead we are concerned with how we can use them to enjoy our own free time. Is there yet time to look away from self-preoccupation to goals worthy of commitment?

Because God has first acted for us, the Christian is called to act with and for God and his fellows in whatever time he has to do so. We need time for reflection and contemplation, to feed our souls, to give us perspective, to enable us to evaluate where to put our trust in any given situation. But we must also make decisions and act in our leisure as well as our work, and it is only as we commit ourselves to the goals of our actions that we lay hold of the freedom we have been given. The interesting thing is, when we do so, we may find that we are enjoying ourselves more than we ever did before when our attention was riveted upon ourselves.

The Joy of Creative Living

For you shall go out in joy,
and be led forth in peace;
the mountains and the hills before you
shall break forth into singing,

and all the trees of the field shall clap their hands.
(Isa. 55:12.)

The kingdom of heaven is like treasure hidden in a field, which a man found and covered up; then in his joy he goes and sells all that he has and buys that field. (Matt. 13:44.)

The fourth implication of a Christian understanding of time for leisure concerns the joy that comes when life is lived "abundantly." Despite the seriousness which surrounds decision making and responsibility, Christian faith also affirms that time is a context in which real joy pervades and sustains those who love life, with all its difficulties and despairs. It is thus that leisure offers us our greatest opportunities to exercise our capacities for joy as well as for freedom, but as freedom is realized in commitment, so joy is found in the love which is the creative source of living—which for the Christian means God's love as it affirms him and enables him to live creatively.

Let us note first that this joy is different from the more fleeting experiences of pleasure and happiness. Whereas pleasures and happiness are positive experiences that are gratifying, joy is more a state of being which pervades all experiences—pleasureable and painful, happy and sorrowful. Joy is a "norm" for our faith and our response to God as creator of a life which is basically good.

Joy may best be understood as "blessedness." On the one hand, pleasure and happiness are normal, natural desires that are good in themselves, but experience has shown that they have limitations. In the case of pleasure this limitation is really a practical matter—it is a relief that experiences which yield pleasure do not last forever, for pleasure turns into pain or disgust when pushed beyond a point or when it lasts too long. Though happiness is more lasting than pleasure, it too is limited because it concerns a certain state of being and life experiences will not let a person grasp and hold on to that state indefinitely.

255

On the other hand, blessedness is a joy of the spirit in which just being, doing, and serving is the focal point. Pleasure and happiness are really both egocentric and represent different levels of self-seeking. The paradox that is recognized in blessedness is that we are most truly ourselves when we forget ourselves; the self needs ends outside itself to which it can give itself in order to realize itself. Happiness and pleasure as goals to be pursued and attained are always elusive; they are rather "by-products" of life.

Thus the ultimate Christian questions are not, "Are you happy in your work?" "Are you happily married?" et cetera. Rather the ultimate question is, "Are you in this relationship all you can be and should be?" To the degree that you are, you are blessed. Probably happiness will be there also, but not always—for the motivation of the Christian is love, and he who loves always suffers, even as God lives in constant love and suffers for it. The ultimate end and destiny of the Christian is the blessedness of life with God in which he suffers with him, but has joy even in the midst of suffering, because he has found his right relationship with God.

Now in distinguishing joy from pleasure, there is no implication here that the Christian guards himself against enjoying anything pleasureable. What is implied is that the person whose life is pervaded with joy sees pleasure in its proper perspective, as a desirable experience which has inherent limitations. In this sense pleasure is neither idolized nor regarded "idly." It is not a goal to be sought, but neither is it a derogatory experience of a rather shabby nature.

Perhaps the most distinguishing quality of joy is that it can never be possessed nor produced. We can go looking for an experience of pleasure and find it after a fashion, or we can achieve a situation of comfort, ease, and security in which we can say we are happy. Joy, however, is not dependent on experience or situation; it comes in relationship to "the Other." Joy breaks through in love—of God, of men, of the world, of life; it often comes to our consciousness when we least expect it, and it is not limited in duration by its own nature. For the Christian who believes that God loves him in spite of everything there is an abiding joy even though all other relationships may have been taken from his presence and though he may suffer physical adversity.

Thus one of the last men to speak to Dietrich Bonhoeffer, the German Lutheran pastor who was imprisoned and executed by the Nazis for his resistance to Hitler, wrote of him: "Bonhoeffer always seemed to me to spread an atmosphere of happiness and joy over the least incident and profound gratitude for the mere fact that he was alive." [15] Though Bonhoeffer expressed in his letters and poems his times of doubt and fear, he was enabled to live his life in prison creatively and his life with others in joy. Neither suffering nor sorrow can shake the capacity for joy.

But what does all this have to do with the vast majority of us who are seldom called to be imprisoned for our faith and who have satisfied our material needs to the extent that we have a leisure problem? We may suggest at least two important possibilities for the person who sees the vision of what time pervaded with joy can mean.

First, he may be freed to enjoy his leisure. Instead of racing frantically in chase of a good time and filling the leisure hours with activity, he may rest in the rhythm of acting and reflecting, giving and receiving. "I have learned, in whatever state I am, to be content," Paul wrote (Phil. 4:11b), not meaning he has passively submitted to circumstances, but that he has found a peace in his conditions. If we are at a party with friends we need not be plagued by the thought that we might have had more fun if we'd gone to the movies, or if we are called to an important political or church meeting we need not fret unduly

[15] Bonhoeffer, *Life Together* (New York: Harper & Brothers, 1954), from the Introduction by John W. Doberstein, p. 13.

about missing our favorite television program. To live in anxiety about what might have been or what we missed is to wish our lives away and miss the joy of creative living.

"In this moment, in this relationship, am I all that I can be or ought to be?" is the question in both work and leisure. Thus our leisure has no preconceived goal of pleasure connected with it which we are required to achieve, but the opportunities to live creatively are opened to us—to increase our skills, express our talents, freely fulfill our obligations, learn new things, dream new dreams, see new visions, enjoy each other in teamwork, serve each other in love, and worship God in spirit and in truth—for their own sakes.

Second, he may be enabled to affirm himself in his leisure. Sebastian de Grazia suggests that the great mass of people do not have the capacity for leisure. The world, he says, is made up of two classes: "One is the great majority; the other is the leisure kind, not those of wealth or position or birth, but those who love ideas and the imagination." [16] De Grazia's purpose in making this distinction is to point out that most people do not want leisure in the sense that the thinkers, artists, and musicians know it, and that their envy of them as "having it easy" is not true. Governed by the truth they seek, these "leisure kind" impose their own disciplines on themselves—they are blessed in that their work and leisure fuse, but they do not have it easy (most of the time). De Grazia quite rightly suggests that we must find ways to support this select group of people so that they can be free to pursue their callings, the benefits of which are everyone's gain. To do so will require some change in political and social ideas.

We would agree with De Grazia's analysis of the state of the "leisure kind," but in his passion on that side he neglects offering any leisure possibility for the rest—the "great majority." At this juncture Paul Tillich speaks cogently to us:

[16] *Of Time, Work, and Leisure*, p. 377.

Spiritual self-affirmation occurs in every moment in which man lives creatively in the various spheres of meaning. Creative, in this context, has the sense not of original creativity as performed by the genius but of living spontaneously, in action and reaction, with the contents of one's cultural life. In order to be spiritually creative one need not be what is called a creative artist or scientist or statesman, but one must be able to participate meaningfully in their original creations. . . . Everyone who lives creatively in meanings affirms himself as a participant in these meanings. He affirms himself as receiving and transforming reality creatively. He loves himself as participating in the spiritual life and as loving its contents. He loves them because they are his own fulfillment and because they are actualized through him. The scientist loves both the truth he discovers and himself insofar as he discovers it. He is held by the content of his discovery. This is what one can call "spiritual self-affirmation." And if he has not discovered but only participates in the discovery, it is equally spiritual self-affirmation.[17]

We need not be creative in the sense of original creativity in order to be re-creative. Too often we abstain from full participation in leisure pursuits on the grounds that we have limited talents or native abilities. We fail to see the re-creative joy that comes from the use of whatever talent, resourcefulness, and imagination that is at our disposal for the sake of inner satisfaction and growth. Re-creation may involve restoration—the resting and recharging of tired muscles, frayed nerves, and overworked brain cells. Above all, man's re-creative activity relates him to the Creator of all things. Re-creation is rest in God. We may rest *from* our labors, but our rest is most truly refreshing when we rest *upon* and are strengthened in our dependence upon God.

Furthermore, we must look also to the areas of interpretation and appreciation as suitable for leisure participation. Our leisure gives us opportunities to participate in the truths which

[17] *The Courage to Be* (New Haven: Yale University Press, 1952), pp. 46-47.

the "leisure kind" have apprehended. But because it is parti-pation, it is nonetheless creative or true leisure. Indeed, enjoy-ment and appreciation must be viewed as a major function of creativity today. To love and affirm the truth and ourselves in that truth is to know the joy of creative living and to live time abundantly. To be open to the love of God and the working of his grace is the source of that joy, and by turning to him in our leisure times we will find that time fulfilled *in* joy.

Conclusion

This is the day which the Lord has made;
   let us rejoice and be glad in it. (Ps. 118:24.)

I came that they may have life, and have it abundantly. (John 10:10*b*.)

Be still, and know that I am God. (Ps. 46:10.)

This is how one should regard us, as servants of Christ and stewards of the mysteries of God. (I Cor. 4:1.)

A Christian understanding of time beckons us to accept all time as God's gift, including our leisure; to live our leisure in terms of the quality of its events; to be willing to commit ourselves to act during leisure; and to open ourselves to the joy of living leisure in the creative love of God and man.

Much, of course, has been left unsaid even in covering the four dimensions of this subject, but it is our hope that the possibility of looking at leisure in a new way has been stimu-lated by this discussion.

George Soule reminded us that technology has mastered the art of saving time but not the art of spending it, and how we allocate our time will call for a different set of values than those dominant in the nineteenth and early twentieth centuries.[18] Surely the work/leisure rhythm is one area where new values

[18] *Time for Living*, pp. 100-101.

must be realized; the perception of what is important in life is another; what it means to "be still" is yet another.

> Lie down and listen to the crabgrass grow,
> The faucet leak, and learn to leave them so.
> Feel how the breezes play about your hair
> And sunlight settles on your breathing skin.
> What else can matter but the drifting glance
> On dragonfly or sudden shadow there
> Of swans aloft and the whiffle of their wings
> On air to other ponds? Nothing but this:
> To see, to wonder, to receive, to feel
> What lies in the circle of your singleness.
> Think idly of a woman or a verse
> Or bees or vapor trails or why the birds
> Are still at noon. Yourself, be still—
> There is no living when you're nagging time
> And stunting every second with your will.
> You work for this: to be the sovereign
> Of what you slave to have—not
> Slave.[19]

We must learn that man is a player who renews his strength by waiting upon the Lord. Rest means the fullness of joy in God's works, so that our own work is not exalted to ultimate seriousness. Perhaps this is what Jesus is saying to us in the account of Martha and Mary. Recall that Jesus rebukes Martha —the one who waits so diligently upon him with service and who became angry at her sister for waiting on the Lord merely by listening to his teaching. "Lord," exclaimed Martha, "do you not care that my sister has left me to serve alone? Tell her then to help me." But the Lord answered her, "Martha, Martha, you are anxious and troubled about many things; one thing

[19] "Time, Gentlemen, Please" by Marya Mannes. *The Reporter* (July 5, 1962), p. 6.

is needful. Mary has chosen the good portion, which shall not be taken away from her." (Luke 10:40-41.)

To a generation of Americans "anxious and troubled about many things" and yet faced with the prospects of still greater leisure the biblical injunction, "Be still, and know that I am God," really means in its full contemporary biblical setting: "Cease, stop, relax, Shut Up! . . . Have Leisure and Know that I am God." Or "Stop what you are doing, you busy little man, who thinks he has no leisure, and choose leisure!"

Furthermore, it will be a hard lesson to learn that not in our possessions do we find "abundant life," but in love, in joy, in experiences of truth. These are the things Jesus Christ has called us to receive. If we live in them in our leisure they cannot but enhance our work and our life as well. In his love he can free us from our anxiety about the future, our boredom with the past, and our conformity in the present, if we live our time in obedience in his spirit. Charles Morgan suggested that, "We have to learn again how to conjugate our lives in the present tense . . . 'I am, thou art, He is' is the sanity of love and faith, and the atom bomb does not affect it." [20]

Christian faith will not do away with the mystery which ultimately surrounds the concept of time. Nor should it. Christopher Fry has spoken of our need "to keep the sense of wonder" alive in a world in which wonder is rapidly vanishing. For the Christian who is aware of the life around him this sense of wonder is part of the joy of his leisure reflection and a guide to experiences in his leisure activity.

Problems we have with us always, but let them not detract from the opportunities galore. The new leisure revolution ushers in a rare opportunity to proclaim the Lordship of Christ over all of time, history, and personal destiny. It should challenge the churches to new shapes of proclamation and witness. The leisure time gift will enable the churches to declare the

[20] *Op. cit.,* pp. 64, 68.

Lordship of Christ across all boundaries of time and space in a truly ecumenical spirit. It is our faith that above, before, below, and behind the mystery of time, life, and leisure—transcending all the dimensions of width, depth, length, and time in our consideration of religion and leisure—there is the God in whom we trust. He is sovereign Lord. And He shall reign forever and ever.

SELECTED BIBLIOGRAPHY*

Adler, Mortimer J. "Labor, Leisure, and Liberal Education," *Toward the Liberally Educated Executive*. New York: The Fund for Adult Education, 1959.

Anderson, Nels. *Work and Leisure*. London: Routledge and Kegan Paul, 1961.

Bell, Daniel. "Work and Its Discontents," *The End of Ideology*. Chicago: The Free Press of Glencoe, Ill., 1959.

Berger, Bennett M. "The Sociology of Leisure: Some Suggestions," *Industrial Relations: A Journal of Economy and Society*. Vol. 1, Feb., 1962. Berkeley: Institute of Industrial Relations, University of California.

Brightbill, Charles. *Man and Leisure: A Philosophy of Recreation*. Englewood Cliffs, N.J.: Prentice-Hall, Inc., 1961.

Caillois, Roger. *Man, Play, and Games*. Chicago: The Free Press of Glencoe, Ill., 1961.

Calhoun, Robert L. *God and the Common Life*. Hamden, Conn.: Shoe String Press, 1935.

Craven, Ida. "Leisure," *Encyclopedia of the Social Sciences*. New York: The Macmillan Company, 1933.

De Grazia, Sebastian. *Of Time, Work, and Leisure*. New York: Twentieth Century Fund, 1962.

* For a more comprehensive bibliography consult Marjorie L. Casebier, "An Overview of Literature on Leisure: A Bibliographic Essay" (San Anselmo, Calif.: Institute of Ethics and Society, San Francisco Theological Seminary, 1963).

Denney, Reuel. *The Astonished Muse*. Chicago: University of Chicago Press, 1957.

Donahue, Wilma, *et al.*, editors. *Free Time: Challenge to Later Maturity*. Ann Arbor: University of Michigan Press, 1958.

Elmen, Paul. *The Restoration of Meaning to Contemporary Life*. Garden City, N.Y.: Doubleday & Company, Inc., 1958.

Friedmann, Georges. "Leisure and Technological Civilization," *International Social Science Journal*, UNESCO. Vol. XII, 1960.

Goffman, Erving. *Encounters: Two Studies in the Sociology of Interaction*. Indianapolis: Bobbs-Merrill Company, Inc., 1961.

Gray, Robert M. and David O. Moberg. *The Church and the Older Person*. Grand Rapids, Michigan: Wm. B. Eerdmans Publishing Company, 1962.

Hartley, Ruth E., *et al. Understanding Children's Play*. New York: Columbia University Press, 1952.

Heschel, Abraham J. *The Sabbath: Its Meaning for Modern Man*. New York: Farrar, Straus & Young, Inc., 1951.

Hodgkins, William. *Sunday: Christian and Social Significance*. London: Independent Press, Ltd., 1960.

Huizinga, Johan. *Homo Ludens*. Boston: Beacon Press, Inc., 1955.

Kaplan, Max. *Leisure in America*. New York: John Wiley & Sons, Inc., 1960.

Kerr, Walter. *The Decline of Pleasure*. New York: Simon and Schuster, Inc., 1962.

Kleemeier, Robert, Editor. *Aging and Leisure*. New York: Oxford University Press, 1961.

Larrabee, Eric and Rolf Meyersohn, editors. *Mass Leisure*. Chicago: The Free Press of Glencoe, Ill., 1958.

Lee, Robert. "Religion and Leisure in American Culture," *Theology Today*, Vol. XIX, No. 1, April, 1962.

Lobsenz, Norman M. *Is Anybody Happy?* Garden City, N.Y.: Doubleday & Company, Inc., 1962.

Lundberg, George A., *et al.* Leisure:A Suburban Study. New York: Columbia University Press, 1934.

Lynes, Russell. "The Pressures of Leisure." *What's New*, No. 208, Winter, 1958. Chicago, Ill.: Abbott Laboratories.

McEntire, Davis. "Leisure Activities of Youth in Berkeley." Berkeley: Berkeley Council of Social Welfare and School of Social Welfare, University of California, 1952.

Martin, Alexander Reid. "A Philosophy of Recreation." Chapel Hill:

University of North Carolina, Second Southern Regional Conference on Hospital Recreation, 1955.

Moustakas, Clark E. *Loneliness.* Englewood Cliffs, N.J.: Prentice-Hall Inc., 1961.

Neumeyer, Martin H. and Esther S. *Leisure and Recreation.* New York: Ronald Press Company, 1958.

Pieper, Josef. *Leisure: The Basis of Culture.* New York: Pantheon Books, 1952.

Riesman, David. *The Lonely Crowd.* New Haven, Conn.: Yale University Press, 1950.

──────. *Individualism Reconsidered.* Chicago: The Free Press of Glencoe, Ill., 1954.

Robbins, Florence G. *The Sociology of Play, Recreation and Leisure Time.* Dubuque, Iowa: Wm. C. Brown Company, 1955.

Rosenberg, Bernard, and David M. White, editors. *Mass Culture: The Popular Arts in America.* Chicago: The Free Press of Glencoe, Ill., 1957.

Russell, Bertrand. *In Praise of Idleness.* London: Allen & Unwin, Ltd., 1935.

Soule, George. *Time for Living.* New York: Viking Press, 1955.

Spike, Robert W. *To Be a Man.* New York: Association Press, 1961.

Veblen, Thorstein. *The Theory of the Leisure Class.* New York: Viking Press, 1899.

Ward, Hiley H. *Space-Age Sunday.* New York: The Macmillan Company, 1960.

Whitman, Lauris B. *et al. A Study of the Summertime Activities of Children in Relation to the Summer Program of the Churches.* The Committee on Children's Work, National Council of Churches, 1959.

Wilensky, Harold L. "Labor and Leisure: Intellectual Traditions," *Industrial Relations: A Journal of Economy and Society,* Vol. 1, Feb., 1962.

Williams, Arthur. *Recreation in the Senior Years.* New York: Association Press, 1962.

Wrenn, C. Gilbert and D. L. Harley. *Time on Their Hands.* Washington: American Council on Education, 1941.

Zelomek, A. W. *A Changing America: At Work and Play.* New York: John Wiley and Sons, Inc., 1959.

Zweig, Ferdynand. *The British Worker.* Middlesex: Penguin Books, A Pelican Book, 1952.

INDEX

Adler, Mortimer, 241, 265
Aged, 24, 203 ff.
Aristotle, 32, 85, 207
Augustine, 190, 200, 235

Barr, James, 225
Barth, Karl, 66-67, 188-89, 227, 229, 235, 251
Bendiner, Robert, 39, 46
Berger, Bennett, 27-29, 31, 215, 265
Berger, Peter, 67
Bergson, Henri, 201, 208
Blue laws, 175, 190-91
Bonhoeffer, Dietrich, 257
Boredom, 21, 23, 25, 108, 113 ff., 124, 145, 203, 237
Brightbill, Charles K., 199, 203, 265
Brunner, Emil, 102-3, 176, 231, 232-33
Bullitt, Stimson, 249-50

Caillois, Roger, 73 ff., 80-81, 265
Calendar, 129-31
Calvin, John, 154, 169
Casebier, Marjorie L., 265
Catcher in the Rye, The, 115 ff.
Christ, 82, 135, 136, 180-84, 187, 189, 199, 223, 227 ff., 233-34, 242, 247, 252, 261-62

Christian faith, 147, 155, 159, 171, 187, 222 ff., 234
Christmas, 136, 140-41, 144
Churches and leisure, 51, 82, 137-38, 166, 169, 173, 188, 194
Commitment, 249 ff., 254
Compulsion, 117 ff.
Craven, Ida, 18, 137, 265
Crestwood Heights, 205, 213-14

De Grazia, Sebastian, 26, 45, 148-49, 199, 204, 210, 239, 250-51, 258, 265
Denney, Reuel, 94, 265

Eliot, T. S., 247
Elmen, Paul, 23, 247, 251, 265
Erikson, Erik, 94

Fadiman, Clifton, 23-24
Feasts and festivals, 130-37, 147, 176, 179
Franklin, Benjamin, 168-69

Gill, Theodore A., 147-48, 227
Goffman, Erving, 81-82, 266
Goodman, Paul, 113
Gresham's Law, 21
Guardini, Romano, 66, 103-4

Heckscher, August, 32, 59, 78
Holy Days and holidays, 127 ff., 149, 192
  American, 139 ff.
  legal, 140 ff.
  Memorial Day, 146
  patriotic, 141-42
Huizinga, Johan, 53, 60, 71-72, 75, 80, 129, 266

Jewish Theological Seminary in America, 89, 217
Joy, 85-86, 90, 93, 124, 129, 236, 254 ff.

Kierkegaard, Søren, 123

Leisure
  activities, 45 ff., 161
  facts and trends of, 36 ff.
  for doctors, 30, 39-40, 239
  classical view of, 32 ff.
  mass, 19, 21, 23, 83, 85
  market for, 42 ff.
  problem of, 17 ff., 25
  theology of, 85, 218 ff., 237 ff.
Levin, Meyer, 117
Lundberg, George, 26-27, 52, 266
Luther, Martin, 138, 142, 146, 184, 194
Lynes, Russell, 20, 266

MacIver, Robert M., 21
Martin, Alexander Reid, 25, 88, 202-3, 266
Mead, Margaret, 29
Meaninglessness, 21, 25, 35, 108, 124
Meyerhoff, Hans, 207, 231
Meyersohn, Rolf, 49
Middle Ages, 56, 137-38, 185
Miller, Arthur, 108, 120, 123-24
Miller, Perry, 159-60, 162, 168
Moonlighting, 40-41
Moustakas, Clark E., 98-99, 248, 267
Muilenburg, James, 201

Mumford, Lewis, 49

National parks, 46
Neibuhr, Reinhold, 223

Outdoor Recreation Resources Review Commission, 50

Perry, Ralph Barton, 153, 157, 164
Pieper, Josef, 33, 34, 72-73, 75, 267
Play, 53 ff., 71 ff.
  business and professional life and, 57 ff.
  children and, 91 ff.
  clubs and societies, 59 ff.
  definitions of, 71 ff.
  leisure and, 76 ff.
  politics and, 58-59, 216
  sex as, 65-66
  worship and, 66
  youth and, 106 ff.
Puritanism, 139, 151 ff., 157

Rauschenbusch, Walter, 89

Sabbath, 138, 142, 155, 174 ff., 227
Salinger, J. D., 115
Sevareid, Eric, 17
Shakespeare, 64, 80, 202
Soule, George, 31, 151, 211, 260
Spike, Robert W., 22, 267
Steinbeck, John, 246
Stewart, George R., 127, 139, 144, 174

Television, 21, 47-48, 242, 251
Thielicke, Helmut, 187
Thrasher, Frederic, 106, 119
Tillich, Paul, 233, 258-59
Time
  free time, 26 ff.
  gang life and, 119 ff.
  God's creation and, 218 ff.
  shorter workweek, 36 ff.
  theological dimensions of, 195, 199 ff.

uses of, 45 ff.
ways of looking at, 206 ff.

Veblen, Thorstein, 19, 66, 267
Vocation, doctrine of, 22, 215

Ward, Hiley, 175, 190, 193, 267

Whitman, Lauris, 173, 267
Work, 19, 22, 27, 28 ff., 41, 86, 139, 175, 215, 250

Young Manhood of Studs Lonigan, The, 114-15